FAITHLESS

PRAISE FOR FAITHLESS

"The mystery of Jane's death and her subsequent revival is at the dark heart of an unfolding biological experiment that will leave readers reeling, and the final reveal is a shocker. Along the way, Ramirez visits the themes of memory and mortality through the lenses of science and occult while playing on universal themes of genetic engineering and ethical issues, trauma, abuse, and malevolence. Clever and suspenseful, the novel pulls the reader in and doesn't let go."

— THE PRAIRIES BOOK REVIEW

"Raul and Jane's mutual respect and a desire to protect each other are the book's emotional backbone. Its action scenes are punctuated by the complications of their soft, sad love. While Jane laments that she doesn't feel easy empathy, her thoughts suggest otherwise: she exhibits clear understandings of those around her, even when she's working to decide who to trust."

— FORWARD CLARION REVIEWS

BOOKS BY STEVEN RAMIREZ

LITERARY FICTION

Let's Get Lost

HELLBORN SERIES

Tell Me When I'm Dead

Dead Is All You Get

Even The Dead Will Bleed

HARD TO KILL SERIES

Brandon's Last Words

Faithless

SARAH GREENE MYSTERIES

The Girl in the Mirror

House of the Shrieking Woman

The Blood She Wore

OTHER BOOKS

Chainsaw Honeymoon

Come As You Are: A Short Novel and Nine Stories

Come As You Are: A Novella

FAITHLESS

HARD TO KILL SERIES BOOK 1

STEVEN RAMIREZ

glass highway

Glass Highway

Los Angeles, CA

stevenramirez.com

Faithless / Hard To Kill Series Book 1 / Steven Ramirez.—1st ed.

Paperback: 978-1-949108-12-5

EPUB: 978-1-949108-10-1

Kindle: 978-1-949108-11-8

Audiobook: 978-1-949108-30-9

Library of Congress Control Number: 2021903806

Edited by Shannon A. Thompson

Cover design by 100 Covers

I don't know you, but I see you in my dreams. You're coming for me. One day you'll find me. And when you do, I'll already be dead. Same as you.

— FAITH REGAN, LAKE ISABELLA

FAITHLESS

PART ONE

WHITE RABBIT

CHAPTER
ONE

WHAT I'M ABOUT to tell you sounds crazy. I died. More on that later. I'm still piecing together the story. Each fragment is like a Post-it I was lucky enough to pull from deep inside my disjointed memory. Or from a trusted friend. Or an enemy. A lot of it's jumbled—maybe even made up. Who the hell knows? But I'm here to debrief. So buckle the eff up.

I used to have a name. Bear with me—it'll come to me. For now, I can tell you I was a PFC—Private First Class—in the United States Marine Corps. Oorah. They deployed me to Afghanistan, along with Lance Corporal Tyler Berry. There were others whose names I can't recall. We joined a squad of men and women—many who'd seen combat. I thought we'd get the lay of the land first. I was wrong.

They sent us north to the White Mountains near the border with Pakistan. The same mountains Bin Laden hid out in when we couldn't find him during the Tora Bora offensive. Now, the Marines were here on a night raid to clean out a nest of IS fighters.

When we arrived in the village at the foot of the mountains, we found we weren't alone. The dead had gotten there ahead of us. I remember glimpses. A cold, driving rain, coming down like glass knives on flesh over us and hundreds of corpses. The worst were the children, smashed like bugs in a coffee can. No one left to mourn the small, still bodies.

Wearing NVG—night vision goggles—we hid behind white stone houses as intense streams of gunfire assaulted us. IS tracer rounds zinging through the air like fireflies on meth. My friend was on my left. We shared the unspoken language of trust, Tyler and me. A knowledge deep in our young souls that one would not let the other come to any harm. I wish I'd done better by him.

Lt. Gorman, teeth clenched, gripped his M4 and peered across the way at a walled compound known as a qalat. That's where the rest of our squad was hiding. A river of fast-moving water separated us, carrying the dead and dying with it. When the lieutenant gave us the signal, my chest tightened and my pulse quickened. I looked at Tyler, who nodded. We advanced, heading to where the shooting came from. Another glorious day in the Corps.

As enemy fire intensified, I took the lead, with Tyler next to me. Using the shadows as cover, we made it past the first few houses. We ducked into a narrow alley as an angry stream of bullets caught Blevins. The impact sent him spinning and falling hard on the wet stones. My instinct was to save him, but he was gone. First tour too. Like me. Guy was motarded—loved this combat shit.

The insurgents hid behind a cluster of dwellings to the right. Blinded by the rain, I focused on Tyler. Though he was a lance corporal, he was never part of the underground where bad information gets passed around like Pokémon cards. And his cutting score was high enough for him to make terminal lance. Tyler was a brother.

In the distance, a haji darted across the path ahead of us. Must've gotten separated from his unit. I was convinced he was the one who'd killed Blevins. Using my NVG, I tracked him as he ran. Rays of moonlight shone from behind dark clouds. Behind him, the steep stone stairs carved into the mountain seemed to rise toward heaven. I didn't know it then, but for me, those steps would lead somewhere else.

I pointed my M4, steadied myself, and fired. It was good. The kill shot sent the bullet tearing out the back of the insurgent's head. The fragments exploded outward in a scarlet bloom between his surprised eyes. Bright blood sprayed everywhere. If I didn't know better, I'd swear he fell in slow-mo. When he dropped, he didn't make a sound.

Lt. Gorman gave us the signal. Time to advance again. I turned to Tyler, closed my eyes, and took a breath. He was shorter than me. But I'm tall for a girl—six feet. It was better he was behind me. I'd protect him. He gripped my shoulder and spoke the last words I would ever hear him say.

"You got this."

I ran full out, firing as oncoming bullets whizzed past. Someone cried out. Veering, I flattened myself against a building. Holding my weapon tight against my body armor. Wishing I could melt into the wall. Tyler was hit. He lay face down in a rush of dark water. I scanned the darkness, hoping to spot a medic.

Across the way, the rest of the squad took heavy fire and returned it in equal measure. I signaled them to cover me. As they let loose a maelstrom against unseen hostiles, I went after my friend. I'm small-boned but stronger than I look. I deadlifted his limp body and carried him to the nearest building.

When I got to the corner, a scorching round struck me in the shoulder. Grimacing from the pain, I drove on. The platoon took out more of the enemy, but insurgents were hiding near the base of the stairs. I could almost feel their body heat. The rain was relentless. Tyler was breathing, but he was in a bad way. I examined myself. I'd taken a bullet under my OTV—bleeding badly. I wished I'd had a QuikClot pack. No idea where the medics were. It looked like we were on our own.

More bullets came at me from the rear like murder hornets. The enemy had moved and was closing in. My one chance was up those stairs. I'd have to leave my friend behind. Maybe the insurgents would think he was dead.

Gritting my teeth against the pain, I dragged Tyler's unconscious body deep into the shadows and propped him up against the bullet-scarred wall. I faced the stairs, my breath ragged. From out of the sky, a single yellow ray of light fell. It showed me the way.

My brother, Bo, stood next to me in the pouring rain, wearing battle rattle. He was four years older than me. And even taller. He resembled an avenging angel as he loomed over me. I knew the look.

"What are you waiting for?" he said. "Run."

Nodding, I gripped my rifle and dashed toward the stairs, firing to the left and right. If I hadn't been injured, I might've made it all the way up. A hail of gunfire cut me down. It struck me in the legs and sent me forward onto the slick, muddy steps. Screaming, I tried getting up, but I couldn't. Bo stood over me, impervious to the bullets raining down on us. His face was wet and shiny, and he was angry as hell.

"Get up," he said.

"I can't."

Big mistake. He grabbed me by the scruff of the neck—the way he used to when I was ten. I remembered falling during the endless training he put me through. He'd stick his face up against mine until his beard stubble chafed me raw. No mercy in those eyes.

"Excuse me?" he said, then glanced back. "Behind you."

Groaning, I turned in time to see a haji approaching fast, about to fire. I found my service pistol, and with one clean shot, I brought him down. Whimpering, I fought my way up the stairs one by one on my belly, using my elbows. My blood mixed with the rain.

The gunfire changed direction. The platoon must've drawn off the insurgents. I was near the top now. Distant voices shouted, punctuated by nonstop shooting. I looked up. Something in a deep mist floated in front of me. The brightness hurt my eyes, and I tore off the goggles. When my eyes adjusted, I looked again.

It was a strange old man, with long, stringy yellow-white hair and a full beard. One eye was clouded over like bad milk. He wore an old gray suit and sandals, and a white scarf. Strings of bright beads hung from his neck. On his head, a red, green, and white turban. During MOS training, I'd read up on Afghanistan and knew what he was.

A malang.

Villagers feared these shamans because of their power, real or imagined. It was said they could summon a demon and make it do their bidding. In this case, a demon being a djinn. And now, here he was. Perched at the top of the stairs in the rain. Unafraid.

"Help!" I said, reaching toward him. "Help me!"

He stared at me with his good eye, tilting his head like a curious dog. I dug way down deep and brought up the little Pashto I knew.

"Mehrbanai wakrai, zama marasti ta arzya laram!"

He didn't react—the bastard. Instead, he waited until I'd reached the top, barely alive and almost bled out. Soon, I'd lose consciousness. Lifting me, he helped me into his house, which overlooked the stairs. Like some fairy tale, a yellow glow poured out of the small, curtainless windows. It was eerily inviting.

The house was rustic but clean, the dirt floor covered in rugs. Candles burned everywhere atop simple homemade furniture. The odor of dinner hung in the air—lamb with saffron rice. As bad off as I was, the smell made me hungry.

The old man laid me on my back in the center of the room and removed my helmet, revealing a shorn head of hair. He peeled off my Kevlar and other gear. It was hard to keep my eyes open. I craved the comforting sleep of death.

After he left me, I became delirious. When he returned, he was carrying an old, chipped coffee mug. I recognized the writing on the side. *USMC. Embrace the Suck.* Had one of our guys befriended him?

He helped me up and offered me the drink. When I smelled the cardamom, I knew it was Afghan tea. I swallowed the pungent, slightly sweet liquid. Coughing, I lay back down. The malang began a slow, dark chant, his voice strong beyond his years. His breath reeked of tobacco and tea. He wiped my face, neck, and hands with a wet towel. The coolness soothed me, distracting me from the intense pain.

A sudden explosion rocked the house, sending the shaman onto his side. Struggling to his feet, he made his way to the window and turned back to me. He pointed outside and said something I couldn't understand. Now, more explosions as missiles from the sky struck the village. Yut, we'd gotten our air support! I should've evacuated with the rest of the platoon. Too late now.

My vision blurred. I could just make out the lined face of the crazy old dude as I slipped away. He gave me a smile through a handful of rotting teeth. As he waved his hands over me, a low-pitch humming—like something out of hell—caused the floor to vibrate. An intense heat radiated from my body like a fever. Then the real fun started.

Spent bloody bullets ascended from my body in slow-mo. Dull and misshapen in the yellow light, the slugs looked like bizarro raindrops in reverse. I tried looking down at my body, but I was in too much pain. The malang continued to chant.

Bullets kept rising, until all of them had left me and came to rest in his hands. A sudden wind blew, shaking the house and taking out the candle flames. Dirt from the floor swirled into a spinning cloud of powder, making it hard to see. The cyclone rose like Lazarus into…

A creature.

It was a thing black like the night—a djinn. Amorphous and cloying, with horrible red eyes. Drifting toward me in a poisonous cloud of menace, it terrified me. I would've cried out, but I was too weak. Instead, I lay there, waiting for the ungodly thing to consume me.

Moaning, I whipped my head from side to side. I was unaware of what was coming as the infernal chanting grew louder. The djinn's burning breath poured over me like demon coal fire. My heart raced to the end. But of what?

The malang shouted a command. Inside a fierce wind, the monster rushed to my side, its hot red eyes boring into me. The cursed thing raised a skeletal finger adorned with a deco- rated black fingernail. The djinn pressed it to my pounding heart. Excruciating pain ignited like fire from my chest and spread to my extremities. My eyes wide open, I released a final breath. And I stopped moving.

I believe I left my body. Because now, the old man and the demon were below me, lingering over me as I lay motionless. My vacant eyes open wide.

That's when I knew I was dead.

WHEN I OPENED MY EYES, I was in water under low lights. I remembered gunfire and people shouting. This wasn't Afghanistan. I didn't know where I was. After the bullet bursts, there was an explosion. Sounded like a grenade. All I knew for sure was, I didn't know shit.

I lay naked in a tank filled with wires and tubes attached to my body. My skin has always been pale. Now, it looked bloodless in the bluish glow of the LED lights lining the top of the unit. I tried moving. No pain to speak of, but I was weak. I called out. What came back was a feeble croak.

It took all my strength to get into a sitting position. I wished I hadn't. Rows of coffin-like tanks identical to mine surrounded me. Each gave off the same eerie blue glow. Besides me, nothing else moved.

I ripped away everything that was in me or on me and climbed out. My legs were wobbly, so I stretched. I half expected to see my brother Bo pissed off. Ordering me to get dressed. Dripping wet, I padded toward a nearby tank. A man in his early twenties lay motionless, his eyes closed.

Blevins.

I could tell it was him by his blond hair. He wasn't breathing. Though he'd been shot many times in the Afghan village, I didn't see a single wound. Unlike my tank, the water in his was black.

Feeling stronger, I returned to my container and dipped my hand. Something flashed on the side of the unit. Kneeling, I found a lighted panel, where a message repeated. MALFUNC-TION. PRESS FOR MORE INFORMATION.

The room was deathly quiet. Shivering, I wandered up and down the rows of tanks. All contained naked bodies—male and female. Like Blevins, they marinated in black water. Some I recognized, most I didn't. And Tyler—where was he?

None of the other containers flashed red. Was I the only one alive? My mind drifted back to the firefight in the White Mountains. I made a careful examination of the places I'd been shot. Like Blevins, no bullet wounds—not even a scratch. No way I'd dreamt the whole thing. Yet now, my hair was long and fell over my shoulders. Way past regulation.

I didn't know what danger lay outside. One thing for sure, I needed clothes. And a weapon. I crossed to the door and peered into the darkened hallway. Nothing but dense shad-ows. The silence put me on edge.

Keeping to the wall, I made my way along the corridor. Something lay on the ground up ahead. It was a man in a guard uniform. I checked to see if he was alive. Negative. Someone had slit his throat in one clean stroke. A pool of dark, coagulated blood formed a halo around his head. I took his clothes and gun.

Gathering up my hair, I tucked it under the cap. Every-thing was baggy on me. The shoes were too big and the pants too short. The shirt was crusted with blood. Also, this guy had some major BO. At least I had a weapon.

Up ahead, I saw a lighted enclosure with elevators inside. I started toward it. Behind me, a rhythmic metallic sound broke through the silence. It was like nothing I'd ever heard before. Definitely not a gun. Raising my weapon, I pivoted. A blond man stood there, tapping a strange-looking knife against a metal post. He was shirtless and barefoot. But it was the eyes—they glowed purple. *What the eff?*

When he came toward me, I fired three times. Every round hit him in the midsection. Stopping, he looked at himself. Stuck his finger into one of the holes. He licked off the blood and grinned. Before I could fire at the psycho again, someone yanked me from behind into the shadows. My strength returning, I pulled free. A frightened guard put a finger to his lips. He took my hand and led me down a narrow corridor. Away from the freak with the purple eyes.

We arrived at a pair of steel doors. Using his ID badge, the guard opened one and slipped inside. Glancing behind me, I followed. We stood in the foyer of a brightly lit hospital wing with an abandoned nurses' station. He pointed at my shirt.

"Are you injured?" he said.

"What the hell was that back there?" My voice sounded rough. Talking made my throat hurt.

"Alpha." His eyes darted like a nervous chihuahua. "They're an experiment."

"They?" I said. "You mean, there are more?"

"Black Dragon might've killed most of 'em."

"I don't know what you're talking about."

"You're not one of us," he said, backing away. "Who are you?"

"That's not important right now."

"Why?"

I broke it down for him Barney style. "We need to leave. There's prob'ly more of those things. I don't know about you, but I'm not dying in here."

"We're not going anywhere," another voice said.

The guard looked past me. *Damn.* As I raised my hands, someone relieved me of my weapon and ID badge. Now there were two assholes. The new one pointed a gun at my head. He had a face like an identikit and wore glasses.

"Man asked you a question," the second one said. "Who are you?"

Using my peripheral vision, I searched for a way out. "I have no idea."

"What does that mean?"

"It means, one minute, I was in Afghanistan. And now I'm here."

"Afghanistan? Dude, she's one of them."

Laughing, Asshole #2 slugged his partner in the arm. Turning serious, he pulled him aside like I wasn't there.

"You know what we have to do, right?" he said.

"Huh? No, no, no. Travis, I can't…"

"We talked about this. I thought you wanted to be a hero."

Enough. While these two superheroes conspired against me, I took the gun away from the second guard and shot him in the head. Stunned, Asshole #1 watched as his friend hit the floor. Grabbing his weapon, I glared at him. He pissed himself.

"Don't kill me!" he said. "Oh jeez. I-I was… Come on, really? I was never going to—"

"Shut up."

I considered killing him anyway. But, like it or not, the gomer was my ticket out of this hellhole. I lowered my gun and grabbed his face.

"We're getting out of here," I said.

CHAPTER
THREE

LIKE AN ABANDONED PUPPY, the guard stared at his dead friend's body.

"Is there another way out?" I said.

Stinking of urine, the goof pointed. "Through there."

"Show me."

He scooted down the hallway past the nurses' station toward a side corridor. We passed a long glass wall. A set of clear doors stood in the middle. Beyond that was a white room with a hospital bed, the sheets crusted with dried blood. I grabbed his shirt, and we stopped.

Inside on the floor, there were three bodies—all men. One wearing a gray suit lay on his back. His heart was missing. Another, also in a gray suit, was on his stomach, his head unnaturally twisted. And the third? He was the worst. Dressed in a black suit, he lay on his side facing us. His eyes were gouged out. And his throat was torn open, as if by a wild animal.

"When did it happen?" I said.

The guard shook his head. "Early this morning."

"And the explosion?"

"That was Black Dragon." He caught my look of confusion. "They're a private security outfit."

"Is that who you work for?"

"I wish," he said, snorting.

Soon, we found an exit. The guard stopped in front of the door and gawked at me like a dog who'd crapped the carpet.

"It's not safe out there," he said. "I need a gun."

I pulled the second weapon from my belt and handed it to him. As he took it, I stuck my barrel in his ear. He piddled again.

"You so much as think about messing with me, and I will end you."

"I-I would never—"

"And stop peeing. You're gonna leave a trail. What's your name?"

"Brandon?"

We took a minute to check our weapons. I pressed the magazine release button. The mag dropped in my hand, and I examined the witness holes.

"I've got six rounds," I said. "You?"

"One."

I wasn't sure I trusted him. Waiting a beat, I gave him two of mine. "Okay, Brandon. Are the elevators I saw earlier the best way out?"

"I know a better way."

He opened the door, and we entered a dark hallway. Up ahead, there were two steel doors. We grabbed the handles and pulled. Inside, the lights were on, revealing a massive concrete room. The center of the floor was made of metal.

One wall was bullet scarred and coated with old blood. In front of it, anchored to the floor, stood a row of steel stands maybe six feet high—tall enough for a man. Each had metal hand and ankle cuffs. At the other end of the room, there was a long table with weapons mounted on it. I identified assault rifles, shotguns, and handguns. The video cameras helped me put it together. Somebody was doing target practice on people. And filming it.

"Where to?" I said.

He pointed at a door across the way. Like the others, it was made of steel and had a small wire glass window. Following him, I stepped on the metal part of the floor.

The guard looked at where I was standing. "Careful."

After we reached the other side, I peered through the little window. The room was dark; small and bare. It didn't look like there was another way out.

"The alpha you saw knows where we're going," he said.

"How can you be sure?"

"Because they're hunters. Why do you think they have those postmortem knives? Once we get through here, we can make a run for it."

I entered first, and the door slammed behind me. Brandon made goofy faces at me through the glass. Furious, I went for the doorknob. There wasn't one. I pointed my weapon at him. But I realized the glass might be bulletproof. With the resulting ricochet, I'd only be hurting myself.

"Why?" I said through the glass.

"Because you're a loose end."

"What?"

"You were supposed to die."

"Why?"

"Travis was right. I am a hero. I bet Amber will have sex with me now." Then to me, "I'll be back."

He shook his wet leg and headed for the exit. *Motherf…* I switched on the lights and made a careful examination of my surroundings. The room was maybe ten by twelve. I guessed it was a holding pen for the test subjects. There was an air vent in the ceiling. Though I was tall, there was no way for me to reach it without a chair.

Outside, a bloodcurdling shriek broke the silence. I peered through the window. The steel doors were open. Something rolled across the floor like a bowling ball and stopped short of my door. It was Brandon's head.

The blond alpha I'd seen earlier burst into the room, followed by a dark-haired companion. Moving away from the window, I pressed myself against the wall. I could stay quiet until they went away. But I'd have no way to get out. And if they found me, they'd kill me for sure.

I reviewed my options and decided. I'd have to trap one inside here and kill the other. I checked the window again. The alphas prowled the room like panthers, then split up. The dark-haired hostile went behind the long table. Blondie dropped to one knee and ran his hand along the seam where steel met concrete.

This was it. I banged on the window. Their heads snapped up, and they leered. Blondie walked up to me and stared at the doorknob. Watching me with crafty eyes, he tried the door. As it opened, I darted to the side and waited.

The alpha stuck his head in, his hand clutching a post-mortem knife. I grabbed his forearm and pulled him inside. The blade skittered across the floor. As I leaped toward the door, blondie tackled me. The door clicked shut. Perfect. Now, I was trapped in here with the creature.

Four rounds left. As the alpha retrieved his knife, I shot him in the neck. The sound reverberated, disorienting me. Hissing, he came at me. I fired again, this time hitting him in the cheek. He shook his head and spat out a mess of bloody teeth. Before he could come at me again, I shot him through the eye. Spasming, he dropped to his knees and fell on his face.

One bullet left.

The sound of machinery caught my attention. The dark-haired alpha peered at me through the window. The knob jiggled and the door flew open. My weapon up, I shoved him out of the way and bolted past.

In the killing room, the metal floor was gone, replaced by a gaping rectangular hole. The alpha stood at the far end, silent. As I moved closer, the smell of burnt flesh assaulted me. Not wanting to, I looked down.

Hundreds of charred bones and bits of clothing lay at the bottom. I recognized remnants of medical lab coats and guard uniforms. And gray suits. When I looked up again, the alpha was in front of me. His hands were empty. I didn't know what he wanted, but he looked sad.

"What is this place?" I said.

"Hell."

He grabbed my hand hard and jammed the gun barrel against his forehead. His hand on mine, he made me squeeze the trigger. The blast echoed, and he fell backward into the pit. I had no clue why he'd spared me. Maybe he knew. I was an experiment too. And he'd shown me my future.

Outside, the last of Brandon lay in front of the steel doors. His weapon next to him. I swapped mine for his and dug through his pockets, looking for his ID badge. That's when I found it—a second mag. Sonofabitch had held out on me. I checked it—it was full. Grabbing the badge, I headed for the elevators.

Inside the enclosure, dried blood covered the floor and bloody handprints decorated the bullet-scarred wall. I made sure I was alone when I walked in. After swiping my badge, I waited for the elevator doors to open and slipped inside.

When I got out, I was in a storage area. Racks of cardboard boxes surrounded me. I examined a container. Medical equipment. As I scanned the words with my finger, I tried to understand what was printed on the side in black stenciled lettering. BASEBORN IDENTITY RESEARCH.

I found an exit and walked outside into the cold, morning light. A guard station stood at the edge of the parking lot.

Whatever this place was, I'd put it as far behind me as I could. I hoped there were no more alphas after me and double-timed it until I was outside the fence.

Staring at a lonely desert road, I had no idea where I was, but the sun was coming up fast. Soon, it would be hot. I took a last look at the dark building complex.

And then, I headed west.

CHAPTER
FOUR

I DIDN'T SEE anyone for a long time. A scrawny coyote appeared from out of a gully, limping. When he saw me, he yipped. The animal remained still as I inched closer. When I was next to him, I saw the bloody rear leg tangled in barbed wire. He let out a mournful howl and sat.

"Easy, boy," I said.

Crouching, I pulled apart the wire, which cut my hands. When he snapped at me, I gave him a scowl. He let me continue. As soon as he was free, he trotted across the road and disappeared into the brush. I tossed the barbed wire and continued walking.

Farther ahead, the scorched shell of a black helicopter lay in the middle of the road. I stopped cold and scanned the desert. When it was safe, I inched closer. The metal was twisted and charred. Next to it, the body of a woman in a gray suit was sprawled on the asphalt. She'd been shot. Crows picked at the flesh, fighting over the eyes.

Peering inside the cockpit, I discovered two more bodies— the pilot, and a businessman burned beyond recognition. I guessed the accident had something to do with Baseborn Identity Research. There was no end to the carnage. Thirsty, I searched the cabin for bottled water. There was nothing except for a few maps and a fire extinguisher.

It was getting warm now, and I was parched. Shielding my eyes, I squinted into the distance. The road stretched for miles. What I needed was to hitch a ride. Dressed in a bloody uniform, that wasn't happening. Behind me, loud music—Ghost Wave's "Here She Comes." A car approached at high speed. Now, voices singing and laughing. I figured they'd ignore me and keep going.

They were close now. I turned in time to see the tricked-out black Camaro, weaving. The distracted driver bore down on me. I couldn't get out of the way fast enough and jumped straight up as the car struck me. I sailed over the speeding vehicle, long enough to make out the occupants. Four men, all in their twenties. I hit the pavement hard and rolled. Up ahead, the Camaro screeched to a stop. Stunned, I remained on my back, the smell of burning rubber gagging me.

My weapon lay to one side, out of reach. The sound of car doors opening. Multiple voices swearing—getting closer. When I looked up, I saw them standing behind me. They gawped, their heads blocking out the sun.

"Do you think he was in that helicopter back there?" someone said.

"Look at all the blood. Let's just go."

"Shut up. Maybe we can…"

A hand touched my shirt. "It's dry. Dude, it's a girl!"

"What the—no way."

Multiple hands were on me now. The simians pawed my shirt and tried undoing the buttons. Someone pulled off my cap, and my hair fell all around me. A sweaty hand slid down my pants on its way to my cooch. Grabbing the fingers, I bent the wrist back farther than it should go. The hostile screamed like a girl. Everyone fell back and stood in front of me. I scrambled to my feet and glared at them.

Wearing tuxedos, they looked like they'd come from a party for rich assholes. Beyond them on the road, there were two wavy black skid marks. I glanced at my weapon. So did they. One of them tried going for it. Despite my injuries, I was faster.

Rolling, I grabbed the gun and sat facing them. They side-eyed each other as I pointed the weapon with one hand and buttoned my shirt with the other. His eyes on the gun, the good-looking one put his hands out in front of him.

"Easy," he said. "We're not going to harm you."

He had a nice smile. His eyes shifted to his friends, then back to me. No one made a move.

"Are you hurt?"

His friend turned to him. This one had small, animal eyes and bad skin. Even in formal wear, he reminded me of a lizard.

"Never mind," the reptile said, and reached inside his jacket.

I caught the gleam of a weapon and put a round through his eye. He dropped where he stood. The others surrounded him, getting on their knees. Trying to save him. Cursing and throwing vicious glances at me.

"She killed him," someone said. He sounded surprised.

I got to my feet and covered the remaining three. Though it was obvious they were scared, they tried acting all macho. I considered whether to shoot them now and be done with it.

"You shouldn't have done that," the good-looking one said. The others pressed forward, but he held them back. "Look, this has gotten way out of hand. We all need to take a step back."

"Screw it," his friend said.

This tool had a neck beard and was shorter and fatter than the others. Asian, and wearing black cowboy boots. Instead of going for his weapon, he trotted back to the vehicle and grabbed something from the trunk. When he turned around, he was holding a shotgun.

The other two stared at me, unsure what I would do. I put them down. My eyes never leaving his, I marched toward Neck Beard. He crouched behind the car door and pointed the shotgun. I fired first. The bullet shattered the car window, leaving a small hole next to his head. Shaking off the glass, he got off one shot. But he missed, and I kept coming.

He didn't take me on. Instead, he got behind the wheel and lead-footed the gas pedal. I emptied the mag, trying to shoot out the tires. But he was too far away. *Shit.* I'd missed my chance. Wouldn't be long before he told someone what happened. Others would come looking for me.

Backtracking, I stared at the three bodies. I dragged them to the side of the road. One of the dead was around my size. I traded clothes with him. To keep the sun off, I kept the guard cap. One by one, I rolled the corpses over an embankment into a gully. The tall weeds would hide them for a while. A pack of hungry crows descended on the bodies like a swarm of locusts. As I continued west, they cawed at me.

"You're welcome," I said.

CHAPTER
FIVE

THE SUN WAS SCORCHING. I was so dehydrated I saw spots. And I was starving. Up ahead, there was a worn white sign. Sitting atop a huge pole, it read CAFÉ in rust-colored letters. I patted my jacket pockets and found a wallet bursting with hundreds. A sign in the restaurant window read No Hipsters.

The owner had locked the door and put out the closed sign. I peered through the screen. Some old dude sat at a table, his head down. A dog lay at his feet. An elderly Latina comforted the man. He ran his hand through his short white hair and looked at me with empty, swollen eyes. Shaking her head, the woman got up and unlocked the door.

"Can't you read?" she said in accented English. "We're closed."

I showed her the money. "I'm starving."

Rolling her eyes, she let me in. The old man stood and pointed at a table. I took a seat. The dog sidled up to me, sniffed my hand, and licked it. I gave him a pat on the head.

The owner brought me cold water, along with chips and salsa. I drained the glass. He returned to the counter, grabbed the pitcher, and set it on the table. Grateful, I drank two more glasses.

"I'll see if my wife can fix you something," he said with a German accent.

A few minutes later, the old woman presented a plate with four hard-shell tacos. I didn't see any meat.

"What are these?" I said.

"Potato tacos."

I picked one up and sniffed it. One bite, and I was hooked. I devoured the meal. Finishing my water, I belched like a boot. I hadn't noticed the Latina leaving my table. When I looked up, the old man was holding a shotgun aimed at my chest.

"Who are you?" he said.

"Good question."

I thought about grabbing my weapon, but the couple had been kind. I didn't feel like they were a real danger to me—not like those posers in the desert. These folks were scared. I put my hands behind my head, interlacing the fingers.

"There's a gun in my right pocket," I said. "You can take it —I won't fight you."

He inched closer. Reaching out his left hand, he took my weapon and backed away. I relaxed and belched again. Laughing, he lowered the shotgun and sat across from me.

"Can't be too careful," he said. "I'm John Zwick. Wife's Consuelo."

With no name, I did the best I could. "Good to meet you."

"Who sent you?"

"No one, I… I was in this awful place—"

"Where?"

"Not far. I think it's a research facility."

His eyes got huge. Ignoring his surprise, I went on.

"Not sure what it is, but it's evil," I said. "When I woke up, I was alone, surrounded by bodies. I heard a lot of shooting."

I lowered my head and rubbed my eyes. Trying to will myself to remember. Faint flashes from the past danced in and out of my head like bent marionettes in a Broadway chorus line. I remembered the malang—and the djinn. But I couldn't tell this guy. He'd think I was nuts and call someone to take me away in a happy suit.

"Those aren't your clothes," he said.

"I ran into some trouble."

"You were at Hellborn?"

I blinked at him stupidly.

"Baseborn Identity Research."

"That's the place."

"*Hellborn* is what a friend of mine calls it. I just come from there. Had a helluva fight."

"I saw. Those three bodies in the hospital? What's it all about?"

"Too complicated. And I don't know you. We had a job to do, and we did it."

"Copy. I passed a helicopter on the road. That part of the situation?"

"The dead guy inside was one of 'em. I'm surprised you made it out."

"Tell me what happened," I said. "Please."

Consuelo approached us, carrying a round tray with a bottle of El Señorio Joven con Gusano and three shot glasses. Without words, she set the tray down and poured out the amber liquid. The little dead worm relaxed at the bottom like he was on vacation in Virginia Beach. A sudden flashback blinded me...

"Drink up, man, it's your birthday!"

A group of us sat at a waterfront bar in Sneads Ferry, North Carolina. We were drinking mescal. Tyler wasn't there.

We'd been stationed at Camp Lejeune, where we had completed infantry training. This was our last night. Next stop, MOS training in Dam Neck, Virginia.

The birthday boy was in our squad in Afghanistan.
It was Blevins.

"Hey, you okay?"

I looked across the table at the strangers who'd shown me kindness. Taking my glass, I downed the contents and set it out, hoping for a refill.

"Old memories," I said.

John nodded. "You kind of zoned out there. What do you know about Hellborn?"

"Nothing." I looked out the window. "Where are we?"

"Perro Negro. North of Los Angeles."

"And the death house back there?"

"Rosamond."

"What's today?"

"December 25th."

Christmas Day. I couldn't recall ever having celebrated it.

"How did you end up there? Were you kidnapped?"

"Can't remember." Then on their reaction, "I'm being serious. I don't even know my name."

"Okay," he said as his wife refilled our glasses. "They've been doin' things in there—nasty stuff. Creating monsters."

"Monsters?"

"Insane humans who carve people up. It's all mixed in with the government. That's all I know."

"How did you get involved?"

The old woman took his hand. "Our son," she said. "Those devils killed him."

I looked at her husband. "And that's why you went there? For revenge?"

"And to rescue someone," he said. "A girl. Not supposed to tell you any more."

Woozy from the mescal, I got up and reached across the table for my weapon.

"I won't hurt you," I said. "But I need answers. And I intend to find them."

Looking at his wife, he handed me the gun, butt first. I slipped it into my jacket pocket.

"Thanks for the food." I threw down five bills. "I better leave."

"What are you fixin' to do?" he said.

"No effing idea."

I should've left sooner. Two black Lincoln Continental town cars screeched to a stop in front of the café. The wheels kicked up clouds of desert dust. Four men in black suits climbed out.

"Get in the kitchen," I said.

John grabbed his shotgun. Taking the dog, the old couple retreated. I drew my weapon and prepared to face whatever was about to walk in. The door burst open, and two hostiles entered with guns. I fired twice.

The bullets struck them in the head, sending blood spray and brains everywhere. As they went down, I backed toward the counter. Wait. There'd been four of them.

Before I could make it to the kitchen, the other two stepped out. Each held an old-timer by the arm. One of them was taller than me. Latino, with dark eyes and dark curly hair. His partner was the neck-bearded prick I'd intended to kill in the desert. I pointed my weapon at the attractive one. Smiling with perfect teeth, he stroked Consuelo's hair with the barrel of his gun. She looked at him with disgust.

"I don't like killing old people," he said.

"Leave them alone." I placed my weapon on the floor. "They have nothing to do with this."

Neck Beard seemed disappointed. Maybe he was hoping I would try something so he could trash the place.

"Fine," Dr. Handsome said.

The Asian glared at him. "What? Raul—"

"Cállate, pendejo."

The one named Raul tilted his head toward his partner,

who came out from behind the counter. He confiscated my weapon and did a quick pat-down, careful not to come anywhere near my privates. From where I was standing, I could've kicked him in the head. But his friend would kill the hostages. Unaware of my murderous intent, Neck Beard pointed the gun at my head. He was enjoying this.

Raul stared at the old man, a curious expression on his face. I thought the hostile might harm him. Instead, he gave him a smile and waved his weapon. When John didn't move fast enough, Raul pushed him to the floor.

"¡Mi amor!" the old woman said. Then to her captor, "¿Y tú? Sinvergüenza."

Though she had told him he should be ashamed of himself, he didn't seem to mind.

"You remind me of my lita," he said. "You too. On the floor."

"Cabrón."

Shooting me an angry look, she complied. he came from behind the counter and walked toward us. He stared at the two bodies near the front door and clucked his tongue.

"Headshots," he said. "I heard you were some kind of killing machine." Then to his partner, "Call it in."

Nodding, the Asian stepped outside. Raul grabbed my arm and shoved me forward through the front door.

"What now?" I said.

"We're taking you with us. That tuxedo looks familiar."

Outside, I yanked my arm away and marched toward a town car. Neck Beard pocketed his phone. He opened the front passenger door and motioned me inside. Raul climbed in behind the wheel while his partner hopped into the other vehicle.

"Kersey isn't going to be happy you killed his nephew," my driver said.

"Which one was he?"

"You're wearing his tux." He started the engine. "And don't try anything, or we'll come back and burn the place to the ground. With your ruco friends inside."

I decided to take his advice.

CHAPTER
SIX

RAUL SAID little as we made our way south on the 14 toward LA. I worried about what would happen to John and Consuelo. These guys were professionals. Death was incidental to the job. Sure, they'd clean up the mess in Perro Negro. But did it include taking out the old couple? I couldn't recall ever being religious, but I said what might have passed for a prayer. *Let the café owners come out of this all right.*

"Are you a security guard?" he said, pointing at my cap. "Vincent mentioned you were dressed like one when they found you."

"You mean, when they ran me over?"

"I'm guessing Kersey's nephew was driving. Lousy eyesight. And he refused to wear contacts."

"That was on him."

"You're a salty bitch, aren't you?"

"Salty and sweet."

"Laugh all you want. Any idea how much trouble you're in?"

I stared out the window, thinking about the alpha who blew his brains out with my gun. "I've seen worse."

"You know what? I believe you."

He switched on the stereo. Latin music blared over the speakers. The sound hurt my ears, so I turned it down.

"What were you doing in the desert?" he said.

"Penance. Where are you taking me?"

"You ask too many questions."

He cranked up the music again, and I thought about how I would get myself out of the situation.

Though traffic going into the city was light, we were stuck on Interstate 5 behind a line of semi-trailers. I gazed out the window at the grayish, hazy landscape. Nothing here looked healthy. I tried remembering if I'd ever been to LA, but I drew a blank—like the rest of my murky past. It was early afternoon when we exited the freeway and wound up on Alameda.

"What's over there?" I said, pointing.

"Union Station. Don't get any ideas."

The road took us into a sketchy industrial area. Train tracks ran along old brown buildings that looked as if they'd been standing a thousand years. No sign of life—not even a hobo. This was a good place to get yourself lost. Or dead.

Raul pulled up behind a building and parked. My body felt stiff. I got out and did a few stretches. The high windows were covered in city grime. To my left, crows picked at a dead mongrel dog. I wondered if they'd followed me from the desert. Four black town cars were parked next to ours. Somewhere far off, a train horn wailed with the promise of escape.

"What now?" I said.

"Now we go in."

Grunting, he pulled open a huge sliding door made of corrugated steel, the wheels screeching across a rusty track. The noise hurt my teeth. The interior suggested an old machine shop. I hesitated as I watched him go inside. When I didn't follow, he shook his head and pulled out his weapon. Giving him a kiss-my-ass smile, I went in after him.

The place was huge and dusty and smelled like stale oil and ancient farts. It looked like no actual work had gone on here for years. Several men, all wearing identical black suits, stood in a half circle, shooting the shit. I recognized Neck Beard. Side-eyeing me, he said something to the others.

"That guy doesn't like me," I said.

"Can you blame him?"

Raul crossed the floor littered with dirt, leaves, and empty Cheetos bags. He approached a man who might've been in charge. The head honcho looked me over. His thinning black hair was slicked back and shiny. Like a foreigner. He wore expensive Italian loafers.

Kersey.

I couldn't stop staring at the squareness of his jaw. He gave me a smile through veneered teeth. Tossing his toothpick, he walked toward me. From the way he moved, I could tell he'd done time. I didn't know what they expected me to do and stood at ease. He stopped about five feet in front of me, a good enough distance in case I tried the roundhouse kick he knew I was contemplating.

"Take off the cap," he said. "I want to see your face."

He spoke with an Eastern European accent he was trying hard to hide. It sounded sort of Russian, but different. I did as he asked, letting my raven hair fall over my shoulders. There should've been music. He grinned, and as the others crept closer, looked me up and down.

"Those clothes don't do you justice."

"Already fantasizing?"

Someone laughed and choked on something. Kersey pivoted. He glared at the tool, who was holding an e-cigarette. Excusing himself, he marched toward the vaper. From his expression, the dude had no clue what he'd done. I glanced at Raul, who stared at the ground. The boss grabbed the device, threw it down, and stomped on it like it was a snake.

"What did I tell you about smoking?" he said.

"It's not smoking. It's…it's vaping. I thought…"

Furious, Kersey stormed across the room and rummaged through a pile of junk on one of the old, splintered wood tables. When he returned, he was carrying a dull metal funnel sticky with hundred-year-old motor oil. He handed it to the butt-munch.

"Put this on," he said.

"What?"

"Put. It. On. Your. Head."

By now, the others had forgotten about me and watched the show. Thinking about running, I looked toward the exit. Neck Beard drilled me with his angry eyes.

Turning crimson, the hapless vaper took the funnel and tried positioning it on his good haircut while his boss waited. It kept slipping off. He worked at it until it was stationary.

"Nice," Kersey said. "Next time you want to vape or whatever, you let me know. Because I'll shove the thing so far up your ass, the smoke will come out the hat."

He swiped at the guy's head, knocking the funnel to the ground. The goof stepped back in line, holding his bright-red ear. Taking a breath, the boss straightened his jacket and returned to the task at hand. Stopping short, he took out his weapon and glanced at the Asian, who trotted over to the open door and pulled it closed. Everyone moved back.

The electricity was off, and we were in deep shadows. A few patches of afternoon light streamed in through the high, dirty windows. A ray surrounded me in a weak, glowing pool. Like I was an angel in a preschool pageant. This guy wasn't doing anything. He just stood there, looking me over.

"I'm Kersey," he said at last.

"Yeah, I heard."

"And you are?"

"Is that your first or last name?"

One of the background hyenas cleared his throat.

"Last," he said. "Why did you kill my nephew?"

"He posed a threat."

He pointed the weapon at me and, with no emotion, shot me in the thigh. The intense, red-hot pain made my leg buckle, and I fell to the floor. He seemed unimpressed.

"And what about the others?" he said.

"They would've raped and killed me. Or maybe the other way around. Who knows with ignorant mooks, am I right?"

"You always shoot people you don't know?"

"Only if they have it coming."

I knew I'd be dead soon and focused on my wound. It was better than looking at this bad actor from a low-budget action flick. Adrenalin should've made my heart race, but my pulse ran steady. Blood seeped through my pant leg, then abruptly stopped. The pain, searing at first, lessened.

Instead of going into shock, like most people, I recovered. When I got to my feet, the slug slid down the inside of my pant leg, where it landed on the floor with a soft chink.

The boss stared at the bullet, shiny with blood. Murmuring, the others came closer. He snapped his fingers. Raul trotted over, and retrieving the slug, delivered it. Kersey held it up to the light like it was a precious jewel.

No longer bleeding, I scanned the room for a way out. Furious, the boss tossed the spent round and fired at me again. This time, the bullet struck me in the shoulder. Though the force threw me back, I didn't fall. I stood there, biting down on the pain. Glaring at him.

It was the same as before. The wound bled for a bit and stopped. Straining to see my shoulder, I shook my arm. A fresh slug hit the floor. Kersey's men gasped.

"You wearing body armor?" he said. Then to Raul, "Cover me."

Putting his gun away, the slick-haired foreigner examined

my shoulder. He stuck his finger in the hole while I watched. I thought about crushing his windpipe, but I was worried he'd go for the head next time. He got down on one knee like he was proposing and felt up my leg. I glanced over at the others. To a man, they refused to make eye contact. Perplexed, he got up and, brushing off his pants, returned to the group.

"Go stand over there," he said.

He waved his gun toward a wall. I did as he asked. Making my way to the other side, I worried that he might shoot me in the back. Though my thigh and shoulder throbbed, it was nothing compared to the initial pain.

"Okay, that's good. Now, turn around."

As I faced the others, he pointed his gun at my head. This was it. No djinn black magic would save me from a bullet to the brain.

"Vincent told me they hit you with the car," he said. "And you walked it off."

"Turns out I wasn't hurt that bad."

"We'll see."

My heart rate steady, I ran through the scenarios in my head.

1. I make a run for it. The sliding door is closed. As I struggle to open it, everyone in the room opens fire on me. I die.
2. I come straight at Kersey. Unafraid, he raises his weapon and puts a bullet in my brain. Same result.
3. I dart sideways toward the three oil drums in the corner. They're too far away. Before I can get behind them, a million rounds take me down. Adios, muchacha.

No more time. I got ready to die.

He squeezed the trigger, and time slowed. Before the bullet left the chamber, my hands were up in front of my face, one over the other. The slug tore through my palms, then veered away from my head.

Kersey shook his head in disbelief. Frustrated, he mag-dumped me. The hot lead struck my chest, arms, and stomach. Screaming, I fell onto my back. With my eyes closed, I saw the djinn coming closer. The bullets floated up—away from me. Someone shouted while strange hands descended on me.

"I don't think she's dead," Raul said.

COLD WATER TRICKLED down my face and neck. I thought I recognized Bo watching over me, one eyebrow arched. It was Raul, holding a bottle of water. Lightly, he slapped my cheeks. I grabbed his wrist to make him stop.

"Can't believe you're alive," he said. "What are you?"

"Help me up."

We locked hands, and he pulled me to my feet. Staring at the spent, bloody slugs all around me, I rested my palms on my thighs. I needed a minute to gather my thoughts. Yeah, I was alive. But I was enraged too. Kersey and the others closed in, all of them armed. I didn't feel like being used for target practice again and gave them the death stare. They shrank back—except their boss.

"The rest of you wait outside," he said.

One by one, the others peeled away and shuffled out. Raul went last, closing the door after him. When we were alone, Kersey gave me a smile. He was no longer pointing his weapon at me. We stood close to each other, playing the quiet game. I used my peripheral vision to scope out my surroundings. That's when I spotted it—a narrow exit in the rear.

"You've had your fun," I said.

"What else can you do?"

"I'm not effing Wonder Woman."

He tried a rabbit punch. I blocked it easily and hit him with a spinning back fist. He stumbled but didn't fall. Straightening up, he grinned through bloody teeth.

"Krav maga," he said. "Impressive."

When he removed his jacket, I rolled my eyes. I'd wanted nothing more than to protect John and Consuelo. But this diddlefest had gone far enough. By now, he had taken off his belt and holster and rolled up his sleeves. He wore an intricate tattoo of a Slavic warlord on one forearm. Raising his fists, he bobbed and weaved like a boxer. It was a lame ploy to throw me off his fighting style.

He attempted a roundhouse kick, but he was stiff. I moved out of range, deflecting his leg with my hand, and punched him in the throat. He went down hard, choking and gasping for air. This was my chance.

Grabbing my cap, I ran full out toward the exit and flung the door open. Neck Beard was waiting for me. I didn't have time for this and front-kicked him in the groin. He crumpled to the ground, wailing. Taking his piece, I bolted.

I had no plan. There was a chance I could make it to Union Station and catch a train to somewhere far away. But I needed answers. And the only way to get them was to remain in LA. Maybe even return to Hellborn. For now, I'd settle on getting out of the immediate area.

Looking ridiculous in the tuxedo and cap, I ran until I reached the train station. I entered the lobby through glass doors with brass trim. The place was deserted. I stood there a minute, marveling at the architecture. The sea of leather chairs. The dark walnut. The colorful tile. Then, another flashback…

I was seventeen, in stressed jeans and a crop top. Standing in the middle of the lobby as throngs pushed past me. All I had with me was my purse. My brother came toward me, his arms out. He had on a combat utility uniform. I was so happy to see him.

"Bo!" I said, waving like I was in summer camp.

Dropping his duffel, he picked me up and spun me around. He kissed my cheek and smiled at the paperback sticking out of my purse.

"Always with the reading. So whadda you say to a Marine?"

"Oorah!"

"Come on, that the best you got?"

"OORAH!" My voice echoed through the lobby, making heads turn.

Bo laughed until he turned red.

Some old guy stood near me, mopping the floor. He stared at me as I made my way to a ticket booth. Before walking up, I checked my pockets to make sure I still had the wallet. A middle-aged African American woman in a dark sweater eyed me from behind the glass.

"I need some information," I said. "Where's a good place to buy clothes?"

She looked me over without judgment. "What are you in the mood for?"

I grabbed my lapel. "Anything but this."

She laughed and told me about the subway lines. When I said money wasn't a problem, she recommended the promenade in Santa Monica. She reminded me it was Christmas Day. Everything was closed.

"I forgot it's a holiday," I said.

"The stores are open again tomorrow. You know, for the sales. Make sure to get there early."

She directed me to the Expo line. I didn't have change. Taking pity, she broke a hundred-dollar bill for me. I turned to leave when I remembered something.

"What kind of architecture is this?"

"Spanish Colonial and Art Deco. Do you like it?"

"Yeah, I do. Thanks for everything."

"Good luck, honey," she said.

I hurried down the escalator to purchase my ticket. One of Kersey's men—the vaper minus the Tin Man hat—waited near the gates to the platform. Halfway down, I turned and ran back up. He yelled after me. I scanned the upper level. Clear.

Desperate, I ran past the ticket booths toward the entrance where I'd come in. The old janitor continued to mop. When Raul and Neck Beard walked in, I moved out of their line of sight. Across the way, there was a sign for the restrooms.

My dress shoes clacked as I darted across and slipped into the women's bathroom. Empty. I locked myself in a stall and climbed on top of the toilet. Holding my weapon in front of me, I waited.

I must've remained crouched for, like, an hour. No one ever came in, except the woman from the ticket booth. I watched her through the slit in the door as she washed her hands and hummed. After she left, I walked out and checked the corridor. No one was there.

Sprinting, I made it to the lobby entrance. At the light, I crossed the street and headed into what was left of LA's rich Spanish heritage—Olvera Street. Everything was closed. Hungry and thirsty, I moved past the shops, restaurants, and stands, glancing over my shoulder. When I'd reached the end, I spotted a Catholic church. La Placita. Would Kersey's goons look for me in there?

I entered through the red door. Services had ended for the day. An elderly Latina rearranged Baby Jesus in the crèche. As I weighed my options, a priest walked in and spoke to the woman in Spanish. From their conversation, they were getting ready to lock up.

When I was alone again, I ducked into a storage room.

Inside, there were piles of hymnals and wicker collection baskets. For the next half-hour, I waited. Outside, the sounds of random footsteps and jingling keys. Soon, the lights went out, and all was quiet. Nothing to do now but wait until morning.

I pushed the door open and did a quick sweep. When I was sure I was alone, I slid into a pew and stretched out to catch a few hours' sleep. For the first time since waking up in the death tank in the desert, I felt safe.

No one came to me in my dreams—not even Bo.

CHAPTER EIGHT

SPANISH-SPEAKING VOICES WOKE ME, and I sat up. A scattering of immigrants wearing their finest filed into the church. I wished I knew what time it was. As they took to the pews, I smoothed my hair and exited without making eye contact.

From the position of the sun, it looked like early morning. Merchants were getting their shops ready. I moved past, taking in the colorful Mexican dresses, leather goods, and toys. I was hungry, and the smell of food made it worse. But there wasn't time. Hoping for anonymity, I kept my head down as I made my way to Union Station.

At the light, I sprinted across the street, not slowing until I was inside the building. There were a lot more people than yesterday. Most were on their way to work. I hurried past the Wetzel's Pretzels and continued down the escalator.

With an all-day pass in my hand, I waited on the crowded platform. Kersey's men were nowhere in sight. In a few minutes, the train arrived. I checked my surroundings one last time and boarded, heading for a seat in the back. At last, I was on my way to Santa Monica.

The trip would take close to an hour. As we pulled out of

the station, I peered through the windows. Someone waited on the platform as others passed in front of him. He wasn't one of the boss's men. This one had on a gray suit. From his demeanor, it was clear he was looking for somebody. Putting him out of my mind, I closed my eyes.

Gently, someone shook me. Snapping awake, I looked up. A cute little Latino boy with missing front teeth grinned at me. His mom, a pleasant-looking woman with wiry hair, gave me a smile.

"This is the last stop," she said.

I took in my surroundings and exited the car with them. As they headed in the opposite direction, the little boy waved to me. A cool breeze greeted me as I walked along 5th Street toward Broadway. I wanted badly to get out of these clothes, but I was starving.

There was a place called Jinky's Cafe on 2nd. Inside, it was dead. I settled on the breakfast special. Thankfully, the server didn't comment on my mismatched outfit. When the food came, I stared at the plate. I couldn't remember the last time I'd eaten bacon and bit into a strip. The taste made me gag.

Grabbing a bunch of napkins, I spat everything out and washed down the sick with coffee. I forked a turkey sausage and took a whiff. Same deal—Puke City. Funny, I had no recollection of being a vegetarian.

The eggs and pancakes went down fine. I thought about the man in the gray suit. He reminded me of those dead guys I'd come across in the hospital at Hellborn. Coincidence? In my head, Bo's voice came over the horn loud and clear. It was as if he was standing behind me, speaking into my ear.

"Prioritize. What is the immediate threat?"

"Not Hellborn."

"Right. Then what?"

"Kersey."

"Chow time's over. Move your ass."

"Copy."

The server dropped off the check. He looked at me like I was a mental patient. I left cash on the table and went in search of clothes.

Reaching my destination, I stopped to assess the situation. The promenade was tree lined, dotted with old-fashioned lampposts and pop-ups. Lots of civilians—some with children. A few cops. There were plenty of stores to choose from on either side. I wasn't looking for anything fancy and decided on Brandy Melville.

As I approached the entrance, I spotted Neck Beard. *How in hell?* He stood next to a trash can, pounding down what looked like a red bean bun. Pivoting, I walked the other way. That's when I spotted Raul.

He was leaning against a lamppost, his arms folded. It was obvious he'd seen me. I pretended not to notice and made a quick detour past a movie theater. He ran after me.

Pushing past clumps of people with shopping bags, I tried getting lost. For a time, I thought I might be okay. I pressed myself against the wall and scanned the promenade. The hostile was nowhere in sight. I ducked into the nearest dress shop.

I pretended to look through the clearance dresses, all the while keeping my eyes on the front windows. A salesgirl who might've been Middle Eastern approached me. She did her best not to judge, but I could tell she wished I'd take my business elsewhere.

"Can I show you something?" she said.

"I'm good."

Raul appeared in the window, his back to me. The girl must've noticed the look on my face as he scanned the promenade, his phone pressed against his ear. She touched my arm and spoke low.

"I know this is none of my business," she said. "But is that guy bothering you?"

I wasn't good at playing the victim and kept it simple. "He's been following me all morning."

Glancing at him, she turned back to me. She was angry. "I'll take care of it."

I kept my eyes on the window. Out of nowhere, two Santa Monica beat cops appeared. As they questioned the suspect, he took out his wallet and showed them his ID.

"Come on," the girl said.

She led me past the register to the storage room. It was packed with returns—dresses and shoes, mostly. I spotted an exit. She nodded, and I walked toward it.

"Thanks," I said.

"Stay safe."

The door led to an alley. I looked to my right. There was the street. When I turned left, Neck Beard grinned at me. Before I could reach my weapon, he hit me with a taser to the neck.

Blackness swallowed me like a bad night in Baghdad.

I WAS IN A DREAM—NOT the one I'd awakened from at Hellborn...

The overhead lights hurt my eyes. Voices chattered over a PA system. I was in a corridor with beige walls and a speckled tile floor. Doctors in medical lab coats and nurses in lavender uniforms moved past like wraiths. They ignored me and everyone else. I had a powerful urge to run.

There was a long line of men and women, and I stood toward the end. All of us were barefoot. We wore skimpy patient gowns with a field of lilacs printed on them. They barely covered our asses. The faces looked familiar. Some were the people I'd seen in the room with the tanks—all dead now.

When I turned around, Blevins was grinning. I think he had a thing for me. He moved closer and stage-whispered.

"Want to see me dance naked?" he said.

"I'd rather chew on broken glass."

I pulled my gown closed and held onto it. Craning my neck, I peered up the line, looking for Tyler Berry.

Two orderlies escorted patients, one by one, into a private room. No way to see inside. People went in but none came out. Roach motel. The line moved quickly. Before long, I was at the front. Nervous, I looked at Blevins.

"When do we leave for Afghanistan?" I said.

"I always knew you were a joker."

An orderly led me through. Behind me, Blevins called out one last time.

"See you on the other side," he said.

When I came to, I was slumped on a steel chair in a storage area enclosed by a chain link cage. My hands and feet were bound with zip ties, my cap nowhere in sight. Someone had tied a bandanna over my mouth. Tasted like ass. Far off, the squeal of tires on cement. Outside the cage, there were diagonal white lines painted on the floor between the concrete columns. Great, trapped in a parking structure.

Kersey stepped out of the shadows, accompanied by Raul and Neck Beard. His face was bruised, which filled me with pride. Tossing his toothpick, he pointed at me. The Asian hobbled over and removed the gag.

"How'd you get the limp?" I said. "Fall off a scooter?"

He made a move to backhand me when his boss raised a warning finger. Groaning with frustration, he rejoined the others. Kersey whispered something to his men, and they left us alone. He paced in front of me, saying nothing. I tried breaking the tension.

"How's the jaw?" I said.

He rubbed it, wincing. "I've had worse."

"I gotta ask. How did you find me?"

"Not hard. One of my people saw you at Union Station."

Shit. "Who was it?"

"Guy who manages the Wetzel's Pretzels spotted you when you walked past. I own the store."

"You're a legitimate businessman?"

"Sometimes. We were with you the whole time, all the

way to Santa Monica." He gave me a secret smile. "The woman on the train who spoke to you?"

"The one with the kid?"

"My housekeeper."

"Un-effing-believable."

He stood in front of me, his hands folded. "Do you have a name yet?"

"I can't remember it."

"Are you telling me the truth?"

Weary, I shook my head and glared at him. "Yeah. It's the truth."

"Okay, whatever your name is," he said. "Here's the deal. I've decided not to kill you."

"What a relief."

He started pacing again. "You're impressive." He laughed. "The thing with your hands. And the bullets. I can't figure out—"

"Oh, do go on."

He placed his hands on the arms of the chair and leaned in. "How would you feel about working for me?"

Well, that was random. "What about your dead nephew?" I said.

He swatted away the thought. "My sister's kid. The skur-wiel has always been a pain in my ass. Thought he knew everything. Between you and me, you did me a favor."

"And the others?"

"Friends of his. Forget about them. I have important business, and I could use someone like you."

"What's the catch?"

"No catch."

I stared at the hole in my pant leg where he'd shot me. "There's always a catch."

He gave me a wide grin. "Smart too. Okay, what we do is not—"

"Legal?"

"You'll make good money, and you'd be repaying your debt to me."

"What about your grieving sister?"

"Let me worry about her."

I thought over the offer. Weird. And yet…

"So, is *Kersey* your real name?"

"It's Buchinsky. I changed it when I came over."

"From?"

"Small town in Poland," he said. "You wouldn't know it."

Anger welled up inside me. If it weren't for the zip ties, I might've taken him out right there. But one thing was for sure. I had no idea who I was or why I'd been kept prisoner in a secret facility. Truth was, I needed answers more than I needed to kill a Polish gangster. Going off on my own might not be the best solution right now. This guy had to be connected. Maybe he could help me.

"Two conditions," I said.

"Go on."

"The old couple at the café? You agree to leave them alone —forever. They're not part of this."

"Done. And the second thing?"

"Untie me, and I'll tell you."

He took out a pocket knife and, looking at me warily, sliced the ties. I stood up and stretched. My body wasn't a hundred percent. To get the blood flowing, I touched my toes a couple of times. When I was done, I looked him in the eye. He gripped his weapon tighter. Funny. Under the smooth, salesy exterior, this mook was scared of me. I could use that at some point.

"I want you to help me find out who I am," I said.

"You were serious about the name thing?"

"You must know people."

He looked up and to the side. "Okay, deal."

"I need you to look into an outfit called Baseborn Identity Research. You're not writing this down."

Reddening, he took out a Montblanc pen and a small black notebook. "They here in town?"

"I guess. I'll let you know when I find out more."

"Are they looking for you?"

I thought about the man in the gray suit at Union Station. "Could be."

We walked up one level. A black town car sat parked across two spaces.

"When do I start?" I said.

"Now. But first, we need to get you some decent clothes. I run a class outfit."

Raul sat behind the wheel. Neck Beard was nowhere in sight.

"Also, you need a name," the boss said. "And papers. Let's see. How about Jane Doe? Catchy, right?"

"Seriously?"

Like a gentleman, he took my hand and motioned me into the front passenger seat. He sat in the back. In a few minutes, we were on Ocean Avenue heading north. We pulled into the Jonathan Club, where Kersey had an important meeting. He climbed out and, giving me one of his game show host smiles, put a fresh toothpick between his lips.

"Be seeing you, Jane," he said.

He strode into the building like he owned the place, and Raul pulled into traffic. Soon, we were heading east on the 10 Freeway toward LA.

"I think he likes you."

"Just what I always wanted," I said. "A rich boyfriend."

PART TWO

SUIT & TIE

THE TAILOR HAD an office on Santee in the garment district. We had to climb four flights of stairs because the stupid elevator was out. Never mind, I needed the cardio. When we reached the fifth floor, Raul directed me down a dark corridor smelling of resin and cigars. A door with frosted glass read MOSKOWITZ & SONS. A buzzer sounded as we walked in.

"I'm curious," I said. "What's with all the toothpicks?"

"Helps Kersey stay off the cigarettes."

Like the rest of the building, the outer office was nothing to speak of. There was old, dark furniture that belonged in a museum. A set of ancient wood filing cabinets. A small desk with a faded green blotter. An old-fashioned black rotary dial telephone. And a ceiling fan out of a Raymond Chandler novel, squeaking with each labored rotation. Near the desk stood a door partway open. Raul walked up to it and poked his head through.

"Nate?" he said.

An impeccably dressed woman appeared. She had on thick glasses, a long, dark wool skirt down to her ankles, a white ruffle blouse, and manicured red nails.

"Brought you a new victim."

"You're recruiting women now?" Her accent sounded familiar.

"You know Kersey."

She came closer to get a better look at me. Though she was past fifty, I considered her attractive. Her face was modestly made up. She wore her graying brown hair pulled back in a short ponytail, resulting in a more youthful appearance. Her hands looked arthritic, the knuckles swollen. She gave me the once-over while clucking her tongue. I amused myself imagining what she must be thinking as she examined the bullet-ridden tuxedo.

"Is this blood?" she said. Then to Raul, "You wait out here."

The back room was jammed with tailor's dummies, bolts of fabric, and suits and dresses in different stages of completion. Long tables held patterns, scissors, giant spools of colored thread on metal spindles, and three industrial sewing machines.

The demure tailor motioned for me to stand next to the window. She adjusted her glasses and began measuring me. When she brought the cloth tape measure near my breasts, I grabbed her hand. I caught the surprised look on her face and let go.

"Don't know why I..."

Unfazed, she continued taking my bust measurements. "You're tall."

"Nate's a cool name." I sounded like an idiot.

"It's Natalia."

"Who's Moskowitz?"

"Former tenants."

"How come you never changed the sign?"

"Why should I spend money?"

"Oh, I thought—"

"You ask too many questions."

"Why does everyone keep saying that?"

When she'd finished, she led me over to a wall next to the fabric.

"Mr. Kersey insists on virgin wool flannel," she said. "The same kind Prada uses. Let's see… Yes, this one."

She pointed at a bolt of black fabric. I'm no fashionista, but to me it looked beautiful. I reached over to touch it.

"Go ahead. You can feel the quality."

A little embarrassed, I slid my fingers on the wool. Though I remembered little about my life, I couldn't imagine having worn anything as nice as this.

"I'll make you five suits to start," she said. "You'll need other clothes. For evening and such. There are shops all around here. Or try Nordstrom."

"What about shirts?"

"White silk blouse with a French placket. Simple but stylish. I'll make you a dozen."

She stepped back and made a face. Shaking her head, she muttered something in a foreign language.

"I cannot let you leave in this condition," she said. "Take off those filthy things. Dressing room's over there."

She pointed. Like a child buying clothes with her mother, I tramped over to the small space. After closing the door, I stripped. *Aw man, no underwear.*

"Uh, hello?" I said. "I don't have any…"

Something flew over the door and landed on the floor. Bra, panties, and knee-high stockings, all with the price tags attached. In another beat, my wallet sailed in.

"Thank you."

I stepped out in my skivvies. The room was cold. The tailor pulled apart a finished black suit at the seams. Working quickly, her concentration was uninterrupted by my presence. She reached across the table and grabbed a white silk blouse.

"Put this on," she said. "And remember, hand wash in cold water only."

I did as she asked. Though it fit tight across the chest, I guessed it was good enough for me to be seen in public.

"I thought you had to sew these," I said.

"I made that one a long time ago. It was a, how do you say…trial?"

She went back to work and, before long, had reassembled the suit. After a quick press, she handed me the pants. I climbed into the toasty fabric. The pants were the right length for heels and fit well around the waist and butt. Picking up the jacket, she helped me into it. The sleeves were perfect. I couldn't believe it had been a man's suit.

"Tak lepiej," she said. "Eh, much better. Now for the shoes."

She dug through a plastic tub in the corner and found a pair of Ferragamo black pumps. *She just has these lying around?*

"I hope you're a nine."

"Close enough."

She handed me a hairbrush and waited as I worked my way through, grimacing from the pain. I tried not to think about all the split ends. She used her fingers to arrange it.

"You have good hair," she said. "Strong and thick."

"I get it from my mother." *Okay, where did that come from?*

She escorted me to a small room. One wall was flat white. In front of it, there was a camera on a tripod and lights with silver umbrellas on either side. After positioning me, she got behind the camera.

"Smile," she said.

When we'd reached the outer office, I thanked her. On an impulse, I gave her a hug. She buttoned my jacket and gave me an appraising look.

"You're a nice-looking girl. Even in a man's suit."

Raul was there, reading something on his phone. He glanced at my new outfit, then let his eyes wander back to the phone screen. Nate walked up to him and, noticing a stain on his lapel, clucked her tongue.

"You should take better care of your clothes, young man," she said.

He side-eyed me. "I ran into some trouble. When will the suits be ready?"

"In a few weeks." Then to me, "I have some girls helping me."

I wasn't used to heels. Walking toward the door, my ankle gave out, and I was suddenly shorter by four inches. Oblivious, Raul kept walking. Struggling, I got the shoe back on and hurried after him.

When we were on the street, I stopped him. I wasn't the kind of girl who fished for compliments. And I was the last person to try to impress anyone, least of all this mook. But come on. Not even an off-color joke for the pretty lady?

"Well?" I said.

"What?"

"For shit's sake, how do I look?"

His eyes traveled from my shoes to my hair. "Better. Let's go." Then when he reached the door, "You have something in your teeth."

"Shut up."

At the car, I hesitated before getting in.

"Forget something?" he said.

"I was told to buy other clothes."

"Like what?"

"Oh, I don't know, Raul. Underwear? Jeans and a few tops? And maybe some different shoes. These heels are killing me."

What I heard him say next sounded like *tan cansona*. I was a pain in the ass now?

Despite the attitude, he agreed with me. We continued walking, and I thought some more about the tailor. How in the world had she become mixed up with a guy like Kersey?

"So, Nate," I said as we passed a men's shop. "What's her story?"

"She came over a few years ago."

"From?"

"Poland."

"I don't get it. Why would she—"

"Kersey is her son," he said.

AFTER TWO HOURS OF SHOPPING, I'd had enough. Plus, my feet were in agony. And I was starving. I dumped my bags in the trunk and got into the car.

"Don't you ever get hungry?" I said.

"I could eat."

We drove for a few minutes through downtown LA, heading north on San Pedro. Raul made a left on 3rd and pulled into a parking structure. I was grateful Grand Central Market was only a short distance away.

It was noisy inside. The smell of the food coming from the stalls was intoxicating. Ignoring the stares, I went in search of potato tacos. After three tries, I found a guy who served them. They weren't as good as Consuelo's, but at this point…

We found seats in the food court and people-watched as we ate lunch. I sneaked a look at my companion's plate. Six little street tacos and a variety of salsas and chopped onions in a nice presentation.

"What are those?" I said.

"Tacos de buche." He caught my expression. "Pork throat and stomach."

Even the sound of it made me ill, never mind the smell. I focused on keeping down my gorge as he happily dug in. A flashback bulldozed my head…

I was a kid again. Outside in the backyard with Bo. Beyond lay the corn maze. We'd been doing calisthenics all morning. Him wearing camo pants and a khaki wifebeater. Me in gym shorts and a tank top.

He offered me a paper plate with a white bread sandwich. When the food started moving, I backed away.

"What is it?" I said, eyeing the plate.

"I made you a sandwich."

"No."

"It's good. I want you to eat it."

"You eat it." I crossed my arms and stuck out my tongue.

"You have a choice, stoopy. Eat this effing sandwich. Or you can drop and give me what you owe me."

A fat, juicy pink worm wriggled its way out from under the bread. Furious, I knocked the plate out of my brother's hand. The worms went everywhere.

I started in on my push-ups while Bo counted me down from a hundred.

"Hello?"

When I looked up, Raul was grinning at me. I hated to admit it, but his smile was infectious. I thought I was a fast eater, but he was ridiculous. He'd pounded down a plate of street tacos in a couple of bites. Instead of food, balled-up napkins were piled on the plate.

"What?" I said. "Stop looking at me."

Keeping my head down, I finished my lunch. When I made eye contact again, he was shaking his head.

"I can't figure you out."

"Likewise."

"And you legit don't remember anything? Or maybe it's an act."

"It's not."

I wiped my mouth and pushed my plate aside. The conversation had taken a dark turn, and it made me mad. I took a breath and drank some water. If I was going to work for these guys, I'd have to find my happy place—fast.

"Look," I said. "I remember some things. Bits and pieces from when I was a kid." I decided not to mention my brother.

"Where are you from?"

"Medellín."

Though I wasn't into the Colombian, I wanted to know his story. His fingers were covered in small scars. Made me think he might've been a fisherman back in the old country. Somehow, I couldn't picture him baiting hooks for a living.

"Where'd you get those scars?"

I knew I was wasting my time. He looked at me, betraying nothing. I was prepared for him to tell me to mind my own effing business. He pointed at me.

"Same place you got that."

Confused, I ran my finger along the right side of my neck, where I found scar tissue I didn't even know I had. Why hadn't I noticed it before? I racked my brain, trying to remember how the mark had gotten there. But like a steel door, my mind remained shut.

"That's... A dog bit me."

"Uh-huh."

"I'm serious. It's one of the few things I can remember. It was a stray. I was playing with it, and—"

"Okay." From his expression, he didn't give two shits.

I redirected. "You think Vincent is still mad at me?"

"For turning his balls into tonsils? What do you think?"

"Teach him to be prepared next time."

"I'll be sure to tell him."

We packed up our trash and walked outside. I checked to make sure there were no men in gray suits lurking. For some reason, he thought it was funny.

"What are you doing?" he said.

"Nothing. Let's go."

The light turned red as we exited the parking structure.

"Hey," I said. "Do you think maybe there's a bookstore around here?"

IT WAS LATE when we left The Last Bookstore. We'd spent a couple of hours, and it was hard for me to leave. I imagined living in a tent beneath the Book Arch Wall. Happily reading and eating take-out. No Kersey. No Hellborn. No djinn.

As we made our way through downtown, I began wondering where I'd sleep. It occurred to me that when I agreed to work for Kersey, I'd neglected to include a no-nudity clause in my contract. We approached a Mediterranean-themed apartment complex overlooking the 110 Freeway, and I tensed. Raul pulled into a visitor space in the underground parking.

"Is this where I'm staying?" I said.

"Nice, huh?"

"Do you live here too?"

He pretended not to hear me. We rode the elevator to the lobby, both of us loaded down with bags. As we approached the front desk, the doorman offered to assist.

"This is Jane," the Colombian said.

The doorman returned to his station. He was a squirrelly-looking man—maybe fifty. With beard stubble, weak eyebrows, and bad breath, he took in every bit of me. I imagined putting his eye out with my heel.

"Last name?"

"Just Jane."

"Okay, Ms. Jane. I'm Dick."

Yes, you are. He unlocked a cabinet and removed a large manila envelope filled with papers. Opening it, he pulled out a smaller envelope. Inside was a shiny new key.

"All of the information about The Borgia is in the envelope," he said. "Your key works on your apartment door and the emergency gate in the parking garage. Don't lose it, or I'll have to charge you twenty-five dollars to replace it."

We rode the elevator to the eighth floor. The hallway was well lit, and the carpet was new.

"The Borgia?" I said. "What is this, a hotel for assassins?"

"They have a steam room."

When we got to my door, I tried the key and walked in. The apartment was small, but clean and fully furnished. There was a modern kitchen, with cupboards finished in dark gray and granite counters.

"Anyone else staying here?" I said.

"I forgot to tell you. You're sharing with Vincent."

"Hilarious."

I toured the living room. A huge TV dominated one wall. Raul set my bags down and headed for the door.

"Wait," I said. "What happens now?"

"Get some sleep. I'll pick you up in the morning. Be ready at eight. And wear the suit."

He was like a machine, and it was getting on my nerves. I was used to Tyler. We were simpatico. This guy was a puzzle.

"Thanks. For taking care of me, I mean."

"Honestly, I was hoping to get you killed."

"Yeah, well. Maybe next time."

He gave me a smile. It was nice. Then he handed me my packet.

"Make sure you're on time," he said and walked out.

Lingering near the door, I took in my surroundings. One thought played over and over like a scratchy tune on an old record player. *What are you doing here?* Sure, I'd busted out of Hellborn. But soon, someone would discover the empty tank, and they'd realize I was alive. These people had murdered John and Consuelo's son. They'd have no compunction about taking care of a rogue test subject.

I wished I could remember. There was no way to tell how long I was a prisoner. Or why I'd ended up there to begin with. I was a Marine fighting in Afghanistan. What in holy hell was I doing in California? And where was my squad? Those others in the tanks? Though I'd seen them in a flashback, only Blevins had been with me in the White Mountains. And he wasn't talking.

Time for a drink.

Exploring the kitchen, I found the cupboards fully stocked with canned and dried goods. The refrigerator was stainless steel. When I opened the freezer, I found beef, chicken, and fish. The thought of cooking up flesh nauseated me. I'd have to ditch those later. Below in the other section, there was fresh milk and produce. And on the bottom shelf, three bottles of an Italian white wine. I wanted something stronger.

Going through the lower cabinets, I discovered the liquor stash. There were bottles of pricey vodka, single malt whiskey, gin, and tequila. I opted for the latter and made a note to stock up on mescal. What the Zwicks had served me at the café was excellent.

A bowl of fruit sat on the counter next to the espresso machine. I cut up a lime and got out the salt shaker and some ice. The Patrón was exquisite. I dumped the contents of the manila envelope. There was a glossy brochure describing the amenities—private gym, indoor swimming pool, steam room, and sauna. I spotted a xeroxed copy of the house regs and a remote for the garage gate.

Glancing at my hands, I noticed the bullet wounds Kersey had given me. They were nothing more than infinitesimal scars now. Another gift from the djinn or whatever. I topped up my drink and wandered into the bathroom. The mirror was spotless, and I made goofy faces at myself.

It was bad enough I didn't know my name—I didn't even know how old I was. I guessed early twenties. Trying to remember school and old boyfriends was useless. There was nothing there but my brother. I was tied to him—he had to be real. But what about the rest of my family? Father? Mother? It was no good. It was as if a dense fog had filled my head. All I knew for sure was the here and now.

I moved closer to the mirror and examined the crescent-shaped scar on my neck. It looked old and resembled a bite, not quite two inches. If my body was capable of rapid healing, why did I have the scar? I rubbed the shiny raised tissue with my finger. A man's voice whispered in my ear, hoarse and slurry.

"Good girl."

Shuddering, I tried shaking off the creepy vibe that seemed to surround me. That voice—it was a thread. But I wasn't sure I should pull it. I took another sip of my drink and stretched out on my bed. What had I gotten myself into? Whatever it was, it couldn't be any worse than what I'd left behind in the desert.

Hellborn.

Had I escaped from hell? I visualized the dark-haired alpha lying in the pit. The intense eyes. The desperation. Whatever program I'd been part of, there was an excellent chance I'd end up like him. Crazy and suicidal.

The trick was to put that off as long as possible.

RAUL PICKED me up at 0800 sharp. I'd washed and pressed the shirt. Instead of the heels Nate lent me, I decided on soft black Italian booties—M. Gemi. Though they were expensive, he sprang for three pairs. They weren't the best shoes to run in if something happened. But they went well with the suit.

We arrived at the Clock Tower Building on Santa Monica Boulevard. I recognized the parking structure where Kersey had held me, but I decided not to say anything. The Colombian walked me into the Art Deco lobby and pointed at the bank of elevators.

"You're not coming with?" I said.

"He's on the ninth floor. Remember, don't ask a lot of questions."

"Anything else I should know?"

"Don't stare at his lazy eye."

"What?"

"You'll be fine."

He brushed the invisible dust from my shoulders. Was macho man flirting? It's always the quiet ones, am I right? Thanking him, I proceeded to the elevators.

. . .

Kersey's office was decorated in muted colors and simple, expensive furniture. I suspected his mother had something to do with the decor. I stood at ease, waiting for him to get off the phone. He spoke in Spanish. Though I wasn't fluent, I knew he was negotiating a rate for a delivery. I caught the word *entrega*. When he'd finished, he set down the phone and looked me over.

"Much better," he said. "You should do something with your hair."

"Like what?"

"Do I look like a stylist? A trim, maybe—what do I know? There's a place downstairs. Mention my name, and they'll take you right away."

I noticed the manicured nails. This guy paid attention to detail, and I was all about the details.

"Thanks for the clothes," I said.

"Don't thank me. It comes out of your pay. Oh…"

He withdrew a bulging white envelope from a side drawer and tossed it over to me. Inside was a pile of crisp hundred-dollar bills.

"That's an advance. I cover the rent and utilities. You buy your food, clothes, and anything else you want. No drugs. If I hear you're doing 8-balls, I swear I'll find a way to kill you."

"Copy. What about weapons?"

"I was getting there. We supply everything. Ammo too."

"Guess I'm all set."

"Not quite."

Coming around the desk, he led me to a side cabinet. He slid the door open and removed a manila envelope, a Glock 19, and four mags. Then he poured out the envelope's contents on top of the cabinet. US passport, Social Security card, driver's license—and a black flip phone I recognized. Raul had the same one. I picked up the device.

"That's a Motorola Razr," he said. "It's the only phone we use."

"Why?"

"They're burners with the GPS disabled."

"Who are we hiding from?"

"You get paid on Fridays. Every two weeks, you exchange the phone for another one."

"Must cost you a fortune."

"I bought a ton of these when the company stopped making them. I have enough for a lifetime. I'm assuming you know how to drive?"

"Sure." I had no effing clue whether I did or didn't.

The photo on the driver's license was the one Nate had taken. Instead of white, the background was now blue. The name Jane Doe was printed on the front, along with a Los Angeles mailing address. The passport had the same photo, this time with a different background.

"Why the Social Security card?" I said.

"I run everything as a legitimate business."

"What's my job title?"

"Security Consultant." He tapped the driver's license. "Anybody asks you if that's your real name—cops or whatever—you say you had it legally changed."

"From what?"

"Karla Nowak. Your parents were from Laski, Poland."

"Laski. Is that where you're from?"

"Your parents are both dead, and you don't speak Polish."

"I could learn. Where did I grow up?"

"All over. Enough with the questions."

He handed me the weapon. There was nothing in the magazine well. I pulled the slide back and peered inside the chamber. Empty. I grabbed a full mag and slapped it in, which loaded a bullet into the chamber. He opened the drawer again and took out a box of ammo. I released the mag, topped it off with an extra bullet, and reinserted it.

"Good," he said and handed me another document. "Concealed carry permit."

"Where's the holster?"

"Gówno. Here, take mine."

He peeled back his jacket, revealing a Bravo Concealment holster, and removed his weapon. We unfastened our belts. He slid off the holster and handed it to me. I looped my belt through it on the right, placed my weapon in it, and buttoned my jacket.

"So what's my assignment?" I said.

"Raul will fill you in. I don't want you to do anything right now. Your job is to watch and learn. And don't let what happens get to you. Women tend to—"

"Please don't."

"Right. Don't let your emotions get to you is all I'm saying. Happens to everybody. You do as you're told, and everything will go like clockwork."

I took the extra mags and papers, and he walked me to the door.

"Check in with me tonight," he said. "Boxwood Restaurant. Nine o'clock. You'll need to put on something different."

"I was starting to like this suit."

"Wear a cocktail dress. Black. Gordon likes things classy. Got any jewelry?"

"I'll pick some up," I said. "Later."

When I reached the lobby, Raul was waiting for me. I noticed his shoes were newly shined. I grabbed a handful of hair and showed it to him.

"I was told I need a haircut," I said.

"That's cool."

"Also, I've got to pick up some fake jewelry. Good thing you bought me that little black dress."

"Dinner at Boxwood, right? He ask you to look classy?"

"He mentioned some guy named Gordon. Is he the owner?"

"You never heard of Gordon Ramsay?" He looked all butthurt.

"I can't remember. How many women are in Kersey's operation anyway?"

"Two. Nate and you."

"Maybe we should start a book club," I said.

At the salon, they cut and flat-ironed my hair into a bob. I was so impressed with the result, I purchased a device from them. As usual, Raul didn't say anything.

He took me to a jewelry store in the promenade and let me go nuts. I picked out high-quality costume jewelry to go with the dress and the gun. Afterward, we stopped for coffee. I spotted the woman from the dress shop—the one who'd helped me. We made eye contact, and she gave me a smile. I walked over.

"I love your hair," she said. "Hey, isn't he the guy who—?"

"Boyfriend. We, uh, we worked things out. I told him next time he tries getting rough, I'll rip off his ball sack and feed it to my gecko."

"Nice." She frowned at the Colombian. "He makes you dress alike?"

I shook her hand and slipped her five bills. Her mouth fell open.

"Thanks for everything."

"Any time, sista."

We returned to our car and headed east on the 10, then South on the 5 toward San Diego. I had no clue what would happen next.

"Friend of yours back there?"

"She thinks you're too controlling," I said.

CHAPTER
FOURTEEN

WE ARRIVED at Otay Mesa Detention Center in the late afternoon. The place was enormous. A chain-link fence topped with razor wire surrounded drab beige and brown buildings. ICE agents processed what seemed like hundreds of newly arrived immigrants. I had no idea what Kersey wanted here. But my orders were to watch and learn, which meant keeping my pie hole shut. Raul pulled into a handicap parking space and turned off the engine.

"Wait here," he said.

While he crossed the parking lot, I scanned the perimeter. A sea of armed ICE agents stood guard over Latino men, women, and children waiting to be processed. The Colombian met a guy in his fifties wearing a Sig Sauer P320 sidearm. His beer gut prevented his shirt from staying tucked in. Our government at work. After a quick exchange, the slob led him into the main building.

Though it was late December, it was hot. Grabbing a water bottle, I got out and twisted from side to side to get the kinks out. My body was more responsive now, better than when I'd emerged from the tank at Hellborn. Three children appeared at my side, smiling like cherubs. One of them—a mop-haired boy—eyed the water bottle. Rolling my eyes, I handed it over. He took a swig and passed it down the line.

Everyone here spoke Spanish with different accents. Some pleaded with volunteer advocates, asking about a court date for their hearing. Others looked after small, crying children. The kids were tired, hungry, and scared. If this was our idea of fixing the illegals problem, we'd already screwed the pooch.

Nearby, a volunteer tried speaking with an agent. Screaming, the tool ordered her to mind her own business. When she made the mistake of touching his arm, he went for his weapon. Everything in me said to clock him, but I wasn't supposed to draw attention. Then, a break. A supervisor showed up and defused the situation.

Raul was away a long-ass time. By the time he returned, the sun had gone down, and I was alone. I noticed him waving me over and followed him into the complex.

Beer Gut led us down a long, well-lit corridor with a grimy floor. A giant Christmas tree stood in the corner, with a pile of fake presents haphazardly arranged underneath. The clacks of our shoes on linoleum echoed as we made our way down what seemed like a city block toward the rear of the building. With each step, the agent's keys jingled like reindeer bells.

We passed through another set of locked double doors, out the back, and into a courtyard. Another guard—some lanky dude with zits and armed with an AR-15—watched over a group of six children. They looked to be as old as twelve and as young as five. *Where are the parents?*

The agent in charge gazed at the children, then turned to us. He seemed weary, his eyes sad. Whatever he was doing was off the books.

"Van's out back," he said. "Be careful."

"Always." The Colombian handed him an envelope. Then to me, "Go back to the car and wait. As soon as I leave the facility, follow me. I'll be in a white van."

"Copy."

"And stop saying 'copy.'"

As the agent in charge escorted me out, a little girl sobbed. An older one told her in Spanish to be quiet. Outside, I got into the town car. I wasn't sure yet whether I knew how to drive and hoped for the best.

The skinny pizza-faced guard walked out, away from the building. Something about him wasn't right. I suddenly recalled an incident in Afghanistan. Before that disastrous night raid, we'd questioned a villager about insurgents hiding among the locals. With huge crooked teeth, he assured us only women, children, and old men lived in the town—no fighters.

This idiot reminded me of the traitorous villager. He made a call, his eyes darting left to right as he spoke. I considered alerting Raul. But being a noob, I didn't know the situation. Maybe everything was normal. I decided to let it go. Just in case, I used my phone to take his photo.

Soon, an unmarked van left the premises. Beer Gut stood across the way and gave me a nod. I checked my mirrors and made sure no one was behind me. Carefully, I backed out. Putting the car in drive, I edged forward. I slammed on the brakes when a stray dog ran out in front of me. Stupidly, he sat in the middle of the road, daring me to hit him. A quick blast of the horn, and he was gone.

I got onto Calzada del a Fuente and followed the Colombian, who by now was traveling east toward Campo Road. The van made its way up the 94, maintaining a steady speed. It was full dark now, and I wondered where we were headed. Okay, so I wasn't allowed to ask questions. But I couldn't help thinking about those kids. I assumed the worst.

We'd made it as far as Jamacha. Out of the darkness, a

black Lincoln Navigator shot past me and forced its way in between the van and me. Raul sped up, with the other vehicle hot on his tail. As I struggled to keep up, I wondered if the pursuers realized I was a part of this thing. Now a burst of gunfire. The van swerved dangerously, then recovered.

"So much for *like clockwork*," I said and punched down on the gas.

FIFTEEN

FISHTAILING, the van skidded off the road and came to a jagged halt in the sand. Raul climbed out of the vehicle—weapon raised—and crouched behind the driver's side door. The Navigator stopped a hundred feet away. Two men with guns emerged.

I sped past. Taking the crest of a hill, I slowed and parked in darkness. All I had was my Glock. I needed better fire-power. As a gun battle raged below, I popped the trunk and spotted a thin metal handle under the carpet. When I yanked on it, I found a cache of weapons—one of which was an AR-15. I checked the chamber, flipped off the safety, and inserted a 60-round mag. Grabbing two smaller mags, I sprinted down the road and took cover behind a tall, twisted saguaro.

A hostile lay next to the Navigator. The other was crouched behind the car door, shooting at the van. Raul remained hidden, returning fire when he could. He had a Glock and nothing else, and I worried that he'd run out of ammo.

Despite the danger, my pulse ran normal. I took a breath and made my move. Walking toward the Navigator, I shot at the attacker. Startled, he fired back. He had a Tavor X95 bullpup—a nasty weapon. The sting of 9mm rounds tore up my arms, making me stumble. Enraged, I charged him.

Surprised, he gawped at me. His hesitation cost him. I killed him with a quick burst of fire to the head. When I was done with him, there was nothing left of his face. I made sure no one else was hiding inside the vehicle. Stepping away, I heard a groan—the other hostile. I finished him too.

"Jane!"

When I looked over, Raul was waving at me. I ran toward him, leaving a trail of spent slugs in the sand.

"You okay?" I said.

Seeing the blood, I knelt to examine his shoulder. He pushed my hands away and stood.

"Never mind that. Check on the kids."

I marched to the rear of the van. The doors were riddled with bullet holes. Inside, I found the little girl from before, frozen and staring at me. She was covered in blood.

"Tranquila," I said, putting away my weapon.

Telling the child to relax was crazy, but what else could I do? I checked her over, starting with her face and neck. The blood wasn't hers. The oldest—a boy with dark hair—lay toward the back. The others stood near him, silent. He didn't move. A young boy of around eight pointed at him.

"Está muerto," he said like it was nothing.

He didn't have to say those words. It was obvious the other kid was dead. The Colombian joined me, nursing a bleeding shoulder and carrying a first aid kit. I dug around inside the box and found a QuikClot pack. He tore off his jacket and shirt, revealing tattoos on his arms and chest. Probing the wound, I couldn't help noticing all the scars.

"Nate's gonna kill us for trashing her suits," I said.

"She's used to it."

"You're lucky. Looks like the bullet entered under the clavicle and exited."

"Stop talking and patch me up."

I cleaned the wound as best I could and applied a bandage to the front and back. When I'd finished, he got dressed.

"What now?" I said.

"I'll make the delivery. You get back to LA for your meeting."

"Screw that, I'm coming with you. What if you pass out? Those kids could—"

"I said no." His eyes were fierce. Then, "Be careful going back."

"You too." I wanted to throttle him for his stupid man stubbornness. "Who were those guys?"

"The competition."

"How'd they find out?"

"Someone at the detention center tipped them off. Kersey will find out who and take care of it."

While the rest of the kids waited near the van, we climbed in to retrieve the boy's body. Outside, I stopped and addressed the others.

"¿Cómo se llama?" I said.

The little girl looked at me, too scared to cry. "Guillermo."

We carried the body a ways off in the desert and left it. On an impulse, I went through the boy's pockets and found a photograph. It had been taken in front of a small concrete house with a corrugated tin roof. Surrounded by grinning brothers and sisters, he looked fearless.

"Take care, Guillermo," I said. "You deserved better."

I returned the photo. Maybe someone would find him and give him a decent burial. Or the vultures would take care of the remains. Either way, he had no more worries.

Raul secured the little girl in the front passenger seat. After getting the others settled in the back, I shut the rear doors. The Colombian said nothing. Instead, he climbed in and drove off, leaving me with the empty desert and a cold, starry sky.

Before returning to my car, I went through the pockets of

the two dead men and retrieved their IDs. Probably fake, but Kersey would want them anyway. I took a picture of the license plate. Walking back to my car, I wondered what it would be like for those kids.

What did Kersey say to me? *Don't let your emotions get to you.* The thing was, I didn't have any emotions. I felt nothing for those children one way or the other. Still, they didn't deserve what was coming. Like the boy lying out there somewhere in the darkness. He'd done nothing to anyone. It wasn't fair. I thought about something my brother said to me once. *Life ain't fair. You want fair, make sure whoever hurts you pays—big.*

It was like this was all a mad dream.

CHAPTER
SIXTEEN

I MADE it to LA with barely enough time to get ready. On cue, Dickles the Clown leered at me from behind the desk as I entered the lobby. I avoided eye contact and double-timed it to the elevator.

When I entered my apartment, my temperature spiked. I checked the thermostat. Sixty-four degrees. Ignoring the sudden fever, I peeled off my ruined clothes and held up my jacket to the light. There was a mess of bullet holes. At this rate, Nate would have to make me a hundred suits.

While showering, I thought about the Colombian. Though his wound wasn't serious, he'd lost a lot of blood. There was no way he was going to make it if he didn't get medical attention. Still, he'd sent me away. Good luck, asshat.

After my shower, I noticed my fever was gone. I stood in front of the steamy mirror, examining myself. Almost no evidence of gunshot wounds. Nothing hurt. I recalled the gun battle in Afghanistan. I couldn't comprehend how I'd survived it. *Maybe djinns are real.*

Seeing everything in my head, I knew where I'd been hit. I probed my arms and sides. Nothing but smooth skin peppered with faint, disappearing scars. I propped a foot on the sink and examined my leg where Kersey had shot me. The skin was completely smooth.

Curious, I walked into the kitchen and grabbed a sharpened knife from the wood block. I rested my left hand on the counter. Waiting a beat, I sliced my palm straight across. The bright blood came right away, oozing over my hand and threatening to stain the granite. As I rinsed off in the sink, the water became less and less red, until it ran clear.

When I checked my hand, the wound had closed. I visualized the djinn with the glowing red eyes. Was I cursed? Or did Hellborn do something to make me like this? I needed answers. I toyed with the idea of returning to Rosamond to uncover evidence of what happened to me and the others in the death tanks. But I had this stupid thing with the boss. In the bathroom, I grabbed the hair dryer and finished getting ready.

Opening my bedroom closet, I was surprised to find more clothes. Nate's army of tailors must've worked overtime because now, I had five more suits and a half-dozen shirts. I grabbed the black cocktail dress and laid it on the bed. Next, came the Ferragamo pumps. Something was missing. During my rushed shopping spree, I'd forgotten to buy a purse. Too late. I opened a dresser drawer to pick out some jewelry and found a rectangular white box. Inside, was a black leather crossbody bag. Big enough to hold my ID, phone, and gun.

"Thanks, Nate," I said. "I owe you."

West Hollywood is one of those places where people go to be seen. Walking into the London hotel, my ankle gave out again, and I lost my shoe. Cursing, I slipped it back on. I checked to see if anyone had caught my act, but people were too busy making deals.

We dined in a private room at Boxwood Restaurant. Besides his suit, Kersey wore an expensive black silk shirt. For a gangsta, he cleaned up pretty nice—had manners too. As I approached the table, he stood and pointed at someone. A server poured two flutes of Crystal. A second one pulled my chair out for me.

"Special occasion?" I said.

My new employer raised his glass. "A toast. To opportunity."

I tried the champagne. It was good. The first server refilled my glass. Both left the room and closed the doors.

"I like the new hair," my boss said. "How'd it go out there?"

"Raul didn't tell you?"

"I want to hear your side."

"Someone followed us. They started shooting and killed a kid. Two men in a Lincoln Navigator." I handed over the IDs. "I'll text you a photo of the license plate."

"You're thorough. I like that."

"Raul thinks someone at the detention center tipped them off."

"Agreed. What we do is big business. And everyone wants a piece. Don't worry, I'll take care of it."

"I'll also send you a photo of this one guard. I think he had a hand in it."

"Thanks. We'll check it out."

"You know they almost killed Raul tonight, right?"

Uninterested, he looked away. "He's a big boy."

"How is he?"

"We got him patched up. And you? You seem to have come out of it okay."

"You knew I would."

"I made the right choice bringing you on," he said. "You're good for business."

He took another sip and pushed the glass aside. I could tell this guy wasn't a drinker. He liked staying sharp. Smart.

He began telling me about the bright future in trafficking illegals, as in children.

The picture he painted, though disturbing, didn't register. Sometimes, my lack of empathy surprised me. I saw things rationally, and my actions as a means to an end. He seemed to be of the same mind.

On any given day, illegals from all over Latin America poured into the country through Mexico, creating opportunity. Some had no identification. Often, parents sent their kids alone, hoping for a better life for them. Those were the ones Kersey—and others like him—could easily divert.

Though he didn't tell me why he wanted the children, it didn't require much imagination. Sex trafficking. Organ transplants. The works. As he put it, everything was on the table. I didn't care about any of it. All I wanted was to find out what Hellborn did to me—and why. This job? A necessary detour.

"You did good tonight," he said. "There's a lot more to do. We can talk about it on Monday."

I'd forgotten it was Friday already. What was I supposed to do for two days? "Any plans for the weekend?"

He put down his fork. "Taking my daughter camping."

"I didn't know you had a kid."

"She's the most important thing in my life."

"I'm trying to picture you pitching a tent."

"Camping's not my thing. But it's an American tradition, right? Besides, I promised Lily."

"Pretty name," I said.

I was about to ask him if he'd uncovered anything about Hellborn when the doors opened. Throwing down his napkin, he stood at attention as if a superior officer had entered the room.

It was a woman. Fortyish, like my boss. She had straight platinum hair down to her shoulders and wore a black satin blazer with black pants. No shirt—not even a bra. On her neck, three gold necklaces. No bag. She moved like a cat as she approached the table, smiling through glossy red lips. He pulled out a chair for her. With perfect posture, she sat and extended her hand to me.

"Griselda Müller," she said. Her accent was German. "And you are?"

"Jane. I like your blazer." Come on, I had to say something.

Looking me over, she fiddled with one of my dress straps and stroked my bare arm.

"Though I suspect it would look better on you."

She reached across the table and took Kersey's champagne flute. When she'd tasted the wine, she gave him a sly smile.

"Little young for you, don't you think?" she said.

"She works for me."

Using her fingers, she helped herself to some of his fish.

"Lucky for you. How did you find her?"

He looked away, embarrassed. Anyone could see he was in love with her. "She came highly recommended."

As they continued their awkward dance, I felt disinvited. Instead of trying to interject, I kept to myself and nibbled at my pasta. Apparently, these two went way back. And they had business together—Kersey business.

"I heard what happened tonight," she said.

She gave me a warm smile, then frowned at my boss. When he answered, I could hear the irritation.

"I'm taking care of it."

She dabbed her mouth with my napkin. Folding her hands, she leveled her gaze at him, her expression deadly serious.

"See that you do," she said. Then in German, "Wir sind eine Familie. Und Familien halten zusammen."

"You don't need to tell me how to run my business."

"Our business." She gazed around the room. "No dessert?"

She rose and straightened her blazer. I noticed her flawless nails as she took my hand.

"It was a pleasure meeting you, Jane." Then to Kersey, "Are you coming to the party?"

"I'll be there."

She looked at me, wearing the cat smile. Pursing her lips, she cupped my chin. My boss seemed okay with the bi-curious flirting. Me, not so much.

"You should come too," she said.

The first server returned, carrying two slices of chocolate cake on a tray. As the German crossed the room, he held the door open for her. On her way out, she tried the frosting. Sucking her index finger, she kept her eyes on Kersey and disappeared.

"My German's a little rough," I said. "What did she say to you?"

"That we're a family. And families stick together."

He looked like a high school quarterback who'd learned his girlfriend was screwing a college man. I almost felt bad for him.

"I don't understand. How do you know her?"

He tried the cake. Making a face, he set his fork down and finished the champagne.

"She's my ex-wife," he said.

SEVENTEEN

BY THE TIME I got home, I'd already decided to return to Hellborn. I changed clothes and got on the road, heading north toward the desert. Driving up the 14, I thought some more about Griselda Müller. What was with all the touching? Wait…

His drink. His food. Me. She was dominating him. And one thing was obvious. Between her and Kersey, she was the stronger one. Cool. Calculating. No nonsense. She was the kind of woman who knew how to work a room. And for all the refinement, underneath the veneer, she was vicious. I liked her.

I recalled a *Star Trek* episode I must've seen when I was a kid. The one where Spock returns to Vulcan to take part in a savage, to-the-death mating ritual. He's promised to some evil bitch who doesn't want him. She fixes it so Spock is forced to fight a rival. If Spock dies, she wins. If Spock lives, he won't want her—she wins.

That was Griselda Müller.

• • •

Two hours later, I was back on the lonely stretch of highway leading to Rosamond. This wasn't the smartest thing I'd ever done. What if there were more alphas roaming around inside? As I got closer, I expected to pass the burned-out helicopter. But the road was clear. And whoever cleaned up the mess repaired the damaged asphalt.

When I arrived, the lights were on inside. A fleet of black Escalades was parked in the lot. A whirring noise in the sky caught my attention. Drones. I watched as they circled the property. Below, men in gray suits with guns combed the area. I thought about turning back, but more than anything, I needed information.

Driving past, I hid my vehicle behind an outcrop of boulders. I made sure I had my Glock and extra mags. But I left my phone and ID in the car. Jogging back, I made a wide circle past the guard gate toward the rear of a side building. It was a moonless night, and no one had spotted me.

A wall of rock stood where the fence ended. I started climbing. In a few minutes, I'd made it to the top. Someone had screwed a stainless steel anchor into the rock and attached a rope to it. John Zwick and his friends, no doubt. I tested the line and made my way down. When I hit the ground, I peered at the sky. Far off, the drones performed lazy circles, their blades whirring like angry cicadas.

For a time, I studied the UAVs, trying to discover a pattern. I visualized a grid, with each drone a glowing white dot. In no time, I had it. Any sec now, they would break formation and head to the other side. Sure enough, the last one soon drifted out of sight. I bolted toward the main building and continued to a side entrance. Pressing myself against the wall, I tried the door handle. Locked.

Though it felt like forever, I'd been there only half an hour. Accepting defeat, I turned to make my way back to the rocks. There was a jiggling noise, and as the door swung open, I moved to the side.

A man in a gray suit stepped out and lit a cigarette. When he saw me in the glow of the lighter, he went for his weapon. I punched him in the windpipe, and he went down. Clutching his neck, he struggled, gasping for air.

Scanning my immediate surroundings, I dragged him inside. I laid him on the concrete floor behind some boxes of medical equipment. All were stamped with the company name and the words LOS ANGELES, CALIFORNIA.

"Tell me what you people are doing," I said.

He reached for his weapon, then realized I had it pointed at his head. Coughing, he got to his feet.

"One of the hypers escaped."

"*Hypers*? Don't you mean alphas?"

"Those were part of the Surrelis trial. We think they're all dead."

"What do you want with the hypers?"

A steady beeping came from inside his coat pocket, and he backed away. "Shit, it's you!"

I couldn't risk him alerting the others, but I didn't want to shoot him. The sound might give me away. I came at him.

"What're you doing?" he said.

"It'll be quick."

Frightened, he took a wild swing at me and connected with air. Using a flying kick, I sent him hurtling against a storage rack. A box fell, knocking the weapon out of my hand. As he went for the gun, I roundhouse-kicked him in the head. Dazed, he sank into a sitting position.

Setting aside my weapon, I hooked my arms under his and pulled him clear of the boxes. I put him in a chokehold. Coming to, he flailed his arms and tried grabbing my head. I tightened my grip, cutting off his air.

In the movies, they always show the hero giving the bad guy's neck a quick snap, thus killing him. Hard to do in real life unless you're The Hulk. Better to suffocate them. Eventually, his body went limp. The beeping continued. I ignored it and held him another beat.

Common sense told me to get out of there. But I still needed answers, especially now that I knew they were looking for me. I had to find a way to move around freely. The dead man was close to my height, so I put on his clothes. Grabbing his ID badge and gun, I hurried to the elevators, a single question burning my brain.

What in hell is a hyper?

EIGHTEEN

I MADE my way to the room with all the tanks. Outside in the hallway, the lights were on. There were bullet scars on the walls and blood spray everywhere. Over forty-eight hours had passed since I escaped, and some dead hypers were still here. People in disposable white coveralls with hoods loaded the last of them into body bags.

No one paid any attention to me. Silently, I moved among them while they disconnected wires and tubes and lifted the corpses dripping black liquid. A technician with a low hairline and caveman features zipped up a bag containing a small Asian woman. I saw him slip his hand in and massage her cold breasts. When he caught me glaring at him, he closed the bag and hauled it outside.

"What're you doing here?"

The voice had come from behind. I pivoted and found an African American man wearing a gray suit. Fifty, maybe. Looked as if he was in charge. His face a question mark, he waited for me to respond. I stood at attention.

"You're supposed to be on four checking the other labs," he said.

"I was curious how they died." I slipped past him and headed for the hallway.

"Hold on."

Listening to the approaching footsteps, I stopped. I felt his hand on my shoulder. He had a tremor. I turned around and faced him. He had gray, thinning hair and appeared out of shape. I noticed the wide wedding band. As he looked me over, he gave me a smile. Not in the usual creepy guy way—not like Dickles. This guy was all right.

He glanced at the pile of body bags. "Sabotage."

"Why?"

"Hell if I know. There'll be an investigation."

"How'd the hyper escape, though?"

"As best as we can tell, there was an equipment malfunction. Come on, I'll show you."

He led me to the tank where I'd awakened. On the side panel, the error message continued to flash.

"See all those tubes? One was designed to deliver a lethal poison, in case there was a breach." He pointed at the panel. "For whatever reason, this one failed. Lucky for her. She must've woken up scared and ran."

Moving past him, I picked up a plastic line. As I examined it, someone smacked the side of the unit hard. Black liquid began flowing into the tank like oil. I dropped the tube and turned around. A gap-toothed technician grinned at me like a feeb with a lightsaber.

"It was stuck, is all," he said, pointing at the panel.

I looked down. No more error message.

"Get back to work," the guy in charge said. Then to me, "You're new. Just get in from HQ?"

I tried to think. My response had better be right, or I'd have to shoot my way out. In my head, I was back in the storage area. I visualized the medical equipment boxes. There was printing on the side—the name of a city…

"No," I said. "LA."

"Oh. Didn't think we had any women specialists there. What are you doing here?"

"I requested a transfer."

"What's your name?"

"Jane."

"Harry Packard." He shook my hand. Despite the tremor, his grip was firm. "I'm the security chief of this facility."

"I figured."

His radio crackled, and he brought it up to his face. "Packard. What'cha got? Over."

"No trace of the hyper," a voice said. "Why'd we wait so long to get up here? Over."

"Orders from HQ. We were on lockdown until Forensics could get here."

"Okay, but it would help if we had her serial number."

The security chief gave me a weary look. "We lost track of it in the system. I'll let you know when I've recovered it."

"Copy. We've packed up all the evidence for transport to LA."

"What about the alphas?"

"All dead, sir. We found a fresh one in the pit. Someone shot him in the head. You think the hyper might've done it?"

"Possible. They're trained to kill."

"Oh, and there's a dead security guard. Headless. We think maybe the alpha did him."

"Cripes. Make sure to ID the guard."

"Already done. Name's Brandon Wheegar. Poor sonofabitch. Anyway, cleaners are en route."

"All right. Keep searching for the hyper. She may be hiding somewhere in the building."

"My guess is she won't last long without the drug."

"We don't know that for sure." He looked at me like he knew something, but I didn't react.

"One other thing, sir. Whoever broke in got their dead out before we arrived. Also, the Russian girl is missing."

Packard rolled his eyes. "That's Zeddemore's problem. Anything else?"

"Trower's dead."

Long silence. "Okay. Packard out." Then to me, "What a shitshow."

The security chief gave me a sad smile. I tried reading him. What I got was a deep weariness—the kind that comes from having seen too much death. And too much BS. Kind of like the military.

He pulled out his phone. The lock screen was a photo of a nice-looking girl in her late twenties, with green eyes and a huge smile. He unlocked the device and fired up an app.

"What does it do?" I said.

"They haven't trained you up on this? What the hell are those people doing in LA? This phone comes equipped with a proprietary antenna."

I watched the screen over his shoulder.

"The app is called Keepr," he said. "It can detect a microchip up to one hundred meters away."

"Microchip?"

"Active RFID. The kind that's embedded in each of those hypers. It's also wired for GPS tracking when the subject is out of range."

"Doesn't it require a power source?"

"Great question. The microchips are designed to use body heat and can store the energy for several days."

He pressed a white circle on the screen. In seconds, the white dot turned red, with glowing concentric circles surrounding it. The phone emitted a familiar beeping sound. As more and more overlapping circles appeared, I slid my finger to my weapon's trigger guard.

"What's it telling you?" I said.

He pointed at the body bags. "That we got a mess of dead hypers." He turned off the app and slipped the phone into his pocket. "We're supposed to leave it on, but it drains the battery."

I loosened my grip on the gun. Staring at the bodies, I pictured myself lying cold and alone inside a plastic bag.

"What if you don't find her?" I said.

"Oh, we'll find her. Listen, if there's anything you need, don't hesitate to reach out. Better get going. We're supposed to wrap this up by 0500."

I took his advice and headed toward the elevators, shuddering over the poison cocktail I'd barely avoided.

Instead of going to the fourth floor as ordered, I returned to the storage area. In the distance, a security alarm blared. Someone using the app must've detected me as I moved away from the lab.

I put on my regular clothes and exited the building through the same door I'd used earlier. Outside, the drones circled. Waiting for the right moment, I sprinted toward the other building. When I reached the rock face, I scrambled up, and still gripping the rope, used it to get down the other side. Scanning the sky for UAVs, I made my way back to my vehicle.

Harry Packard must've figured out I was the hyper they were looking for. I didn't even know what a hyper was, much less what being one meant. Though I was more than a hundred meters away, they could track me using GPS. Somehow, I had to lose the microchip.

Sabotage, Packard had said. Someone put an end to one of Hellborn's dark experiments. And they killed all the test subjects—but not me. Whoever was responsible, they wanted me found.

And without a doubt, they wanted me dead.

CHAPTER
NINETEEN

BEFORE HEADING BACK TO LA, I stopped at the café in Perro Negro. It was dark inside. I got out and peered through the front door. There was a light on in the kitchen. Maybe Consuelo was back there. Someone closed in behind me.

"Turn around. Real slow."

I recognized the voice—it was John. Calmly, I faced him.

"It's you," he said and lowered his shotgun. "Thought you were dead."

"I didn't mean to frighten you. I wanted to make sure you and Consuelo were okay."

"Let's go inside. Got a name yet?"

"Jane."

He led me around to the rear. There was a small ranch-style house, separated from the café by a well-tended yard. John unlocked the front door, flipped on the lights, and waved me through. It was a charming place, simple and warm.

"Where's the dog?" I said.

"Asleep in our bedroom."

In the living room, there were photos of his deceased son

on the mantel. One caught my eye. John and a young man standing in front of a rustic house in the woods. Both wore jeans, flannel shirts, and hiking boots. Each held a fishing rod.

"Where was this taken?"

"We have to speak softly. Consuelo's asleep." He gazed at the photo. "We have a cabin in Lake Isabella. That was the last time we were there as a family. You're welcome to use the place. Want a drink?"

"Maybe some water."

I followed him to the kitchen, where a cuckoo clock hung on the wall. He poured me a glass of tap water, and we sat at a small dinette table. He looked tired.

"Did they clean everything up in the café?" I said, taking a sip.

He rubbed the back of his neck. "Yeah. Real professionals. I'm still wondering why they didn't kill us."

"You don't need to worry. They won't be back."

"You know these men?"

"No, but…"

"You made a deal." For a civilian, he was pretty sharp.

"I had no choice."

"Well anyway, Consuelo will be relieved. We haven't slept much since—"

"Look, John. I could use some information."

"I'll tell you what I can."

"I went to Hellborn tonight and—"

"What?"

"It's okay. The place was crawling with these—"

"Gray-suits. That's what Dave calls 'em."

"Friend of yours?"

"What did you find out?"

"They're looking for me—hard. They wanna kill me."

"Why?"

"You ever hear of Surrelis?"

"It's an experimental drug."

"When I escaped from there the first time, I ran into one of those monsters you told me about."

"Cutters?"

"They call them *alphas*."

John blanched. "Those things killed most of our team. How did you get away?"

"Bullet to the brain. The gray-suit I spoke to said the woman they're looking for is part of the Hyper program."

I told him about how I awoke in the lab and escaped. He knew the place I was talking about. He and the others had passed through there while looking for someone named Sasha. They'd seen the test subjects twice. The first time was when we were still alive and unharmed.

"The gray-suits refer to us as *hypers*," I said. "I don't know what it means."

"Me neither. But whatever you are, it sounds like they don't want you around to be discovered. You're the last one. It was the same with the Russian girl."

"They mentioned her. And also someone named Trower. Who's he?"

John got up and went over to a cabinet. When I saw the mezcal, I knew he was about to tell me something bad—dead worm at the bottom of a bottle bad.

He poured two drinks and sat. His was gone before I'd raised my glass. He took his time telling me about the mission. I guessed he had PTSD.

"So, the Russian girl—Sasha," I said. "They planned to kill her too?"

He didn't answer for a long time. Then, "They wanted the child she was carrying."

"An alpha child?"

"She wasn't like the others. Wasn't a cutter, I mean. That's why she was important to them."

"Where is she now?"

He took a minute to refill his glass. *Why are you stalling?*

"She didn't make it," he said.

I finished my drink and pushed the glass aside. The ticking of the cuckoo clock filled the silence.

"Do you think your friend Dave would know any more about the Hyper program?"

"Don't think so."

"Twice, I heard someone mention Black Dragon. What's the deal there?"

"Private security outfit. They organized the rescue."

"Would they know anything?"

"Jane, be careful. I'm not sure you should be talking to Black Dragon or Dave Pulaski or anyone else."

As soon as he'd spoken the name, he regretted it. It was in his eyes. Must've been the mezcal. I pretended not to notice.

"You think Dave might be in on it?" I said.

"No. I trust him with my life. But I know him. Once he signs on, he'll dig until he finds something. He might talk to the wrong person. And that would be it for you. And him. And also… Never mind."

"I appreciate your concern. I better go. Say hi to Consuelo for me. I miss her potato tacos. Thanks for the drink."

He watched me from the doorway as I slipped into the cold December night. I wondered if I'd ever see either of them again. Something caught my attention. It was the same whirring sound I'd heard at Hellborn. I looked up. A dark object moved low across the ink-black sky—a drone. I went back to the house.

"I need to borrow your shotgun," I said. "I'll explain later."

John went inside. When he returned, he was carrying the weapon and a box of shells. He handed me a slip of paper and a house key on a scuffed-up Power Rangers keyring.

"It opens the door to our cabin," he said. "I meant it when I said you could use it. This is the address."

"Thanks. Who else knows about this place?"

"No one. The deed's in a safe deposit box. And the utilities are paid automatically."

"The whole thing is turnkey?"

"Ever since our son was killed, we've taken precautions."

"I promise to get the gun back to you," I said.

On the road, I kept well behind the drone. It appeared to be heading west. I'd already gone five miles when it made a wide arc and turned back. I pulled over on the deserted road. Grabbing the weapon, I got out of the car and waited. As the UAV passed overhead, I took aim.

It was black and hard to see against the dark sky. Two glowing red eyes appeared. I waited until the thing was directly overhead and fired at the lights. The buckshot struck the machine at an angle, sending it spinning wildly to the ground. I finished it off with two more blasts and stomped on the camera lens.

After returning John's shotgun, I got on the road. Part of me wanted to find Dave Pulaski. But John was right. I had to be careful, now that Harry Packard knew what I looked like.

It was when I reached the freeway I remembered the microchip tucked away somewhere inside me. I had to tell Kersey. If Hellborn could track me by satellite, it could put his entire operation at risk. But he was out of town for the weekend. I would tell him on Monday. In the meantime, I'd lay low.

Nothing for me now except books and takeout.

TWENTY

I DON'T DREAM MUCH. When I do, it's about Afghanistan and the malang who saved my life. I opened my eyes to shards of piercing light through the blinds. A new day. I cricked my neck and rose to go through my morning routine.

Lying in a metal coffin for who knew how long had left me weak and out of shape. The first thing was to stretch. It's hard to explain, but I had a keen awareness of my joints now. They didn't hurt. But I understood the connections and precisely how it felt to move them. Another hyper trait?

Next, a series of exercises I normally do one after the other. Side straddle hops. Wide-grip push-ups. Crunches. Hand-to-knee squats. Standing calf raises. Standing toe raises. Back extensions. And finally, another set of stretches to cool down.

I had a vague recollection of my brother taking me through the grueling routine I came to hate. Him dripping with sweat in the blistering sun of our backyard, and me grunting like a piglet. Yelled at. Denied water. Struggling to get through the last of the crunches without puking. Good times.

When I'd completed the routine, I checked my pulse. Slightly elevated. But I was warm—hot, in fact. I hoped I wasn't sick and made a mental note to purchase a thermometer. I'd also need a pull-up bar. And a BOB—body opponent bag—and other equipment for my martial arts workouts.

My vision blurred for a sec, then cleared. But the fever persisted. Stripping, I got into the shower. I thought maybe I wasn't used to exercising and had overexerted myself. Yet I'd done intense workouts for years with no negative side effects. More hyper crap? I kept the water cold, letting the luxurious stream wash over me until I felt normal again.

After getting dressed, I was hungry af. I checked the fridge and found a carton of eggs. I stared at them like they were those greenish things in *Alien* that squirted facehuggers. I couldn't remember ever having cooked. *How hard can it be?* I dug out a pan and switched on a burner.

When I cracked open the first egg, part of the shell landed in the pan. Outstanding. I tried the second one. This time, pieces flew everywhere, inside and out. And the yolk went all over like a kid with yellow finger paint. I stuck my hand in, attempting to get the shell out. As the hot mess sizzled, I burned myself and let loose a string of expletives worthy of a boot camp DI. Screw breakfast—I'd rather starve.

Disgusted, I turned off the burner and took a breath. I found some energy bars in a cabinet. As I pounded one down, I checked my phone. There was a text message from the boss. He wanted to see me asap. Which was perfect because I was supposed to tell him about the thing with the guy in the place.

Oh, we'll find her.

That's what Harry Packard had said to that other mook. Though I'd taken out the drone, I worried about the security chief locating my serial number so he could track me. As a precaution, I'd left the town car in a lot one klick away from the apartment building. The last thing I wanted was a gray-suit showing up at my door. Heading over, I kept to little-used streets and alleyways—the kind frequented by hobos and stewbums.

Kersey wasn't the kind of person who enjoyed small talk. Neither was I. As soon as I walked in, he pointed at a chair.

"I have another job for you," he said. "Raul will give you the details."

"There's a problem."

"I didn't hire you to bring me problems."

"This is for your own good."

He rolled his eyes. "All right, let's have it."

"There's a tracking device in me. I need someone to remove it."

His eyes went dead, his mouth contracting into a dangerous slit. He took out his weapon and pointed it at a spot between my eyes. I might've blinked.

"How long have you known?" he said, lowering the gun.

"Since Friday. I went back there."

"To the place in the desert?"

After talking to John Zwick, fragments of the Baseborn Identity Research story began floating in my head like puzzle pieces in lazy water. When they'd assembled themselves into a coherent picture, I told Kersey everything I knew. I was a hyper. But there was another program involving alphas and a pregnant Russian girl who, according to the official narrative, was dead. Dave Pulaski and Black Dragon had conducted a covert operation to rescue her. That same night, someone— not Black Dragon—poisoned the other hypers.

Kersey leaned against the desk, his weapon nowhere in sight. He gnawed on a fresh toothpick. "This is a science fiction movie."

"How else do you explain what I can do? Whoever's in charge of the Hyper program is looking for me. I know because I met the security chief."

He shook his head. "You're bad for business."

"That's not what you said last time."

He didn't answer right away. After a beat, he returned to his desk and, looking something up on his phone, made a call.

"I need a favor," he said.

Another quality I admired about Kersey was he enjoyed solving problems. And despite his misgivings, it was clear he intended to protect me. He explained the situation to the person on the other end. Grabbing a Post-it, he wrote something down and handed it to me.

"They're expecting you," he said. Then on my reaction, "What's with the face? This guy checks out. Used him for years."

"Whatever you say."

"After your appointment, get ahold of Raul. He'll brief you on your assignment."

As I crossed to the door, Kersey took a seat at his desk. Despite the rough edges, I was starting to like him. I would've said goodbye, but he was already engrossed in something on his laptop.

So I left without saying anything.

CHAPTER
TWENTY-ONE

WILSHIRE BOULEVARD WAS A MESS, and I cut over to 6th. I thought a black Escalade might be tailing me, which meant Harry Packard was on to me. In my head, I pictured a grid. That traveling blip was me, and I was surrounded by menacing red dots. 6th Street dead-ended at San Vicente. I jogged south and merged back onto Wilshire. When I checked the rearview mirror again, there were no Escalades.

The medical building was on Barrington in West LA. I used the underground parking, and instead of taking the elevator, walked up the five flights of stairs. I couldn't shake the feeling I was being followed, though. In the lobby, I crossed the marble floor and consulted the directory. There, I found Dr. Arjun Chowdhury. Before stepping out of the elevator on 4, I scanned the hallway for gray-suits.

Expensive furniture and plants filled the waiting room. Three men in suits sat on comfortable-looking leather chairs. Across the way, a woman in a colorful print dress and too much jewelry judged me. Ignoring her, I approached the receptionist. She was a young woman with flowing coffee-colored hair and dark eyes. Hard to tell her ethnicity. Apparently, my training had prepared me to home in on things like a person's weight, height, and race.

"I have an appointment," I said.

"We've been expecting you, Ms. Doe."

"Do I need to fill anything out?"

"It's all been taken care of. You can enter through there."

I went to where she pointed and stepped through a door. A kid with flaming red hair and who smiled way too much waited for me.

"Follow me," he said. "Did you have any trouble finding our offices?"

He didn't give me time to respond and continued blabbing like an over-caffeinated tour guide.

"And how's your day going?" He grimaced like he was squeezing one out. "I don't know if they told you. We don't validate."

He stopped at a patient room and gestured like a courtier in a Molière play. I guessed he was a struggling actor.

"Dr. Chowdhury will be with you in a moment," he said.

The room was typical. Examination table covered in white butcher paper. Cabinets with supplies. Sink. And one plastic chair. A box containing electronics sat on the counter. I didn't know what kind of doctor this guy was and had to trust that Kersey wouldn't screw me over.

I stood near the tall, narrow window and watched the traffic below. A black Escalade pulled up in front of the building. It was identical to the ones I'd seen at Hellborn. A gray-suit climbed out of the passenger side and did a quick visual sweep of the area. Whoever was behind the wheel didn't budge. My instincts told me to get out of there.

A knock interrupted my concentration. A slender, middle-aged Indian man of medium height entered. He wore rimless glasses and had on a medical lab coat.

"Ms. Doe?" he said. "Please remove your jacket and take a seat."

Eyeing my gun, he pointed at the table. I glanced out the window again. The Escalade was gone. I was nervous about sticking around and concentrated on getting rid of the microchip.

Using both hands, Chowdhury palpated my neck. Next, he lifted each eyelid and, using a penlight, peered closely. His breath smelled like toffee.

"Curious. You seem to have a kind of bluish iridescence. I'm not an ophthalmologist, but normally, the macula is yellowish."

"Maybe I'm special, Doc."

"Indeed."

After listening to my heart and lungs and testing my reflexes, he stepped back.

"You seem in perfect health," he said. "Temperature's a little elevated, however. Have you been exercising?"

"This morning."

"Let's see if we can locate the microchip."

"That's what I'm here for."

He opened the box on the counter and removed an odd-looking black device resembling a giant teething ring. When he switched it on, the LCD screen illuminated and gave off a single beep.

"What is that thing?" I said.

He handed it over. "They use it to scan for microchips in pets. I had someone pick it up this morning."

I stood at ease as he ran the device up and down the front and back of my body, starting at the head. The device didn't make a sound. He took my hands and extended them, palms up.

"Often, chips are inserted between the thumb and forefinger. Were you conscious for the procedure?"

"No."

He scanned each hand. Nothing. Packard had said his phone used a proprietary UHF RFID antenna. This piece of junk wasn't capable of detecting that kind of tech. Disappointed, Chowdhury returned the device to its box.

"I'm afraid we have to perform a full body scan," he said.

He stepped into the hallway. When he returned, a young Asian woman also wearing a lab coat accompanied him.

"My assistant will show you the way."

"How does this work?"

"Once we know the location, I'll perform the surgery," he said. "Shouldn't take long."

The whole-body scanner looked like something out of a sci-fi movie. It was sleek and cylindrical. White, with a patient table in front. The assistant asked me to change into a patient gown. I didn't like being without a weapon, but I needed this thing out of me. When I was ready, she had me lie on my back on the table headfirst. Before she could hit the button sending me into the machine, I sat up.

"This thing isn't gonna make the chip explode, is it?" I said.

Her laugh was musical. "Nothing to worry about."

Before I knew it, I was inside. The scan took less than a minute. When I went for my clothes and gun, she touched my hand.

"Not yet. You don't want to get blood on your suit," she said.

The girl escorted me to another room for the surgery. I laid everything on a chair. Chowdhury reviewed the results of my scan on a computer monitor.

"Where was it?" I said.

He extended his index finger and touched a spot on the left side of my head where the outer ear met the skull. It had never occurred to me to examine myself there. Running my finger over the area, I sensed the outline of something long and cylindrical.

The doctor directed me to lie on my stomach on the table. While sterilizing the site, he explained the procedure. He'd inject me with lidocaine, then use a scalpel to make the incision. The device was located near the surface. Chowdhury would use forceps to remove it. The needle stung as he injected me with the local. I felt something warm—blood— and heard him gasp.

"Is there a problem?"

"The wound—it's closing!"

I tried laughing it off. "I've always been a quick healer. Have the forceps ready. Make a longer incision and get in there as fast as you can."

He didn't say anything. I waited for him to continue, but he was flummoxed.

"It's fine. I'm used to it."

Before he could resume, a faraway gunshot startled him, and he dropped the scalpel. Outside, a woman screamed. That's when I knew.

The gray-suits had found me.

CHAPTER
TWENTY-TWO

OUT IN THE HALLWAY, two more shots—closer this time. A weapon with a suppressor doesn't silence the bullet the way most people think. But it does change the quality, making it seem farther away. That's what this gunfire sounded like to me.

I slid off the table and shoved the doctor out of the way. Using the chair, I secured the door. After getting dressed, I grabbed my weapon. Outside, rapid footsteps and men's voices. The happy wannabe actor ululated. Another shot, followed by a thud as something fell against the door.

Using the gun, I waved the terrified doctor and his assistant to either side of the door and signaled them to crouch. There was a metal tray on the counter. In it, were a disposable scalpel and forceps still in their wrappers, cotton balls, and a bottle of Betadine. I grabbed everything and shoved it into my pocket. Outside, the footsteps faded away. I turned to the doctor and his assistant.

"Stay here," I said. "Secure the door like this after I'm gone."

I removed the chair and grabbed the door handle. Chowdhury grabbed my arm.

"Jane, are you planning to perform the surgery yourself?"

"Maybe."

"You must be careful not to sever the posterior auricular vein."

I scanned the room. The computer monitor the doctor had used earlier was mounted on the wall next to the cabinets. Under it was a stand with a keyboard and mouse.

"Show me," I said.

He brought up a browser with jittery hands and did a search. An anatomy diagram showed a right profile of the human head. Blood vessels were indicated in blue. I nodded as he pointed at an area below the ear.

With my weapon up, I opened the door. Chowdhury's assistant let out a frightened squeak as the dead ginger fell toward me, one eye blown to shit. I scanned the hallway in both directions and dragged the body out of the way. The door made a snick as it closed behind me.

As I passed a supply closet, the door opened a crack. When they saw my gun, the two female assistants hiding inside almost screamed. I put a finger to my lips and closed the door.

I looked up in time to see a shadow from around the corner. When the gray-suit appeared, I was ready. I fired even before he saw me. Because I didn't have a suppressor, the gunshot echoed, making my ears ring.

Earlier, there were two men in the Escalade. *Where's the other one?* I continued toward the waiting room. All the patients must've gotten out, but not the receptionist. She lay dead in her desk chair, shot in the face, with a blood spray on the wall behind her. The hostiles must've figured killing me was a one-man job. Big mistake.

When I exited the elevator in the lobby, I put away my weapon, brushed back my hair, and hurried to the exit leading to the parking structure. As I trotted down the stairs, I kept an eye out for the Escalade. I found it on the third level, taking up two spaces in a shadowy corner. The driver was younger than me and sat behind the wheel, texting. I stuck the barrel of my Glock behind his ear.

"Get out," I said.

He let the phone slip from his fingers onto the seat. I stepped back as he opened the door and stood at attention, his hands at his sides. I thought he might lose his water.

"Take out your weapon and lay it on the ground. Good. Now kick it over here."

His nervous eyes were on me the whole time as I pocketed the gun. The squeal of tires caught my attention. A woman in a BMW rounded the corner. Grabbing the kid's face, I planted one on his lips. When the car was out of sight, I flung him away and took his phone. I switched off the device and slipped it into my pocket.

"I need answers," I said. "What is Baseborn Identity Research?"

"What?"

I trained my gun on his heart. "Are you deaf?"

"It's…it's a… They're scientists. Working with the government."

"What kind of research is it?"

"Military—I don't know. I started last week."

"What are hypers?"

"A, a new kind of…soldier. Look, I don't—"

"Soldiers who can't be killed?"

"I guess?"

"Who runs the program?"

When he tried looking away, I grabbed his mouth and stuck the barrel between his eyes.

"Caroline Sheldrake!"

"What about the alphas? Who's in charge of them?"

"Walt Freeman used to be, but he's—"

"Dead?"

"Murdered."

I recalled the burned-out helicopter in the desert, and the businessman's body inside. Walt Freeman? I considered my situation. This kid didn't know anything. Still, I couldn't let him walk.

"Tell me the passcode to your phone," I said. Then when he'd given it to me, "Close your eyes."

After hiding the body in the back of the Escalade, I returned to the building. There was an accessible bathroom off the lobby. As I walked in, sirens blared in the distance. Soon, the cops would be all over the place. I locked the door and set out the things I'd need on the counter. In my hurry, I'd forgotten the lidocaine. *Screw it—pain is gain.*

I washed my hands and probed for the microchip. Once I'd located it, I assembled the scalpel and sterilized the blade with Betadine, as well as the forceps. Before starting, I cleaned the area behind my left ear. I visualized the diagram Dr. Chowdhury had shown me, trying to imagine where the vein lay. Taking a calming breath, I picked up the scalpel. Out of nowhere, I heard Tyler's voice in my head. *You got this.* Yeah, right.

With steady hands, I made a quick lengthwise cut, trying to get as close to the outer ear as I could. Warm blood flowed down my neck. Grabbing the forceps, I forced the incision to stay open as I dug around for the microchip. The pain was worse than I expected. I saw stars.

Blinking away the perspiration, I kept at it until I felt something between the blades of the forceps. Gently, I removed the foreign object. The incision began to close as I wiped off the remaining blood with fresh Betadine-soaked cotton balls.

Holding it up to the light, I squinted at the devilish device. It was an inch long and slender. Clear with electronics inside. A tiny serial number was printed on the glass. Filled with sudden rage, I threw it on the floor and pounded it with my heel until it was dust.

When I exited the bathroom, LAPD officers wearing ballistic helmets and body armor poured in through the front door. I waited for them to head to the elevators, then double-timed it to the exit. No one had warned me about West LA parking. I'd ended up on the lowest level.

While checking my vehicle for explosives, I spotted a tracking device. It was underneath, attached to the gas tank. *Nice try, Packard.* I removed it and stuck it on a nearby sewage pipe.

Outside, cop cars, fire trucks, and ambulances lined the street in front of the building. Exiting the structure, I shot across lanes and accelerated into traffic, going the opposite way. I'd managed to evade the gray-suits. But soon, there'd be more. At least I'd gotten rid of the microchip and the vehicle tracking device. By now, they had my license plate number. Only one thing to do.

Lose the car.

PART THREE

SHE RIDES

CHAPTER
TWENTY-THREE

I DIDN'T KNOW LA well and ended up in Koreatown. When I spotted a Gas-N-Gut, I pulled in and called Raul. We arranged to meet at a place called Beer Belly on Western. The phone I'd taken from the young gray-suit lay next to me on the seat with the battery removed. It wasn't anything like the burners we used. I had the urge to turn it on. But if I did, the hostiles would track me.

There was an electronics repair shop across the street. My shirt collar was covered in dried blood. Made me look like a victim of a vampire attack. Tucking it in, I jogged over. An Asian man in his fifties was facedown behind the counter, working on an iPad. Next to him was one of those Japanese lucky cats sitting in a bowl of loose change, its paw waving up and down.

"Can you help me remove a SIM?" I said.

"Busy. Come back after lunch."

I laid down a hundred-dollar bill. Nodding, he opened a drawer. He placed a SIM card removal tool on the counter. I handed him the phone, and he extracted the card. Using a loupe, he examined it.

"This one not the regular kind," he said.

"What do you mean?"

He handed me the loupe and the SIM. As my eye focused, the manufacturer's name materialized on the front of the card —CLAYBORN ELECTRONICS.

"Have you got a bag?" I said.

He slipped the phone, SIM, and extractor in a Ziploc bag and handed it to me. I thanked him and left.

Inside my car, I reinserted the battery and switched on the phone. The lock screen displayed a photo of the kid with a blonde girl who looked like a model. Both wore hiking shorts and stood on a mountain peak overlooking a valley. I entered the passcode. Right away, I noticed the Keepr app icon on the home screen.

I accessed the phone's settings to look up the owner's name, then changed my mind. I didn't need to know who I'd killed. Instead, I opened the Messages app. The gray-suit had communicated with a contact identified as *LC*. From the tone of the conversation, LC was the kid's rabbi.

> Missed registering for winter quarter.

> Focus on the job, school will happen.

> Girlfriend thinks i'm an auditor with the firm lol.

> Better she doesn't know.

> What if i run into the hyper?

> Three to the head. Termination guaranteed.

> I'm scared.

> You got this.

I dropped the phone. *LC... Lance Corporal? No way — Tyler Berry?*

Something didn't add up. A man from my former squad was a gray-suit? Not even possible. Tyler and me, we were... I wanted answers, but there wasn't time.

Resigned, I switched off the phone and put everything in my pocket. The Colombian would be at the restaurant by now. As I found my way, a tuneless voice loop played in my brain like a doll with a busted pull-string.

Three to the head. Termination guaranteed.

Raul and Neck Beard were waiting for me in the parking lot. The Asian looked pissed—nothing new. I grabbed my garage gate remote from the glove compartment and joined them.

"What happened?" the Colombian said.

"Ran into some trouble. What have you got for me?"

He tilted his head at a Ford Mustang Shelby GT500. My brother had taught me all about muscle cars. They were his passion. This one was all black and new. A flashback interrupted the conversation...

Bo and me in the garage. I was thirteen. We had our heads stuck under the hood of a yellow Plymouth Hemi 'Cuda Convertible.

He showed me how to take out the old spark plugs and gap the new ones. The smell of motor oil and gasoline hung in the air.

"I enlisted," he said.

When my head cleared, I looked at Raul. "Yeah, that won't attract any attention."

Neck Beard waved his stubby arms at me, his voice going high. "Are you loco? I'd kill for these wheels."

I ignored him. Then to the Colombian, "How'd you get it so fast?"

"Belonged to one of the crew you popped in the desert."

"Guess he won't miss it, then."

We exchanged keys, and he handed mine to Neck Beard.

The Asian slouched toward the town car, which seemed horribly uncool compared to my new ride.

"What happens to the other vehicle?" I said.

"We have a place in Glendale. They'll switch out the plates and registration."

I started the Mustang and revved the engine. It sounded awesome—Bo would've drooled over it. Raul crouched in front of my open window.

"You want to tell me about the people who found you?" he said.

"Nope."

"In my experience, it's best not to keep Kersey in the dark. It'll come back to bite you in the ass."

"I've got it under control."

He flipped up my bloody collar with his finger. "You sure?"

When I didn't respond, he pointed behind him at the colorful mural on the restaurant's front wall.

"You should try the duck fat fries. They'll change you."

"I don't eat...duck," I said. "Listen, I'm heading back to my apartment. Meet me there in an hour."

He tried to say something. I placed a finger on his lips.

"One hour."

Sweet. Now I was giving the orders.

CHAPTER
TWENTY-FOUR

CAUTIOUSLY, I approached my building's parking garage. The whole time I had the microchip in me, the gray-suits could've found out where I live. Why hadn't they come after me here? I remembered Harry Packard saying they'd lost my serial number, yet they managed to track me down. Dismissing the thought, I parked and made a quick sweep of the garage. I was alone except for a young mom hurrying two small children into a Volvo.

After a quick shower, I dressed in different clothes. The doorbell rang; it was Raul. Lingering there, he couldn't help checking me out in my black tank top and yoga pants. *He's a breeder. Good to know.* Ignoring his sly grin, I stuck my head out and scanned the hallway.

"What are you doing?" he said.

"I thought you might've brought Vincent."

"He's busy cleaning up your mess."

I let him in and went into the kitchen. When I offered him a drink, he declined. Incredulous, he stood over the range and stared at the pan with the dried, scummy eggs I'd neglected to clean up.

"I didn't know you cooked," he said.

"It's a new recipe. Eggs À La Blow It Out Your Corn Pocket."

Disgusted, he grabbed the pan and ran hot water in the sink.

"Never leave a pan in this condition," he said. "You'll ruin it."

I grabbed a bottle of water from the fridge and took a seat on a barstool. With care, he washed and dried the pan. While he was at it, he cleaned up the range. I was enjoying this.

"And you don't want to leave eggs sitting out. That's how foodborne bacteria spreads."

"I'll try and remember that."

He sat next to me, close enough for me to feel the heat coming off his body. For no reason I could think of, I was nervicited.

"How's the shoulder?" I said.

"We need to talk about the assignment."

"And we will. But first, tell me about Griselda Müller."

"After he and Kersey married, they went into business together. Later, they had a kid and got divorced."

"But they still run the operation together."

He waggled his hand. "Sort of. Kersey is under the impression he runs it. Griselda thinks otherwise."

"Well, she does have the bigger balls. And Lily? She lives with the mother?"

"In Bel Air."

I got a sudden cramp in my leg and began walking in a circle. The Colombian eyeballed my ass on his way to the living room. He checked out the stack of books on the coffee table.

"I never got to see what you bought the other day," he said.

"Apparently, I'm passionate about books."

He picked one up and leafed through it. It was Immanuel Kant's *Critique of Pure Reason*.

"This makes no sense to me." He put it back. "Let's see what else you got."

Crouching, he recited titles from the spines.

"*Shakespeare's Sonnets and Poems. Pride and Prejudice.* Vonnegut's *The Sirens of Titan.* He turned to me. "*The Little Sister* by Raymond Chandler."

There were a lot more he ignored. He pointed at the two stacks.

"You read all these?"

I played dumb.

"Who's your favorite author?"

"Raymond Chandler."

He scratched his ear. "Figures."

My phone vibrated on the kitchen counter. It was our boss. The call came through as *Mr. Majestyk.* Cute.

"Where are you?" Kersey said.

"At my apartment with Raul."

"Turn on the news. Then the two of you get your asses over here."

In the living room, I stood in front of the TV, searching for the remote. The Colombian found it on the sofa and handed it to me. On the screen was a dizzying menu of options, which included Netflix, Amazon Prime, and Hulu. Grabbing the remote, he brought up a local news station.

A commercial had just ended, and a BREAKING NEWS banner appeared along the bottom. Clutching her notes, a female news anchor looked gravely into the camera.

"Back-to-back shootings in Los Angeles today," she said. "First, we go to Saul Bernstein in West LA."

The station cut to the front of the medical building I'd visited. A middle-aged reporter wearing a sport jacket stood in front of the camera, surrounded by a crowd of nosey onlookers.

"At approximately nine-fifty this morning, a heavily armed man entered this busy medical building on Barrington

Avenue and opened fire in the offices of Dr. Arjun Chowdhury.

"'Heavily armed'?" I said. "He had a handgun."

Raul side-eyed me. "Cállate."

"Three people are confirmed dead—two employees and the shooter."

The reporter continued for another few minutes, describing the scene in lurid detail. The accompanying footage showed bullet-scarred walls and bloody carpeting.

"Saul, do they know who killed the gunman?" the news anchor said.

"It's unclear at this time. Employees claimed they were hiding and saw nothing."

"Have the police confirmed whether the shooter acted alone?"

"No. But a full search of the premises and surrounding buildings is underway."

"Any clue as to a motive?"

"They didn't take anything. A police spokesperson promised more information as it becomes available."

"What about the doctor? Did you get a chance to speak with him?"

"We tried interviewing Dr. Chowdhury. But as you can imagine, he and his staff are in shock over the attack. LAPD has advised us to wait until they've taken statements."

"Okay, thanks," the news anchor said. "That was Saul Bernstein reporting. And now, let's go to Echo Park, where Victoria Muñoz is standing by. Vicky, what's going on?"

A young Latina stood in frame, holding a microphone. Behind her, a crowd of window-lickers hooted and flashed victory signs as a news helicopter hovered overhead.

"The scene is one of sheer chaos," the reporter said. "A short time ago, a black Lincoln Continental town car was discovered parked in the middle of this quiet street in Echo

Park, west of Dodger Stadium. And inside, the body of the driver, who had been shot several times.

"Although there are no details yet, police have described the killing as an execution. I have to warn you. What we're about to show you may be disturbing to some viewers."

Now, a pre-recorded video shot with a handheld camera. As the reporter described the scene in voiceover, I recognized Neck Beard behind the wheel. He sat motionless, his eyes to heaven. The windshield was shot out.

The Asian's body was covered in glass, the face and chest drenched in blood. I imagined the killers forcing the car over and firing through the smoked-out windows, unaware of who was inside.

"That should've been me," I said.

"Vicky, any idea whether this and the other shooting are related?"

"The police are denying any connection."

"Are there any witnesses?"

"No. But the police have released this photo of a man seen near the area. They're calling him a person of interest."

A picture appeared on the screen. It had been taken on a phone from far away. Though the face was blurry, he resembled someone I knew.

"As in the other attack in West LA, the police do not have a motive for this killing," the reporter said. "And they urge anyone who may have witnessed anything to come forward. Victoria Muñoz, ABC7 Eyewitness News, reporting."

The news anchor came back on. "In other news…"

I switched off the TV and fixed myself a drink. It was a matter of time before they found the gray-suit in the parking structure—the one I killed.

Though I wasn't sure how well Hellborn cleaned up their messes, something else weighed on me—the man in the photo. After reading the text conversation earlier, there was no doubt in my mind who he was. Tyler Berry.

And he'd meant to kill me.

CHAPTER
TWENTY-FIVE

RAUL WAS TOLD to wait outside, and I walked in alone. Even after I'd eliminated his nephew in the desert, Kersey had managed to move past it. But now, he looked ready to feed me to a monitor lizard. I slumped into a chair in front of the desk like a sixth grader in the principal's office.

"Tell me everything," he said. "Starting with the doctor's office."

I ran it down to him, including the part about my self-surgery.

"These men, what did you call them?"

"Gray-suits."

"And using the microchip, they followed you to West LA? Why didn't they try grabbing you sooner?"

"They didn't have my serial number. Now they do."

"And you destroyed the chip. Without it, they're blind, right?"

What if you don't find her? Oh, we'll find her.

"Correct."

"What about Vincent?"

"They must've spotted him on his way to Glendale and assumed I was driving."

"Makes sense. By then, they had the plate number. Do you think they know about me?"

"Anything's possible."

He rubbed the back of his neck. "I'd shoot you now, but what's the point? Waste of a good bullet. What else can you tell me about Baseborn?"

I shared everything I'd learned so far. In Rosamond, Harry Packard and his specialists had scoured the premises, searching for me. Wearing a gray suit, I thought I'd fooled him. Obviously, I hadn't.

"I shot down a drone," I said.

If Packard didn't have my serial number at the time, then how was the UAV able to tail me? Was it possible he was lying and wanted me to escape? But why? Nothing made any sense. And now, Neck Beard was dead.

"I think Packard might wanna keep me under surveillance," I said.

"At the doctor's office, they tried killing you."

"Welcome to my world."

Kersey opened a desk drawer and pulled out a pad. Using his Montblanc pen, he sketched three boxes—two on top and one below. He wrote my name in the third box.

"You mentioned there were two programs at Baseborn," he said.

"That I know of. Alpha and Hyper."

I came around the desk and looked over his shoulder. He wrote *Alpha* in the first box and *Hyper* in the second.

"Who did you say ran Alpha?"

"Walt Freeman."

"And Hyper?"

"Caroline Sheldrake."

He wrote the names above their respective boxes and leaned back, tapping his pen on the pad. Concentrating, he scratched a line between Freeman and Sheldrake, going back and forth until the ink saturated the paper.

"I wonder if there was a thing between these two," he said.

"You mean, like a rivalry? Packard told me someone sabotaged the Hyper program. Maybe it was Walt Freeman."

He drew a line from each of the top boxes, connecting them to mine. On the Sheldrake line, he wrote *Harry Packard*. On the other, he put a question mark. He handed me the pad.

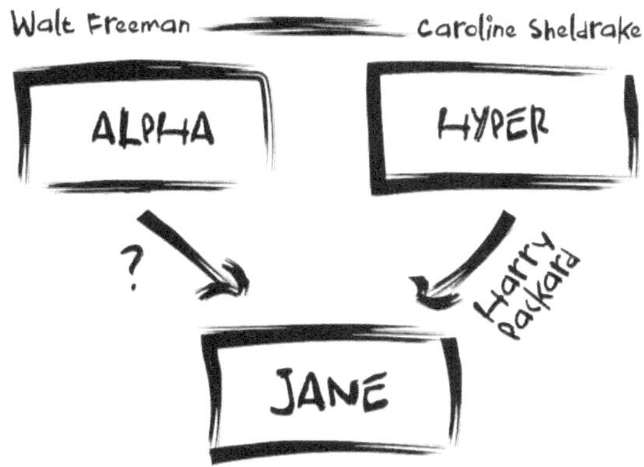

"Let's assume Packard is only interested in watching you," he said. "Whoever tried to kill you—"

"Is working for Walt Freeman. But he's dead."

"Looks like someone took over the mission."

At Hellborn, when the gray-suit on the radio told Packard the Russian girl was missing, the security chief mentioned another name—what was it? Kersey got up and stretched. I laid the pad on the desk and returned to my chair.

"On the news, they showed a photo of a suspect leaving Echo Park," he said. "Any idea who he might be?"

"I wish I did." There was no way I'd tell him about Tyler Berry. I'd track down the shitbag myself.

"What do we know about Harry Packard?" he said.

"Married with a daughter."

"Shouldn't be too hard to find."

"Which reminds me. Any new leads on Hellborn?"

"I, uh. I haven't started yet." Then on my death stare, "I am running a business, you know."

"Fine. As soon as you have an address for Packard, I'll go there and have a heart-to-heart."

"Sounds dangerous. Maybe for now, we watch him."

Screw that. If Packard didn't want me dead, then he must know who did.

That's Zeddemore's problem.

"Zeddemore!" I said.

"What's a zeddemore?"

"It's the name I was trying to remember. Whoever he or she is, they're mixed up in this too."

Kersey put his phone in his pocket like he was going somewhere. "It would be nice to have a first name. Ask Raul to come in."

I went to the door. Outside, the Colombian was chatting with someone—the vaper from the machine shop. When the mook saw me, he gave me the greasy eye. Back in his office, the boss smiled at us the way a Doberman grins at an intruder. Before tearing him a new one.

"Vincent is dead," Kersey said. "You two are partners now."

"Partners?" How did I not see that coming?

"From now on, you'll do all your assignments together. Pretty soon, you'll be finishing each other's sentences."

I had plans to track down Harry Packard and kill Tyler Berry. There was no way I was taking the Colombian with me. He'd only slow me down.

Kersey walked past us to the door. "I have another meeting."

"Wait," I said. "What about the assignment?"

"Raul has all the details. Oh, the New Year's Eve party. I'll text you the address."

He looked me over in my good haircut and black suit. "Wear something expensive."

After the boss had gone, I turned to my new partner. "All I do now is shop."

When he opened his mouth to speak, I stuck a warning finger in his face.

"Whatever you're thinking, keep it to yourself," I said.

CHAPTER
TWENTY-SIX

I MADE Raul park in the remote lot next to me to avoid the gray-suits. We hoofed it to my place so I could change clothes. I left the bedroom door partway open. He waited outside while I stripped and lowered a black-and-white tie-dyed bodycon mini dress over my head. I caught him watching me through the crack. The look on his face wasn't pervy, though. He was annoyed.

"Something on your mind?" I said.

"Why didn't you tell Kersey sooner about the doctor's office?"

I sat on the bed and put on my sandals. "I was gonna."

"He lost some good men because of you!"

I placed the phone and weapon in my crossbody bag. "What are you saying?"

"You're dangerous."

I gave my hair a quick brushing, put on lip gloss, and walked past him. "You're just now figuring this out? Come on. We're taking my car."

"Why?"

"Because yours looks like the one Vincent died in. And I

have no intention of making it easy for the gray-suits." *Or Tyler Berry.*

He exited the apartment ahead of me. "What's with the dress?"

"Like it?" I said. "It's new."

It took us minutes to reach South Alvarado Street. The place was crawling with immigrants, loud music, and the smell of great food. Raul directed me to a parking lot on 8th near MacArthur Park. I followed him back to Alvarado.

The place we were looking for wasn't far. At 7th, we crossed the street and headed toward a gaudy-looking store-front. There was an orange-and-blue sign over the entrance— CHICO'S MONEY TRANSFER. ENVIOS DE DINERO. CHECK CASHING.

The interior looked like something out of a demented circus. Against the bright orange walls with royal blue trim stood a wall of bullet-proof glass. Behind it, a line of girls in orange polos helped nonnative customers send money to the old country.

We stood to one side, conspicuous as hell. The Colombian in his sharp black suit and me in the hormone dress. He gave the girl at the end a wicked smile, making her blush. As we approached a door with one-way glass, she pressed a button under her station.

When the buzzer sounded, we went in. A short hallway led to a large room filled with tables and money-counting machines. I stopped for a sec to observe the operation.

Asians and Latinas wrapped stacks of cash in money bands labeled *$500*. These they loaded into plastic storage containers. There had to be hundreds of thousands of dollars in here. Two armed guards stood at opposite ends of the room. Security cameras recorded the employees' every move.

We continued toward an office in the back. There, a small bald man with glasses and a pencil mustache sat on a stool. His arms were short—more like flippers. He wore a short-sleeve white perma press shirt, black pants, and shoes with thick rubber soles. Using a loupe, he examined a British passport.

"Hey, Perry," Raul said.

The man answered without looking up. "Finally got yourself a girlfriend like I told you?"

"It's not like that."

Ignoring the Colombian, he set the loupe aside and looked me over. "I like the dress. What's your name, sweetheart?"

"Jane." Side-eyeing my partner, I extended my hand. "Nice to meet you."

"Perry Rochambeau. Likewise. Kinda tall, ain't-cha? You keeping our boy happy?"

I fake-laughed like a tart. "Oh, yeah."

"Very good. Here's a little tip for free. He's partial to thongs. And herb butter. Least, that's what I heard."

Burping, he opened the top drawer of his desk and removed a manila envelope. He poured out several passports on the green blotter. Raul nodded to me, and we started going through them. I noticed my partner taking his time with one in particular. When I looked over, I saw the grinning, hopeful face of the boy who'd died in the shootout in the desert—Guillermo. Raul laid the passport on the desk.

"We won't be needing this one," he said.

"What happened?"

The Colombian looked at his hands. "He didn't make it."

I thought Perry was an okay guy until he said, "I still have to charge you."

After concluding our business, we returned to the parking lot. A bunch of teenagers wearing hoodies, distressed jeans, and skater shoes were crowded around the Mustang, oohing and aahing. Though they were white, they tried acting all ghetto. Their fingerprints were all over my car. A short punk pulled repeatedly on the driver's side door handle.

Raul leaned over. "Want me to—"

"I got it," I said. Then to Ant-Man, "What're you doing?"

"Wait, what?" He side-eyed his skeezy pals. "Okay, you're tall. Damn, girl. You a bad kitty too, I bet."

The others cat-called, which only encouraged him.

"Move away from the car."

He looked away, then tried taking a swipe at me. I grabbed his hand and twisted his arm, driving him to his knees.

"I said, move away from the car."

I let him go and kicked him in the ass, making him face-plant. He scrambled to his feet and joined his shocked friends. They ran. When the hobbit was far enough away, he cursed me, which made me laugh.

The Colombian nodded approvingly. "At least you didn't shoot him."

"Where to?" I said when we were on the street.

"Echo Park. Get over to Alvarado. Then a left."

I continued north. "So, Chico's. Kersey uses them to launder money?"

"Hardly. The money transfer part is legit. You'd be surprised how much cash flows out of this country every day —legally."

"And Perry Rochambeau?"

"Best forger in the business. What's with the face?"

"I need a stupid dress for the party."

"No problem. After we drop the passports, we can head over to The Grove."

"Is there an Apple store there?"

"Yeah, why?"

"No reason," I said.

CHAPTER
TWENTY-SEVEN

THE GROVE on Fairfax was overrun with customers eager to spend money on clothes, makeup, and overpriced food. Me, all I wanted was an effing dress. And shoes to go with it —jeez.

I settled on an Hervé Léger black mini cocktail number that hugged me like a drunk producer at an afterparty. With clothes shopping out of the way, we headed to the nearby Apple store.

"Kersey doesn't like us owning electronics he hasn't personally vetted," Raul said.

"Which is why you're not gonna tell him, partner."

While I shopped, the Colombian stood near the entrance, scanning the area for gray-suits. I had to admit, he wasn't bad company. He did what he was supposed to and never complained. I'd worn a dress to appear less conspicuous in La La Land. But it had the opposite effect.

Some asshat in his forties, with a fake tan and veneers, worked his way over to me and pretended he was looking at the merchandise and not at my rack. He had on a black wool sport jacket and a colorful silk shirt. The top buttons were undone, revealing a forest of chest hair ample enough for mattress filling.

"I was admiring you from over there," he said.

"Get lost."

He pretended to take offense. "What? Am I to assume you don't like men?"

I gave him a tight smile. "See the guy over there by the door? Boyfriend. And where he comes from, you even look at another man's woman, and… Well, I'm sure you can imagine the rest."

He laughed. "Ten years of Brazilian Jiu-Jitsu. I think I can handle myself."

"I dunno. Might be tough without any hands or feet. I guess you could try bleeding on him."

He stood there for a sec, incredulous. When I refused to blink, he slunk out of the store.

"Bitch," he said.

When I was alone again, some tool in a company T-shirt dropped what he was doing and rushed over to assist me.

"I need a laptop," I said. "But I'm not sure what kind."

The eager employee walked me through the choices. After seeing everything, I settled on a MacBook Pro. No, I didn't need a monitor or a mouse and keyboard. AppleCare? I guess. Computer bag? Why not. iPad? Save it for the fanboys.

He escorted me to the register and rang everything up. I paid in cash and walked out, hauling my stuff. We decided to grab a snack at La Piazza. Not the best food in the world, according to the Colombian. But I was in the mood for pizza.

We sat on the terrace, facing outward, in case any hostiles were prowling the premises. After we ordered, Raul got a call and stepped away. When he returned, the food was sitting on the table. He watched me as I took an enormous bite of my veggie pizza.

"What?" I said.

"You don't even have the slightest remorse?"

"For?"

"Vincent."

"What brings this on?"

"It occurred to me, ever since we found out, you never even— Forget it."

"Look. I don't feel things the way other people do."

"What you're saying is you're a psychopath."

"High functioning. Okay, I don't go around killing people unless they're a threat. But I don't empathize with them either. Too much drama."

"What does Kant say?"

"Good question. He wrote about a *communicability of feelings*. It's the closest he ever got to the idea of empathy between individuals." I took another bite. "Some people are wired to feel things. I'm not."

"You must have cared about someone at some point in your life."

A flashback sputtered to life like an old movie reel…

Bo and me in the corn maze. I was four. Laughing, we chased each other through twists and turns and dead ends. Someone called to us, and we came out.

A woman stood at the back door, her hands covering her face. She was weeping and…

The pictures faded like hot breath on cold glass.

"I can't remember," I said.

The Colombian's expression changed. Something in the eyes. As if for the first time, he understood.

"What do you need a computer for anyway?"

I was silent as the grave.

"Whatever it is, you can trust me. We're partners, remember?"

He touched my arm. My instinct was to pull away, but I didn't. At this moment, I craved a connection. A reminder that, despite everything Hellborn had done to me, I was still human—still a person.

"Tell you later, okay?" I said. "Was Kersey checking up on you?"

"Friend of mine called. Owns a restaurant. He's having money problems."

"Place any good?"

"Fantastic. Asian fusion. But there's more competition now."

"Why don't you ask Kersey to back him?"

He got to his feet and pointed at my pizza. "Want a box?"

Wow, guess I'm done. "It's okay. I'll prob'ly let it sit out, leaving myself open to all kinds of foodborne bacteria."

He threw down some cash. "Sounds about right."

"Shut up," I said. "I was totally kidding."

TWENTY-EIGHT

AT THE APARTMENT, my first order of business was to set up the laptop so I could start my research. I knew guns, not computers. Raul offered to help. After I connected to the building's Wi-Fi, he advised me to purchase software to mask my IP address. Sitting at the kitchen table, I fired up a VPN connection. When I brought up Google Chrome, he stopped me and showed me how to open an incognito window.

"Really?" I said.

"Extra precaution." He brought over a couple of waters from the fridge. "I thought Kersey was supposed to help you."

"He hasn't done squat."

He pulled up a chair next to mine. The heat from his body was distracting, not to mention his scent. Sandalwood and citrus.

"What is it you're trying to find out?"

"Everything."

I typed *baseborn identity research* in the search field. Google came back with more than a page of hits. At the top was the company's website, followed by listings of all their locations. It surprised me to learn they had offices in Toronto, London, and Tel Aviv. The LA location wasn't too far from where we were. But no reference to the Rosamond facility. I continued to dig.

Raul retreated to the living room, where he found the sports equipment I'd ordered from DICK'S. With everything going on, I hadn't had time to get to it. I think he was bored because he began ripping open boxes.

I followed one trail after the next. Thanks to a Wikipedia article, I learned Baseborn Identity Research was a spinoff of another firm formerly headquartered in Virginia. Robbin-Sear Industries was a privately held bioscience technology company founded in 1990 by Dr. John Robbin and Dr. William Sear.

The Department of Defense awarded them a contract to provide vaccines to American troops during the Gulf War. They made products for Hepatitis A and B, typhoid, and malaria. Soon, they began manufacturing serums to protect against chemical and biological agents. Later, they expanded their program, looking for ways to inoculate soldiers to prevent the effects of PTSD from occurring. There were no more details on the research. Both founders had died from cancer, and the company no longer existed.

Returning to Baseborn's website, I brought up a page listing their senior executives. The Chairman and CEO was Walt Freeman. He looked to be in his fifties. Overweight, with thinning gray hair. His bio said he used to be the COO of Robbin-Sear. No mention of his recent demise in the desert.

Other execs included Eamon Trower, Chief Security Officer. *Trower…right. The guy with his throat torn out in the hospital at Hellborn.* Dr. Caroline Sheldrake, Head of Research, was among the company's officers. She was an attractive woman, maybe sixty. With brown hair down to her shoulders, glasses, and thin, determined lips.

The problem was, I had no clue what I was looking for and decided to take a break. It was almost five. I'd purchased a bottle of the El Señorio Joven con Gusano and poured out two fingers into a shot glass. After adding ice, lime, and salt, I made one for my new partner.

In the living room, Raul had already assembled the body opponent bag. Gloves, wraps, and a rolled-up mat lay next to it. Now he was on the sofa, watching television. I glanced at the pull-up bar in my bedroom doorway.

"Thanks for doing all that," I said, handing him his drink. "Are they speaking Italian?"

In an old hotel, a bumbling idiot tried to open an ancient dumbwaiter, which was voice activated. He was supposed to say the password, but he'd forgotten it.

"It's an old movie from the seventies called *Calma e Pazzo*," he said.

"*Calm and Crazy*. What's it about?"

"Not sure. This guy, Marcello, lost half his brain in a parallel universe."

"Experiment gone wrong?"

"And the dumbwaiter acts as a portal."

I took a seat next to the Colombian, and we watched together. Eventually, the guy remembered the password—*Asa Nisi Masa*—and climbed in. After a bunch of cheesy visual effects, he arrived in a garden. A pretty, barefoot girl picking mushrooms saw him and screamed, which made him scream.

"I could use another drink," I said.

In the kitchen, we took the conversation elsewhere. I refilled our glasses and ran down everything I'd learned, starting with the body inside the helicopter in the desert.

"Walt Freeman ran Hellborn," I said. "Before that, he was the COO of another company that was also into some pretty weird shit."

"Like what?"

"Officially, the company made vaccines for the military. But they'd started developing a new drug to prevent PTSD in soldiers. I found a subreddit where someone who supposedly worked there as a security guard spun up a conspiracy theory. It was all about zombies running around Northern California. Some backwater town called Tres Marias."

"Sounds like *Night of the Living Dead*."

"Right? Here's the interesting part. They claim Baseborn Identity Research took over the project. And they mentioned a drug called Surrelis, which I now know was used to create the alphas at Hellborn."

"And these alphas—"

"Are as real as those scars on your fingers."

"Hijueputa. And they had you on the stuff too?"

"We were in the Hyper program."

"Who would know about that?"

"Caroline Sheldrake. She's Head of Research, based in Hampstead, Virginia. I wish I could talk to her."

Suddenly, I was feverish. As I set down the glass, my vision blurred. I closed my eyes and leaned over the kitchen island, my hands gripping the edge.

"What's wrong?" Raul said.

"I don't know. I feel hot. Maybe it was the mescal."

He touched my forehead. "You have a fever. Has this happened before?"

"There's a thermometer here somewhere."

Vaguely, I waved at the kitchen cabinets. One at a time, he flung the doors open until he found a CVS bag. After inserting the batteries, he took my temperature and showed me the display. 102°F.

She won't last long without the drug.

"Wait here," I said.

I stumbled into the bathroom. Grabbing different clothes, I slammed the door shut and ran the shower. Standing under the steady stream of cold water brought my temperature down.

When I was well enough, I dried myself off and put on my tank top and yoga pants. Raul was at the kitchen table, paging through *One Hundred Years of Solitude*. He grinned at my drowned-rat hair.

"Better?" he said.

"Good to go." I touched his hand. It was warm. "Promise me you won't tell Kersey."

"What if it happens again?"

"I'll figure something out."

"Fine." He got up to leave.

"You can borrow the book, if you want."

"I read it in school."

"So, you'll be at the party tomorrow?"

"Of course."

I followed him to the door. "Good. I mean, see you there."

"In case we don't connect, be careful with Griselda. She's the kind of woman who can charm you to death. Literally."

"Copy—" Catching myself, I laughed. "Understood."

He lingered. For a hot sec, I thought we had a moment. But before things could escalate, he walked out. *Just as well.* Last thing I needed was to get mixed up with my partner. It's no good in the Marines, and a terrible idea here. The important thing was to stay focused. And alone.

The door hadn't been closed ten seconds when there was a knock. I opened it and found the Colombian looking at me with smoldering eyes. He didn't say anything. Instead, he came at me like a battle tank with no brakes.

Kicking the door shut, he grabbed me by the waist and pulled me close. His scent made me dizzy. I forgot myself as he kissed my lips and neck. Though my pulse remained steady, my mind was an open door.

In seconds, we were naked in bed. Our breath heaving. Our bodies throbbing as one. A vague knee jerk from the past startled me—warned me he might get violent. I had an impulse to defend myself, but I didn't. Instead, I forced myself to trust him.

He didn't hurt me. It was the opposite—he was sweet to

me. Without words, we devoured each other. No thought of the past or future. Only the now. I didn't know where this was going, and I didn't care.

When it was over, we lay silent in each other's arms. I listened to his steady breathing. Ran my fingers over the tattoo of a skull on his chest. Touched his bandaged shoulder. And kissed his eyes.

Then, he was sweet to me again.

TWENTY-NINE

THOUGH I DIDN'T ASK him to, Raul stayed with me and left early the next morning. I remained in bed, wondering how our night of passion had happened. One minute, we were partners doing our job. And the next…

I told myself I'd let my guard down because of the fever. I was disoriented and, what, vulnerable? Bullshit. I'd wanted it as much as he did. Another thought crossed my mind—one I refused to accept. I was attracted to the Colombian the first time I laid eyes on him.

Whatever. It happened, that's all. Better to put it in the rearview mirror. I took stock of my situation, wondering what would become of me. *Three to the head.* Was that my fate? Strictly speaking, I should be dead already, like the others. The fact that I was alive meant I might have a purpose. I ticked off my priorities.

1. Stay alive.
2. Kill whoever wants me dead.
3. Remember my name.

None of these would be easy. If this were the Marines, I'd

have my squad, with somebody else giving the orders. I had no one—it was all up to me. Realistically, how long could I elude the gray-suits? They were everywhere. And LC?

I had to get to Harry Packard—I didn't see any other way. But what if Kersey was wrong, and it was Packard who had ordered me killed? Maybe Tyler Berry was working for him.

For the next two hours, I went through my workout routine, adding martial arts to the mix. Later, I opened the fridge and made a face. The last thing I wanted was a repeat of my one and only kitchen nightmare.

With everything I was carrying the day before, I'd taken a chance and parked in the building. Before exiting, I walked the parking garage. As I drove past the gate, I scanned the street for Escalades. Not a one in sight—my luck was holding out.

At Starbucks, I continued researching Hellborn over coffee and a veggie breakfast sandwich. Searching on "baseborn keepr" took me to the Clayborn Electronics website. This was the same firm that designed the SIM card in the dead gray-suit's phone. Based in Maryland, they were a subsidiary of Baseborn Identity Research. Naturally. I felt like I was in an endless loop, so I tried something else.

The subreddit I'd found earlier had mentioned a town up north called Tres Marias. According to the lore, an outbreak had occurred in a secret lab on Old Orchard Road. When I searched on it, a Wikipedia page popped up. It displayed photos of an average-looking town, with history, geography, demographics, and a bunch of other nonsense I had no patience for.

A couple of hours later, I left the store and returned to my car. I opened my purse and stared at the stolen phone. Did I really want to do this? I must've sat behind the wheel for ten minutes. After weighing the pros and cons, I drove to Griffith Observatory.

The view of the city below was magnificent. I reinserted the SIM and turned on the phone. Scrolling through the list of contacts, I found LC. When I made the call, *Private Number* glowed on the display. Someone answered on the first ring.

"Hello?" I said. Silence. "Hello?"

"This is LC."

"Tyler? It's me."

Another long silence, followed by the sound of a door closing. Then a familiar voice. "How're you doin'? It's been a minute."

"Tyler, what's going on?"

"I can explain everything, but not on the phone. We need to meet."

"I saw you on the news. Were you the shooter?"

Another pause. Then, "Naw, man. I was there to protect you."

"From?"

"Harry Packard."

"He's not the one trying to kill me. Hello?"

"Are you okay?"

"I guess. Been getting these—"

"Temperature spikes?"

"How'd you know?"

"I used to get them too. They call it *hyper karma*. It's because you're not on the drug anymore."

"Wait, are you?"

"I got my hands on some Riactis. Keeping it on the down-low."

"Tell me how to get it."

"Sure, when we meet."

"So you got away too? I didn't see you at the site in the desert."

"They split us up. Don't you remember? I stayed in Virginia."

"I can't remember anything. Are we the only ones left?"

"There are others. In Hampstead."

I tried putting everything together. More hypers were in the program somewhere outside Richmond. Walt Freeman didn't kill all of them. But how was Tyler involved?

"And you escaped, right?" I said. "Like me?"

"It's complicated. I'll tell you everything when we meet."

An overwhelming sense of loneliness blanketed me. I'd left Tyler Berry wounded in a village in Afghanistan while I crawled off to die. How was it that he was here in LA?

"It's crazy, right?" I said. Tears blinded me, and I was powerless to stop them. "Tyler, who am I?"

"I don't understand."

"You know you're Tyler Berry. But me—I can't remember my name—please."

"I can't. Not over the phone. Tell you when I see you."

"When?"

"Tonight." He gave me an address. "Listen, there's something I need to tell you. Stay away from Packard. He's dangerous."

I wiped my nose. "I think maybe he let me go."

"It's all a game with him. He's not stable. And he's hunting, like those alphas. When he finds you, he'll kill you—guaranteed."

"Tyler?"

"Gotta go," he said. "Stay safe."

I couldn't move. For a long time, I sat in my car, replaying the conversation. Was that Tyler? Maybe he was dead like the others, and someone was impersonating him. But the voice. No, it had to be him. A sudden rage filled me. I wanted to tear out the throats of all the gray-suits. Then I'd find Caroline Sheldrake and make her tell me who I am.

There was a good chance they'd already located me via

the phone. Though I didn't want to, I removed the SIM and threw it away. After placing the device under my front tire, I rolled over it repeatedly until there was nothing left.

Speaking with Tyler had convinced me there was a way out of this. When we met later, he would give me the drug and tell me who I was. There was no way I would survive without trusting someone.

I decided to trust Tyler Berry.

GRISELDA MÜLLER'S house sat atop a hill in Bel Air, overlooking the twinkling lights of the city. At the gate, I found a cluster of men in European suits and pointy shoes, talking and smoking. They were foreign and spoke in a language unfamiliar to me. As I drove up, one of them walked over and signaled me to lower my window. From where I was sitting, I could see his holster.

"Jane," I said. "I was invited."

Smelling of sweat, he looked me over like a cut of meat. He turned to a companion and said something I didn't understand. Chortling, his buddy made a call.

"How do I know you're not cop?" The sweaty dude's accent was incomprehensible.

"Why would you say that?"

"See the car over there?"

I craned my neck. Across the street, two men in cheap suits sat in a nondescript Ford Taurus, watching the gates. Could they be any more obvious?

"I'm not a cop. I work for Kersey."

I handed him my driver's license. He gave it a cursory

look. His friend ended his call and nodded. Sweaty-balls returned my license, his eyes drifting to my cleavage.

"You let the Polish pig put his hands on you?"

Laughing, he signaled one of the others to let me through. I'd had enough of these ass clowns.

"You understand Russian, right? Idi na hui." *Go eff yourself.*

His face went slack. Without looking back, I drove on.

This was supposed to be a party, but there were few cars at the top of the hill. Two bodyguards brandishing AR-15s patrolled the front. I found a spot and parked. Earlier, I'd practiced walking in heels and made it all the way to the entrance without a problem.

I'd agreed to meet Tyler around midnight. Some warehouse off Venice. My plan was to stay here for a bit, then go home to change before driving to Culver City.

The house was large and modern, with lots of glass. Drippy white Christmas lights hung from the eaves. The front door was unlocked. Pop tunes from the nineties played over a stereo system. Walking in, I found Griselda wearing a tight-fitting, black, strapless satin dress. She was holding court, surrounded by men in dark suits with their cookie-cutter wives or girlfriends.

Kersey stood off to the side, dressed in a floral jacquard dinner jacket. The man he was with was a stranger to me. His face was hard-looking, and his longish blond hair hung loosely over his shoulders. He smiled at me through crooked teeth. A filterless burning cigarette dangled from his left hand. Whoever this guy was, he was ex-military for sure.

I'd made it as far as the living room entrance when Raul met me. I hardly recognized him. His long, dark hair was slicked back, and his suit looked new. Instead of the requisite white shirt, he wore one made of black silk. I had a sudden urge to tear off his clothes.

"You look nice," he said.

"You too."

"Any trouble getting past security?"

"There was one guy. I had no choice but to insult him."

"Didn't think you spoke Serbian."

"I'm pretty sure he understood my Russian. Who's Kersey talking to?"

"Babić. Griselda's security chief."

"And all those men work for him? Why all the muscle?"

"She worries about her daughter."

"What's the game plan?"

"There are important people here tonight. See those two over there? The mayor and his wife."

"Impressive. And the others?"

"Politicians and Silicon Valley types, mostly."

"And then there's Babić."

The guy looked more like a thug than security. On cue, he glanced at me and said something to Kersey. My boss turned, wearing a weak smile. Were those two talking about me now?

"We'd better go in," the Colombian said.

I grabbed his sleeve. "About last night."

"No worries. One-time thing—I get it."

"That's not what I was gonna say. I'm glad it happened." I squeezed his hand. "Wish me luck."

Taking a breath, I entered the room and walked past an enormous Christmas tree to where Griselda stood. She handed off her drink and glided toward me.

"I am so pleased you came," she said.

She air-kissed both my cheeks. Not waiting for me to reciprocate, she took my hand and presented me like a debutante in a Jane Austen novel.

"I'd like you to meet the mayor. Mr. Mayor, this is Jane."

The man was good-looking. Short. Maybe sixty. Latino. I'd never seen teeth so white. He introduced me to his wife.

As the chit-chat dragged on, I looked for a way out. A little girl sat alone on a long sofa. She was blonde and wore a brown-and-pink party dress with pink bows and matching shoes. Excusing myself, I walked over and took a seat next to her.

"I like your dress," I said. "I'm Jane."

Extending her hand, she gave me a smile. "Lily. You look nice too."

"Thanks. You're Griselda's daughter."

"Uh-huh." She turned and pointed. "That's my dad over there."

"I know. I work for him."

Her eyes got huge. "Really?"

"Yep. Started a few days ago."

"Do you know my grandma?"

"I do."

Not far off, Nate, wearing a black off-the-shoulder dress, was in conversation with several other women.

"Your dad mentioned you guys went camping. How was it?"

"Great. He taught me how to fish."

"Catch anything?"

"No. But I saw a condor."

I looked around the room—all adults. "This can't be fun for you."

She shrugged. "It's my job."

"You have a job?"

"Uh-huh. Mama said I'm here to remind everyone she's a mom *first and foremost*."

"Is that right?" I noticed Griselda watching us. "Hey, wanna give me the tour?"

"Okay."

As she took my hand to show me around, someone announced dinner. I made a pouty face. She copied me, and we both laughed.

"Guess we'll have to do it another time," I said. "Are you having dinner with us?"

She sighed. "I ate already." She put out her hand. "It was nice meeting you, Jane. Ciao. It means *See you later*. I'm studying Italian."

A kind-looking older woman wearing a uniform took Lily's hand. As they walked off, the child gave me the best little wave.

We sat at a long table in a dining room with paintings hanging all along the walls. I didn't know shit about modern art, but everything looked expensive.

Griselda had made up place cards. I sat to her left, with Babić next to me. The mayor sat on her right. His wife was somewhere farther down. Our host had stuck Kersey at the opposite end of the table with his mother and a bunch of random stiffs. Raul was nowhere in sight.

"I see you've met Lily," Griselda said.

"She's adorable. How old is she?"

"She turned eight last week."

"She seems mature for her age."

"So, Jane," the mayor said. "What do you do?"

"Oh, I work for—"

"She's employed by my ex-husband," Griselda said. She took my hand, intertwining our fingers like sisters. "I'm making it my mission to steal her away."

She and the mayor shared a laugh. I glanced at Kersey. The man looked miserable.

"You should watch out," Babić said, eyeing the German. "Griselda always gets what she wants."

Our host laughed. "And why not? What is life but for the taking? Wouldn't you agree, Mr. Mayor?"

He grinned in appreciation. "It's the code I live by."

"What do you know? Me too. Divorce that wife of yours, and let's you and I get married."

Awkward and red faced, he laughed. Soon, everyone joined in except me. At the far end of the table, a glass broke. Someone shouted, and the room fell silent. A woman in a white sequin dress stood next to Kersey. She shook her finger at him and shouted in a Slavic-sounding language. Nate tried taking her arm. The distraught woman yanked it away and continued her tirade. Exhausted, she broke down in tears. Nate and another man—possibly the husband—escorted the woman from the table.

"What was that all about?" I said.

Griselda gave me a curious smile. "My former sister-in-law, Marta. It's not her fault. She lost her son recently."

She sighed dramatically, and I could see where her daughter got it from. "I suppose she blames Kersey."

"The poor woman," the mayor said. "Will she be all right?"

We'd gotten as far as the second course when I felt a fever creeping up on me. By now, I knew the warning signs. Blurry vision. Flickers of light behind the eyes. Clammy skin. Head on fire. *Hyper karma*, Tyler had called it.

Fearing a scene, I excused myself and asked a server to point me to a bathroom. Inside, I locked the door and splashed cold water on my face and neck. I tried to slow my breathing, but it was no good. My temperature was spiking. I stumbled out and made my way to a closed door behind the dining room. When I opened it, I discovered the kitchen. Raul and a bodyguard sat at the table, eating dinner. Lightheaded, I moved toward my partner.

"What is it?" he said, getting to his feet.

"It's happening again." I sank into a chair. "See if you can find some ice."

Ignoring the kitchen staff, I laid my arms on the table and rested my head. A moment later, a soothing cold. The Colombian had placed a wet towel on the back of my neck. With his other hand, he pressed his palm to my forehead.

"What's wrong with her?" the bodyguard said in a German accent.

"She has the flu." Then to me, "You're burning up. We need to get you home. Can you walk?"

"I can try."

He helped me to my feet. I took one step and collapsed on the floor.

"Jane!" His voice was a million miles away.

When I opened my eyes, Kersey and his ex-wife were standing over me. Raul was at the sink, preparing another towel with ice. Griselda looked at her ex-husband, genuinely concerned.

"Should we call 911?" she said.

Crouching, he took my arm and signaled the Colombian to grab the other one. Next thing I knew, I was vertical. My legs were like rubber, my head like a coal boiler in a runaway locomotive. Griselda handed Kersey my purse, and the men helped me out the back door.

Outside, the cold air soothed me as they brought me to my car. Last thing I remembered was Raul helping me into the passenger seat. And Kersey's voice, thin and distant.

"Whatever this is, I hope she's not contagious," he said.

THIRTY-ONE

WHEN I CAME TO, I was lying near naked in my tub. Panicked, I imagined drowning in black water and sat up straight. *How long was I out?* Raul was next to me on his knees, his shirt sleeves rolled up and holding a towel. I took it from him and pressed it against my cheek.

"How long?" I said.

"Maybe half an hour."

I gave him a lazy smile. "You took my clothes off?"

"I didn't want to ruin the dress."

"Some dinner. Kersey's sister lost it. What if she finds out it was me who killed her son?"

"She won't."

He helped me out, and I dried myself off. I picked up the thermometer lying on the sink. The last reading was 108°F. He took it from me and checked my temperature again.

"It's down to a hundred," he said.

"That's normal for me. Hey, what time is it?"

"Eleven-thirty."

"I'm supposed to meet someone."

"Who?"

I felt I could trust the Colombian and told him about my conversation with Tyler Berry. I explained what hyper karma was and how it affected me. And I mentioned Riactis, the drug that might prevent the condition.

"Sounds sketchy," he said. "What if this guy is lying, and you walk into a trap?"

"What do you suggest?"

"Let me call one of the guys. He'll drive over and scope it out."

I had to admit he was right. I didn't know if the person I'd spoken to was Tyler. Besides, I wasn't feeling well. If everything checked out at the warehouse, I would find a way to arrange another meeting.

"Sounds like a plan," I said. "By the way, what did you end up telling Kersey?"

"I convinced him you have a virus. He told me to look after you for the next few days."

I went to get clothes and underwear. Raul sat on the toilet seat, holding the thermometer and staring at the floor.

"Don't you have a call to make?" I said.

After showering, I put on jeans and a black tank top. Something smelled good. In the kitchen, I found my partner finely chopping red bell peppers and zucchini. He was blindingly fast. Now I knew how he'd scarred his hands. I took a seat at the island.

"I was hungry," he said. "The food at Griselda's wasn't good."

"What're you making?"

"Frittata. Want some? It's vegetarian."

"You bet—I'm starving."

He poured me a glass of white wine. "You didn't have any basil. I had to improvise. It'll be ready soon."

He whisked eggs and milk in a clear bowl and folded in the ingredients. Then he poured the mixture into a hot skillet. I laughed to myself, thinking about my misadventures in cooking. Soon, the food was ready, and we ate at the table. I sniffed a forkful and tried it.

"Aw man," I said.

"Good, right?"

"Rah. I mean, yeah. Okay, are you gonna explain how it is you can cook like this?"

He took a swallow of wine. "I used to be a chef."

"In Medellín?"

"Grew up in an area called Perpetuo Socorro."

"*Perpetual Help.*"

"Not the best place to practice the culinary arts."

"Gangs, right?"

"You have no idea. I held out as long as I could. But we were poor."

"Were you a…what is it? Sicario?"

"Hitman? No. But I was into all kinds of other shit. Drugs. Kidnapping."

"Nice."

"A corrupt cop double-crossed me, and I was almost killed. That's when I realized I had to change my life. Got a job as a dishwasher. Worked my way up to kitchen porter."

"And kept going until you became a chef?"

"That's right. But my old life followed me. I thought if I came here, things would be different."

"But then you fell in with Kersey."

"Griselda was my sponsor. I met him through her."

"Did you and she ever—"

"She was married to Kersey. He liked me and promised to invest in a restaurant."

"Your friend's place?"

"We were going to be partners. But Kersey never came

through. Said he was trying to build up his operation. And with my background, I would be *a valuable asset to the organization.*"

"When was this?"

"Maybe three years ago."

I finished my wine and refilled our glasses while Raul cleared the table.

"He's never gonna help me with Hellborn," I said.

"I wouldn't think so. He might track down Packard, though. Kersey wants you to stay. And he'll fight anyone who threatens to take you from him."

"Even Griselda?"

I considered my options. My research hadn't panned out, and I needed answers. Tyler was my only real chance at finding out the truth. But... He'd warned me Packard was dangerous—maybe even crazy. I liked to think I had a natural sense about people. I'd met the security chief, and something didn't fit. Being conflicted was a bitch. While I sat there mulling things over, Raul got a call. The conversation was brief. Afterward, he gave me a look that was muy serioso.

"What?" I said.

"Good thing you didn't go to your appointment. Graysuits all over the place."

"Shit. That means Tyler Berry—"

"Is a fake."

As we cleaned up the kitchen, I tried coming up with Plan B. Like it or not, I would have to trust Packard. What choice did I have? My partner washed the knives by hand and placed them reverently in the wood block. I stroked his hand.

"I'm hot," I said.

"I'll get the ice, and we can—"

"It's not that kind of heat."

Grabbing his face, I kissed him. We didn't make it to the bedroom. Instead, we shut out the world and did it six ways from Sunday. Standing up. Kneeling. On the counter. Then, exhausted, we crawled into bed and slept. I dreamed of Afghanistan and everyone trying to kill me. This time, it wasn't Tyler who had my back.

It was Raul.

CHAPTER
THIRTY-TWO

IT WAS EARLY when I woke up. I decided to skip the workout and took a shower instead. After getting dressed, I headed to the kitchen, where I found Raul cooking in pants and a wifebeater. He was arranging croissants and fresh fruit on a platter.

"Trying to make me fat?" I said.

Slipping my arms around him, I rested my head against his back. I felt safe, and I didn't want the feeling to end.

"I like that you're taller than me."

"Stop distracting me. I need to practice, or I'll lose my edge."

I kissed him. "Oh, I don't know. I thought your edge was pretty okay last night."

A bottle of whiskey stood on the counter. I grabbed it and read the label. OLD FAITHFUL BOURBON. AGED 1 YEAR.

"I don't remember buying this. Does it go good with whatever you're fixing?"

"I was going to make us bourbon and salted caramel popcorn for later."

"Don't got no popcorn." I unscrewed the cap and took a whiff.

"It's not for drinking," he said, laughing. "Strictly cooking."

Something dinged. Grabbing potholders, he opened the convection oven and removed four little red ceramic cups with ridges on the sides. These, he set on the range to cool. Each contained a cooked egg in what looked like heavy cream, surrounded by fragrant herbs and peppers.

"What do you call this?" I said.

"Oeufs en Cocotte. Eggs in pots."

I took a bite of toasted rustic bread. He brought over a pot for each of us and placed them on the table with the rest of the food. We ate everything. My belly full, I drank coffee and tapped my empty cocotte with my fork.

"Okay, I'm pretty sure the kitchen didn't come with these little pot thingies."

"I brought over some stuff from my apartment."

I dropped my fork. "You do live in this building." Laughing, I shook my head. "Jerk."

"They're called ramekins. I don't get to use them much."

Something buzzed—my phone, which was on the counter. When I picked it up, I saw a text from Kersey.

Found packard - be careful.

I reread the message. Though I hadn't planned on getting the Colombian any deeper into the plot, I didn't want to do this alone.

"I need to see a guy," I said.

Sitting at the table with my laptop, I used Google Maps to find the address Kersey had provided. Packard lived in the boonies somewhere.

"It's about forty miles," I said. "Simi Valley."

"Home of the Ronald Reagan Library."

I tried gathering my thoughts. Today was New Year's Day.

Like Christmas, nothing was open. Most likely, Harry Packard would be at home relaxing with his family.

"Feel like taking a ride?" I said.

Raul sat across from me. I was starting to recognize his moods, and I'd seen this one before. Not angry, but not happy either.

"Are you sure you want to do this?" he said.

"He won't be expecting me."

"What are you going to do, kill him?"

"All depends."

"You told me he has a family. Are you willing to put them in danger?"

"Said the guy who kidnaps children."

I'd stepped in it. A wall went up between us—me and my big effing mouth. The Colombian grabbed the rest of his clothes and headed for the door. I ran after him and grabbed his arm.

"Don't go."

He looked into my eyes and touched my cheek. I took his hand and kissed it.

"I'm going to tell you something," he said. "And you have to promise me—swear—you won't say anything to anyone."

"And if I don't?"

"I'll make you eat a Fatburger."

"Okay, I promise."

"Get the mescal."

In the kitchen, I poured two drinks straight up. Raul put on his shirt and shoes and sat on the living room sofa. Joining him, I handed him his drink.

"Those kids we took the other night?" he said. "It's not what you think."

"I don't understand."

"Kersey has done some nasty shit in his life. But he's trying to make amends."

"By employing a forger?"

"Think about it. If he was trafficking kids, why would they need passports?"

"I don't know. Because he's sending them out of the country?"

"He's giving them new identities."

"You mean, like Witness Protection? That sounds a little—"

"He found families all over the country willing to take these kids in and raise them as their own."

"But what about their real parents?"

"Every child we've handled came over by themselves. In exchange for a new life, they have to let go of everything. And their birth parents have to forget them."

"How does a parent forget their child?"

"They do it to save them."

"Doesn't Kersey employ coyotes? How do they end up in detention?"

"Sometimes, the kids get caught coming over. And it's up to us to get them out."

I finished my drink. "So Kersey's a good guy now?"

"Funny, right?"

I glanced at my phone. "I need to go. Are you in?"

"Let me take a shower and change clothes."

He headed out, leaving me on the sofa. Someone was staring at me. It was my body opponent bag with the snarly expression.

"What're you lookin' at?" I said.

CHAPTER
THIRTY-THREE

IT TOOK us forty-five minutes to reach the sleepy suburb of Simi Valley. We exited on Tapo Canyon Road and made our way to Wisdom Court. Instead of turning there, I parked on an adjacent street. We walked in, wearing our black suits.

Harry Packard's house stood at the end of the cul-de-sac. The white two-story structure was enormous, picturesquely set against the foothills. A black Volvo XC90 was parked nearby on the street. The plan was for Raul to enter through the back and peacefully detain any family members while I dealt with Packard.

When I signaled my partner, he jogged around the side of the house. I stood in the driveway, facing the front door. Inside, a dog barked. It took less than a minute for the security chief to show up. Wearing jeans and a flannel shirt, he wasn't surprised to see me. I expected him to walk outside. Instead, he left the door open and returned to the house. My Glock in hand, I followed him in.

I found my partner in the foyer, his hands behind his head. A woman in a ponytail and yoga pants held a gun on him. I recognized her from the security chief's phone. Also armed, Packard stepped forward and demanded my weapon. He waved us toward the kitchen.

"I forgot to tell you," he said. "My daughter's a cop."

We sat and placed our hands flat on the kitchen table while our captors kept their guns trained on us. I wasn't worried about getting shot. But there was no way the Colombian was dying in Simi effing Valley—not on my watch. A wire fox terrier appeared at the door. When he saw me, he pranced over and gave me a friendly bark.

"What's his name?" I said, scratching the dog behind his ear.

Packard side-eyed his daughter. "Max."

"Hey, Maxie."

"I'm guessing you didn't come over to play with my dog. What are you doing here?"

"I need answers. Where can we talk?"

He lowered his weapon. His daughter stared at him, her mouth falling open.

"It's okay, Mags. This is—"

"Jane," I said. "And that's Raul."

Reluctantly, she extended her hand. "I'm Maggie."

"A cop, huh?"

"LAPD."

After an awkward beat, I followed Packard to a door off the kitchen. Inside, there was a spacious home office with a view of the hills. Framed pictures of jazz musicians performing at various clubs and concert venues filled the walls.

The security chief took a seat on the black leather sofa. I stood at ease, facing him. Hanging behind him on the wall was an award for outstanding service. It was signed by Eamon Trower, Chief Security Officer at Baseborn Identity Research and recently throatless.

"Why did you let me go the other night?" I said.

"We knew how to find you."

"Yeah, about that."

"You removed the microchip?"

"You never answered my question. Why did you release me?"

"It wasn't safe."

"Because someone on your team is trying to kill me? Are they?"

"It's complicated."

I pulled up a chair. "Try me."

Packard told me everything he knew about the Alpha program. He confirmed what I'd suspected all along. Walt Freeman and Caroline Sheldrake were in friendly competition. Each was trying to win a contract with the Pentagon to produce super-soldiers.

The CEO's approach had been to create fighters who didn't fear death—who would pursue an enemy to the ends of the earth. The problem was the drug they were using. Surrelis turned the alphas into vicious hunters who killed at random and without a conscience. All except for the Russian girl. She was different.

The security chief also confirmed there were early experiments in Tres Marias, which led to an outbreak. The town's mayor contracted with Black Dragon Security to restore order. They did, but at a high cost. Freeman wasn't responsible for the mishap, though. The blame rested with a deranged morphine-addicted project manager working for Robbin-Sear Industries.

Caroline's program was more successful. Mainly because she went down a different path, using genetics to achieve the same goal. Her approach was to alter her test subjects, giving us a miraculous ability to heal from virtually any kind of wound. Though we still had our emotions, we were trained soldiers—hypers—who would follow orders without question.

I brought up the operation to rescue the Russian girl,

laying out my version of the truth. Freeman's only hope for a breakthrough was through the unborn child Sasha carried. When she died, the Alpha program died with her. The CEO must've become desperate and, consumed with a need for revenge, triggered the Hyper program's termination protocol.

"Not buying it," Packard said. "I knew Walt. He was a savvy businessman. As CEO, why would he hurt his own company?"

"To get back at Caroline."

"Wrong again. Sure, they had their differences. But Walt had great respect for her."

"Okay. But if Walt Freeman is dead, then who's coming after me?"

He didn't answer right away. "There are some—not my people—who aren't playing by the rules."

"No shit. You reported to Eamon Trower, and he's dead. Who's your boss now?"

"Caroline Sheldrake."

I recalled my last phone conversation with Tyler. *Stay away from Packard. He's dangerous.* I wasn't sure I trusted him—or anyone else associated with Hellborn.

"What's your plan?" I said. "Kill me?"

"Hell, no. I've been instructed to take you to Virginia, where you'll join the other hypers."

"And if I refuse?"

"You'll die. I'm guessing you've already experienced hyper karma."

I played dumb.

"Wild, random temperature spikes?"

"Yeah, so?"

"In time, they'll get worse. Soon, you won't be able to control them. Eventually, your body will burn itself out."

"How can I stop it from happening?"

Though I already knew the answer, I wanted to see if he'd confirm what Tyler had told me.

"It's imperative you get back on the drug regimen."

"I've heard of Surrelis. What was I on?"

"Riactis."

"Why not hand over the drug now?"

"If it were up to me, I would. Caroline wants you back. She's dangling a carrot."

I got up and crossed to the window. The backyard had a koi pond and a garden with trellises. Nothing was in bloom. A crow, perched on the wall, observed me with one shiny black eye.

"Why can't I remember who I am?" I said.

"I don't know. Maybe the drug affected a part of your brain. We don't know all the side effects yet."

"Is that the truth?"

"I'm not a scientist."

"Most of my memories are gone, except for the firefight in Afghanistan."

He looked at me with an odd expression. Whatever he was thinking, it was nada de bueno.

"Jane, I hate to be the one to tell you this," he said. "You were never in Afghanistan."

THIRTY-FOUR

I GLARED AT PACKARD, convinced I'd heard it wrong.

"I prepared for the mission," I said, getting to my feet. "I'm a Marine. I completed MOS training. I'm—"

"All those things are true. You trained but never deployed. Those so-called memories? They're not real."

"Come on, I was there—in the shit. We were on a night raid in a village near—"

"The White Mountains, I know. It was a simulation."

"No, that can't be. You're effing lying to me."

"Jane, I'm telling you the truth. They ran all the hypers through it. Repeatedly, for months."

A high-pitched keening erupted in the middle of my head. It was like a screech straight out of hell. I closed my eyes until it passed. Meanwhile, the security chief continued to push the false narrative.

"One of our divisions developed a proprietary virtual reality headset," he said.

"Let me guess. Clayborn Electronics."

"You've done your homework. I never tried it. But they say it's like you're there, as you said, in the shit."

"But I got shot."

"Brain sensors allow you to experience sights, sounds, smells…and intense pain. The technical team borrowed research on stroke patients. It's called *coactivation*. They use amphetamines to activate neurons in the brain. I'm not sure how it all works."

"This can't be right."

"Don't feel bad. Over the better part of a year, they modified the game to make it more realistic. And with each new release, they ran the hypers through an improved, more detailed simulation."

"And my ability to heal?"

"Now we're talking real science. You might want to take a seat. It's called gene editing. Ever hear of CRISPR?"

I gave him a blank stare.

"I don't understand it either. But they found a way to copy the healing properties of the axolotl. It's amphibious and lives in Mexico. It can grow back almost any tissue without leaving so much as a scar."

"And that's in me now?"

Feeling disoriented, I sank into the chair. Packard got me a bottle of cold water from a small refrigerator. I finished it in one long swallow. It was hard to see him through my hot, desperate tears.

"What's my name?" I said. "My real name?"

"I don't know." Then on my reaction, "I'm not messing with you. Those records are sealed. We refer to the test subjects by their serial numbers. Yours is 5089774603."

"Who does know? Caroline Sheldrake?"

He nodded. Wiping away the tears, I got to my feet.

"Thanks for telling me the truth. Hey Harry, you ever serve?"

"Twenty-year veteran of the US Army."

"Trench monkey?"

"Snake eater."

"Special Forces, nice. Gulf War?"

"You know it."

I was lost at sea, looking for anyone who could help me. Though I still wasn't sure about Packard, I had no one else. Besides, he'd shared a lot, even things he didn't have to tell me. I decided to trust him a little longer.

"I made contact with someone named Tyler Berry," I said.

He narrowed his eyes. "When?"

"Yesterday. I was supposed to meet him last night. Never made it."

"Under no circumstances are you to communicate with him again. Understood?"

"Why?"

"Because he can't be trusted."

"Funny. He said the same thing about you."

Packard walked over and, with a grave expression, took my arm. "Jane, there is no Tyler Berry."

"Okay, now you're making me crazy. He was in my squad in Afghan— Eff me."

"He's part of the simulation—there's no such person."

"But I spoke to him on the phone."

"You need to listen—he's not real."

My head was swimming. Someone resembling Tyler Berry was seen leaving the scene of a shooting in Echo Park.

"I saw a photo of him on the news."

"I can explain. Come on."

He logged in to his laptop and accessed a password-protected portal off the Baseborn Identity Research website. After a couple of failed attempts, he located the right link and brought up a slick datasheet describing a VR game called *DireWolf*. I leaned over his shoulder and studied the background.

"Look familiar?" he said.

"The White Mountains. Do you know the storyline?"

He shook his head, so I ran it down for him—even the part about the malang and the djinn. When I mentioned the floating bullets, he laughed.

"We purchased *DireWolf* from a defunct game company," he said. "Caroline hired a new group of developers who tailored it for the Hyper program. There's a psychology behind convincing test subjects their ability to repair damaged tissue is supernatural."

"Easier to swallow than thinking you're Frankenstein's axolotl."

He scrolled down the page to a list of the game's characters. Each had an avatar. Among others were "Lt. Gorman" and the malang, here referred to as "Creepy Old Dude." Then I spotted him—"Lance Cpl. Tyler Berry." He was exactly as I remembered him.

"That's the man from the news," I said.

"Who you saw—the man you spoke to—is not Tyler Berry. His name is Wilson Zeddemore."

Zeddemore. "I remember you mentioning his name when we met."

"He's the LA security chief."

"How'd he end up in the game, though?"

"Interesting story. Seems Walt liked Wilson. When he found out about *DireWolf,* he got his protege hired to play Tyler Berry in the new game we were developing. Zeddemore loved it. Man's a bit of a narcissist. They used his face, voice—everything. Except they made him look like a fresh, young Marine. After they wrapped production, everyone in the LA office started calling him *LC.*"

"Lance Corporal."

I'd had enough and headed for the door. The security chief followed me, his weapon in hand.

"Okay, you know it's no good shooting me, right?" I said.

"I was hoping you'd come with me voluntarily."

"To Virginia? What about Zeddemore?"

"I can't promise you'll get all your questions answered. But you might find out who you are."

I looked into Packard's eyes. Something told me he wanted to help. It was the sense I'd gotten from him the first time we met.

"Can't believe I'm saying this," I said. "Okay, I'll go with you."

When we entered the kitchen, I found Raul supervising Maggie as she cooked something on the stove.

"Don't over-stir," he said. "That's how you ruin a good risotto."

I walked up to the Colombian. "Are you kidding me right now?" Then to Packard, "How does this work?"

"I'll arrange for a jet to fly us to a private airfield outside Richmond. From there, we'll travel by car to HQ for a meeting with Caroline. First order of business, get you back on Riactis."

"What's going on?" Raul said.

"I have to leave LA. Take my car. When you get back, tell Kersey what happened."

"Are you sure you can trust this guy?"

"Guess I'll find out. You better go."

We followed my partner to the front door. There were narrow leaded-glass windows on either side. Out of habit, I took a peek through the sheer curtain. I grabbed Raul's hand before he could open the door.

"What is it?" Packard said.

Furious, I pivoted. "This was your plan?"

"I don't understand."

I pointed at the window. "Keep me occupied until they arrived?"

The street was filled with black Escalades. Like army ants,

gray-suits moved into position, their weapons pointed at the house. Several had shotguns.

Toward the front, an African American gray-suit stood behind an open car door. He was in his late thirties and resembled an older Tyler Berry.

It was Wilson Zeddemore.

THIRTY-FIVE

THE SITUATION LOOKED HOPELESS. There were at least fifty gray-suits with their weapons aimed at the house. Zeddemore used his command voice.

"Harry Packard. We know you have the hyper. Send her out, and we'll call it a day."

When Packard turned around again, my gun was in his face.

"I had nothing to do with this. Zeddemore's acting on his own."

"Why?"

"Wish I knew."

Zeddemore let out a sharp whistle. "Not waiting out here forever."

I held my weapon on Packard for another beat, then decided to give him a chance.

"We need more guns," I said.

"On it." The security chief signaled his daughter to follow him.

I turned to Raul. "Any ideas?"

"If we can get out through the back, we can hop the wall and make it over to the next street."

"They'll be waiting for us outside."

"Most likely."

Packard and his daughter returned, wearing body armor and black MICH ballistic helmets. They carried long guns and a gym bag. Maggie gave us each a Kevlar vest and a helmet. After suiting up, I chose an AR-15 with a bump fire stock that would allow me to shoot almost continuously.

She opened the gym bag and handed me a 100-round drum mag. To the others, she gave out extra mags and shells. Packard ordered his daughter and my partner to cover the rear of the house. Taking a breath, he cracked the door.

"Wilson, this is insane," Packard said. "You need to stand down."

"Come on, man. We all know you let her escape. We've been watching your house for days."

"I don't understand why you're doing this."

"I have my reasons."

"Leave now, or innocent people might get hurt."

Zeddemore laughed. "That's on you." He gazed at the sky. "Such a beautiful day. Shame to spoil it. Give her to us, and we'll be outta here right quick."

"Not happening."

The sound of breaking glass caught my attention. Soon after, a gunshot. I grabbed my phone and called Raul. He picked up on the first ring.

"You okay?" I said.

"More are coming."

"Find a way over that wall. I'll meet you at the car."

"What are you going to do?" Packard said.

"Distract them. Call 911."

"What?"

"Do it."

As he dialed, I flung the door open and walked out. I kept going, firing quick bursts at the gray-suits hiding behind car doors. Zeddemore disappeared behind a vehicle, where he continued to shout commands. The other hostiles opened fire on me.

A barrage of bullets struck me in the arms and legs. The pain was intense. But I kept going, taking out as many gray-suits as I could. A slug glanced off my helmet. When I'd gone through the hundred rounds, I dropped the weapon and switched to my Glock. A gray-suit peeked out from behind a car bumper. I put him down.

When I reached the vehicle where Zeddemore had been hiding, no one was there. Behind me, glass crunching, followed by a gun burst and a grunt. I glanced back. A hostile lay dead. In the distance, Packard lowered his weapon. We gave each other a nod.

By now, all the gray-suits were dead. Except for Zeddemore—he'd escaped. Someone said *Holy shit*. I looked to the side. A teenage boy stood on his porch, using his phone to record everything. When I pointed my weapon at him, he disappeared into the house.

"Jane!" It was Packard. "We've had your apartment building under surveillance for days. If we could find you—"

"So can Zeddemore. I'll contact you again."

I scanned the cul-de-sac and jogged to my car, leaving a trail of spent slugs behind me. The Colombian was waiting for me behind the wheel with the engine running as approaching sirens wailed.

"I checked for tracking devices," he said. "The car's clean."

"What would I do without you?"

I peered out the window. No drones or Escalades in sight. While my partner found his way back to the freeway, I removed my helmet and body armor and tossed them in the backseat.

"Is Maggie okay?" I said.

"She's fine. Not sure about Packard."

"He's good. Zeddemore got away, though."

"He won't stop hunting you."

"I am aware."

The LA security chief might get another shot at eliminating me, but what about the other hypers? If I were Caroline Sheldrake, I'd protect them with my life. There was no question—I had to go to Virginia. With or without Harry Packard. I wanted answers. But more importantly, I needed the drug. Right now, none of that was possible.

"I have to get out of LA," I said. "Will you help me?"

PART FOUR

I JUST WANNA GO HUNTING

REMOVING the microchip had paid off. We weren't followed as we returned to The Borgia. Safely inside my apartment, I changed into street clothes. Raul had gone to his place to get luggage for me. When he came back, I switched on the TV, and we watched the inevitable breaking news.

The reporter Victoria Muñoz faced the camera on the Simi Valley street we'd just come from, microphone in hand. Packard and his daughter stood next to her, their stone-like faces betraying nothing. He had on a suit, and Maggie wore her police uniform. Behind them, cops combed the area while paramedics gathered up the dead in body bags.

"New Year's Day," the reporter said, her expression solemn. "Normally, a time to spend with family and friends. But today on this quiet street, gunfire erupted, turning the neighborhood into a war zone. One neighbor describing the scene as *a massacre*."

She addressed Packard, moving the mic back and forth as each took turns speaking.

"You are?" she said.

"Harry Packard."

"Mr. Packard, you told me earlier armed assailants arrived here this morning, looking for you?"

"Correct. I work for Hermes Security Partners. We're a software company based in San Francisco."

"Why do you think you were targeted?"

"We've patented some amazing stuff. Competitors have been trying to steal our IP for years."

"When you say *competitors*..."

"Foreign agents. That's all I can tell you at this time."

The reporter turned to Maggie. "And you are this gentleman's daughter?"

"Maggie Packard."

"I imagine, as an LAPD police officer, you were prepared for this kind of thing?"

Maggie took her father's hand. "You try to be. But it's never easy once the shooting starts."

"And you protected your father?"

"Yes, of course. He made me who I am."

The security chief slipped an arm around his daughter. "Thank God she was here."

The reporter turned to the camera. "According to a witness, a woman with an assault rifle appeared on the scene and returned fire. Miraculously, she escaped. We've obtained amateur video. But first, a warning. What we're about to show you may be disturbing to some viewers."

They cut to a shaky video recorded on a phone. *Effing neighbor kid.* The camera panned from the gray-suits firing toward the house to me. There I was, marching forward. Taking down hostiles with my AR-15. As multiple rounds struck me, I kept moving. The helmet made it impossible to see my face. The station switched back to the reporter.

"Mr. Packard, any idea who the woman is?" the reporter said.

"None whatsoever."

"Thank you." Then to the camera, "There you have it. A

deadly shootout. And a mystery woman who, as one fright-ened neighbor put it, *saved us*."

Now a freeze frame of me in my black suit, holding an assault rifle. I looked like a badass.

"Victoria Muñoz, ABC7 Eyewitness News, reporting."

I switched off the television.

"You're a hero," Raul said.

"Stop. It's interesting Packard claimed to work for Hermes Security."

"It's gotta be fake, right?"

"It's more than fake. Hermes is a deity known as *the divine trickster*. The ancient Greeks believed he was the one who invented lying."

In the kitchen, I searched for Hermes Security Partners on my laptop. A link came up at the top of the page. When I clicked it, a professional website appeared. Their headquarters were located on Market Street in San Francisco.

"When these guys make shit up, they do it right," I said.

We spent the next few minutes packing. I planned to take as little as possible and included a few books and my laptop. I stood at the front door, taking in the apartment.

"Nice while it lasted."

"Where to now?"

"Let's go see Kersey," I said.

When the elevator opened on the ground floor, Raul stepped out first. I tried following, but he pushed me back inside.

"What's wrong?" I said.

"Zeddemore."

"He's here?"

"Go back up to 2 and take the stairs to the garage. I'll meet you there."

"What're you gonna do?"

He grabbed my bags. "Distract him."

As the doors closed, Raul called out to Dickles in a

friendly voice. What in hell was the Colombian planning? In another beat, I was on 2.

I got out and ran toward the emergency exit. When I opened the door, I spotted a gray-suit on the stairs. Carefully, so as not to make a sound, I closed the door. Grabbing my Glock, I pressed myself against the wall. His footsteps got louder, then faded as he trotted past my floor and up the stairs.

When I was sure he was gone, I entered the stairwell and hurried down. At the bottom, there were two doors—one leading to the lobby and the other to the garage. I peered through the small window in the first door.

Zeddemore stood at the front desk. All I could see was the back of his head. As he questioned the doorman, Dickles stared at him, slack-jawed and clueless. I had no idea he was such a talented actor.

Meanwhile, Raul regaled the doorman with some stupid vacation story, his luggage next to him on the floor. Fed up, Zeddemore left the building. I continued to the garage. Soon, Raul joined me, and we were on our way.

"What were you doing up there?" I said.

"Telling Dick about my last trip to Cancún. You know, the great booze, the cute girls…"

"Unbelievable. What did Zeddemore say?"

"He kept asking about you. Your favorite doorman insisted no one fitting that description lived in the building. He even asked to see some ID."

"Remind me to send him a fruitcake next Christmas."

As we exited, there were no Escalades in sight. Now, I had something new to worry about. Zeddemore wouldn't stop here. What if he figured out who I work for?

"Kersey's next on his list," I said.

CHAPTER
THIRTY-SEVEN

WE ARRANGED to meet Kersey far away from his office. Raul suggested Phillipe's on North Alameda, near Union Station. From what I'd heard, the place was legendary. It opened in 1908. Their specialty was French dip sandwiches—beef, pork, lamb, and so on. When I reminded him I was a vegetarian, he told me the place was noisy. We could talk without being overheard.

While everyone else chowed down on animal flesh, I stuck with iced tea. The place was bursting with locals and tourists. It was hard to hear each other. We sat on four-legged stools at a long table. When the food came, we got down to business.

Kersey had seen the news footage. Surprisingly, he took it well. I told him about Zeddemore showing up at The Borgia and that Kersey should expect a visit.

"I can handle him," he said between bites. "What do you need from me?"

I scanned the room. "There's no way I can go back to my apartment. Zeddemore's people are everywhere."

"Finding you a new place won't be a problem."

"I appreciate it. But LA's too dangerous right now. I can't stay here."

"Where will you go?"

"The less you know, the better."

"You'll need money. I can let you have five stacks."

"I could also use weapons."

"Okay. Raul's coming with me. Meet us at the machine shop in two hours."

I gave him a smile. "Why are you being nice to me, Kersey?"

"Griselda likes you."

"And?"

"I don't want to lose you, okay? But right now, you're too hot to handle."

"Literally," Raul said.

"What?"

I gave my partner the stink eye. "Private joke."

"I figure you owe me," Kersey said. "And some day, if you make it out of this thing alive, I'll collect."

"Fair enough."

We finished our lunch and walked out. Standing under the iconic brown-and-white awning, I happened to look up. That's when I spotted them.

"Wait," I said.

Kersey looked up, shielding his eyes with his hand. "What is it?"

I pointed at the sky. "Four o'clock."

South of us, a cluster of black drones hovered over Union Station. Zeddemore must've worked something out with the transportation authority to use their airspace. Kersey spat out his toothpick.

"The sooner I'm gone, the better," I said.

I sat in my car, thinking about my next move. When I began this adventure, I had three priorities. Stay alive, kill whoever was after me, and learn my name. The first depended on the second. But now, there was a new wrinkle. I needed a magic elixir called Riactis to keep myself from going all supernova. Without Packard, how was I supposed to get it?

Time to head over. When I arrived at the machine shop, Raul and Kersey were waiting for me. My boss handed me a black nylon money belt. I put it on, making sure the pouch rested against the small of my back. Under my black cashmere sweater, no one would be the wiser.

"I threw in a couple extra thou," he said.

"What about weapons?"

"Raul and I talked it over. We don't think you should drive the Mustang. I got you another set of wheels. Come on, I'll show you."

Raul rolled back the door to the machine shop. Inside, I found a brand-new all-black Dodge Challenger SRT8. This thing had a 470-horsepower engine. More than sufficient for outrunning gray-suits.

Kersey handed me the keys. "It's one of mine. What can I say? I love American cars."

I circled the vehicle, checking out the rims and the rest of the trim package. The car was tight.

"You're going to experience some drag," he said. "Pop the trunk."

I did as he asked. He lifted the carpet and showed me a compartment. Instead of a spare, I found a custom plastic locker. Inside, were long guns, handguns, and ammo. He'd included body armor and a new MICH ballistic helmet.

"You thought of everything," I said. "Thank you."

"Thank your partner. The helmet was his idea. I also threw in some extra burners."

I loaded the rest of my stuff in the backseat. Hugging Kersey made me smile. The last time we were this close, I'd punched him in the throat.

"How do I reach you?" I said.

"Call Chico's Money Transfer. Ask for Crispin."

"Who's that?"

"It was my Confirmation name. They'll put you through."

"Guess I should go."

Kersey noticed the awkward glances between the Colombian and me. "I'll wait outside."

When the boss was out of sight, Raul took my face in his hands and kissed me with everything he had. I held onto him, knowing we'd never see each other again.

"I want to come with you," he said.

"Too dangerous. You were lucky to make it out of Simi Valley."

"And you won't tell me where you're going?"

"It's for your protection. You and Kersey."

He kissed me again. "Be careful, Jane. I'm not sure if we'll ever..."

I placed a finger on his lips and kissed him for the last time.

"Keep an eye out for gray-suits and drones," I said.

Leaning next to the Challenger, I waited until they'd gone. I climbed in and started the engine. The throaty sound of sheer horsepower echoed all around me. I pulled forward and stopped outside. After locking the door, I got on the road.

There was more I'd wanted to say to Raul. But there wasn't time. At least, now I knew for sure who was after me. Packard had lied to the reporter about who he was and about Zeddemore. Keeping it in the family. And I was sure Maggie wouldn't say anything. Cop or no cop, she was loyal to her dad.

Damage control would be swift. Since no civilians were harmed, an army of Hellborn lawyers would descend on the cops. They'd get them to agree the incident was a random act of violence. To make their case, Hellborn would give the police chief some BS about the government and national security. And they'd find a way to suppress the video.

I got on the 5 and headed north. With a full tank and plenty of weapons, I was set. In less than two hours, I'd be in Perro Negro. I could already smell the potato tacos. But there was something more pressing than food.

It was time for John Zwick to tell me everything.

CHAPTER
THIRTY-EIGHT

SOMETHING WAS WRONG. Approaching the café, I saw a group of Latino farmworkers gathered in front. Some peered through the windows. Another banged on the door. It was nearly dinnertime, and the restaurant should've been open.

I cruised past and parked in the rear next to the house. Across the way, the screen door leading to the kitchen was unlocked. In the distance, men's voices and truck engines starting up. Hoping for a different outcome, I peered inside. The faint odor of death assaulted me, making me gag.

When I walked in, I found John and Consuelo. They lay next to each other on the floor, their arms at their sides. Both were badly beaten. Each had been shot once through the back of the head. Easier to kill someone that way. You don't have to look them in the eye. The dog lay a little ways off. Same fate.

I went to examine the bodies when a noise in front caught my attention. I crossed to the dining room entrance. The silhouette of a straggler darkened the front door. He continued banging while cursing in Spanish. I waited for him to give up, then returned to the kitchen.

Kneeling, I examined John first. Rigor mortis hadn't set in

yet. I checked for a pulse. There was none. When I got to Consuelo, I was relieved to find a faint heartbeat. Crouching next to her, I peeled back an eyelid. She looked at me, unable to move.

"Consuelo, who did this?" I said.

The bullet had entered her brain from the left side and exited out her face near the eye. She tried speaking. What came out was a bubble of foamy blood in a gurgle of words I couldn't understand. Maybe if I called 911, they could save her. As I pulled away, she gripped my arm.

"Ellos saben."

"What do they know? Is it about me?"

"No. Ellos saben que…"

"Consuelo, what do they know?"

Choking on blood, she stopped moving. Whoever did this had come looking for information. I found a dishrag and wiped the fingerprints off everything I'd touched. Then I returned to the house. The front door was open partway. I listened for any sound. Drawing my weapon, I waited a beat before going inside.

This was Zeddemore's doing. After killing the elderly couple, they ransacked the house. *What led them here?* The answer chilled me. It had to be the drone I shot down. He must've gotten ahold of the surveillance video from the night I came to see John.

Ellos saben.

But if this wasn't about me, then what was he looking for? Closing my eyes, I arranged the sequence of events in my head.

1. Zeddemore finds out someone broke into Hellborn, but he doesn't know who.
2. He views the surveillance video, which leads him here.
3. To get to me, he tortures John and Consuelo.
4. One of them lets slip something he wasn't expecting—a secret.

I heard a noise behind me. Pivoting, I pointed my gun straight ahead. It was a Latino boy, maybe ten or eleven.

"Who are you?" he said, his voice warbling.

"Friend of the Zwicks."

Putting away my weapon, I approached him. When he tried running, I grabbed his jeans jacket and crouched to eye level. I ignored the squirming.

"I promise I won't hurt you," I said. "The old couple is dead."

"What? Did you—"

"No. I'm looking for the people responsible. Can I talk to you a sec?"

I led him into the kitchen where I'd shared a drink with John. The kid sat while I poured him a glass of milk. I took a seat across from him.

"Why are you here?" I said.

"I mow their lawn. And I do other stuff for Tita."

"Consuelo's your grandmother?"

"She's everybody's grandmother."

"Did you notice anyone hanging around here earlier? Men in gray suits?"

"When I rode my bike. They were on the road in these huge black cars. They came from the east."

Hellborn. "Did you get a good look?"

"One of them was black."

"Did he see you?"

"I guess. But who cares about a kid?"

"Good point. Anything else you can remember?"

He thought for a sec. "His face."

"The black man?"

"Un pedazo de gasa." He touched a spot under my eye. "Here."

"A piece of gauze."

The boy took my hand. "Is something going to happen to me?"

"Finish your milk," I said.

I walked the boy to the front door. His bike lay outside on the lawn. At this moment, I had one thought—keep him safe.

"Here's what I want you to do," I said. "Go home. Don't say anything about me. Do you promise?"

"Yes."

"If your parents ask about Tita and her husband, tell them you knocked on the door, but there was no answer. And here's the most important part. When the police question you, stick to your story. If they find out you know something, they might tell the bad guys, who will kill you and your family. Now say it back to me."

"I came over like I always do. I knocked. There was no answer. I went home."

"Look them in the eye when you say it. Same with the cops. And remember, you can never change your story. You better go now."

He ran outside and got on his bike. Before riding off, he turned back and looked at me, his eyes defiant.

"You're gonna get them, right? The ones who did this?"

"You can count on it," I said.

In the kitchen, I washed the glass and put it away, careful not to leave any fingerprints. If the police were suspicious, they might try making the kid talk. I'd told him the cops might inform the gray-suits to scare the kid. The more I thought about it, the less it sounded like a lie.

I began going over the sequence of events again. There was something I forgot. It was no use wasting more time here. The best thing was to hole up somewhere until I could figure things out. Somewhere far from this place. *John's cabin—I still had the key.*

Outside, I made a call. It rang twice before someone picked up.

"Packard."

"It's me."

"Jane? Where are you?"

"Zeddemore's on the move. And he's injured. Any way you can track him?"

"He's gone off the grid. Let me bring you in."

"Not yet."

"How's the hyper karma?"

"I'll manage."

"I wish you'd let me help you."

"I'll be in touch," I said. "Say hi to Maggie."

By now, it was getting dark. It would take me less than two hours to make it to Lake Isabella. When I was far enough away, I called 911 to report two bodies at the café. After disposing of my phone in a dumpster, I got on the 14 north heading toward the 178.

As far as I knew, there were no drones in sight.

CHAPTER
THIRTY-NINE

IN THE BLACK OF NIGHT, I took a dirt backroad into the forest. John's place was in Wofford Heights. The house stood among the trees where the road ended. It was beautiful —a custom log cabin with a large entryway and dormers. I pulled my car around the back and parked in the one-car garage. Though it was chilly, there wasn't any snow on the ground.

Carrying my groceries, I entered through the kitchen. I set them down and, exploring the rest of the house, found an open-plan living room with a massive fireplace. The cabin was decorated with Craftsman furniture and accessories, making for a warm, safe place.

After bringing in my bags and putting everything away, I was hungry. I read the instructions on the vegetarian chili I'd bought and poured two cans into a pot. To avoid burning my dinner, I kept the fire low.

It was late by the time I finished cleaning up the dishes. The name John had mentioned—Dave Pulaski—niggled at my brain. Though it was a long shot, maybe he could help me figure out what Zeddemore had been after in Perro Negro. Besides the cabin's address, John had given me the Wi-Fi password. Sipping tap water at the kitchen table, I activated the VPN and started a search for John's friend.

A page's worth of names popped up. There were over ten on LinkedIn and a bunch of others on Facebook, Instagram, and Twitter. One had died of old age in Washington State. I guessed the Dave Pulaski I was looking for wasn't on social media. And there weren't any others who looked promising. Sitting back, I closed my eyes.

John had never said where his friend was from. Somehow, Dave had learned about Hellborn and the Russian girl. Then he and Black Dragon mounted a rescue operation. Why? What was in it for him? John went on the mission because the bastards had murdered his son. What was Dave's deal?

At his house, Packard confirmed that an outbreak had occurred in Tres Marias. And Black Dragon was involved in the cleanup. I did a quick search on Google Maps. The town was located south of Redding, seven hours from Lake Isabella.

What if Dave was from Tres Marias and had sought revenge for what happened? Maybe he'd lost family members. I recalled what John had said about his friend. *Once he signs on, he'll dig until he finds something.* Did that include risking his life on an impossible mission to save a girl he didn't know?

I continued my research, concentrating on the town. There were some recent news articles—one from the website of KRCR News in Redding.

TRES MARIAS — Nearly six months after the town suffered an outbreak of Marburg hemorrhagic fever, California's governor issued an emergency proclamation, ordering agencies to rebuild infrastructure devastated in the catastrophe. More than half of the town's population perished, opening the way for looters to destroy homes and commercial property.

"These funds will give the survivors back their lives," he said in a news conference. "It is our hope that, soon, Tres Marias will once again be a beautiful place to live. An event like this should never have happened. And you can be sure we are investigating the source of the outbreak."

The governor said he planned to set aside competitive bidding requirements in an effort to speed the recovery.

What if this was a cover story? As a rule, I avoided conspiracy theories. But if Hellborn was involved, then something else might have happened to the town. Unable to unearth any more information, I read for a few hours and went to bed. It wasn't long before I dreamt of the malang from *DireWolf*.

How many times had I crawled up that stone stairway in the rain? As always, he stood alone at the top. But now, the figure wasn't an old man. It was Zeddemore, wearing his gray suit. Colored beads draped around his neck. A bloody piece of gauze stuck to his face. Instead of reaching out his hand, he pointed his weapon and fired at me.

Three to the head.

I'd slept later than I intended and awoke to the sound of chittering outside my window. Two squirrels were chasing each other through the yard. After my morning exercise routine and a shower, I tried making breakfast.

Raul could crack an egg with one hand. There was no way I was attempting that. I heated a pan and poured in a little olive oil. Taking my time, I broke an egg and poured in the contents. I was so proud of myself, I did it two more times.

While I ate, I recalled my dream, marveling at having never deployed. If my memories were the result of a VR game, then how was it Bo had made an appearance? Though I couldn't remember my name, I knew in my soul he was my brother.

I had scattered childhood memories of him at different ages. He was real. Growing up, Bo had always protected me. Taught me to be strong. Could it be, thinking the game was real, I brought him in there with me? Was it even possible? Another mystery. Better to focus on the task at hand.

Alone in the middle of a forest, I longed to hear Raul's voice. But I didn't want to risk contacting him. I was eager to get on the road and went to the rear windows to check on the weather. A lone fawn stood in the backyard, staring at me, her huge ears pinned forward. Chances were, I'd never come back here.

I remembered seeing camping equipment in the garage. Along with tents, lamps, and cooking gear, I found a child's purple knapsack. I wondered if this had belonged to John and Consuelo's son. In the kitchen, I grabbed a few bottles of water and some energy bars. Locking the back door, I followed the fawn into the forest.

I hiked for two hours and never saw another soul. My boots fit more or less, but I could feel a blister coming on. Up ahead, the fawn paused between two trees and stared at me with large, gentle eyes.

Instead of approaching, I sat against a tree and took a swig of water. When I tore open an energy bar, she came toward me, pausing every few feet. I took another bite. She stood next to me now, nudging my hand with her wet nose. I gave her my food. Then another flashback…

I was seven or eight, sitting on the ground outside the corn maze. A gray fox nibbled pieces of jerky out of my hand. When I looked up, my brother was grinning at me.

"Why do they always come to you?"

"Because they know I love them," I said.

A gust of wind brought me back. It carried the sound of a stream burbling in the distance. As I listened, my temperature spiked. Effing hyper karma again. I tried getting up, but I was woozy.

Startled, the fawn scampered into the forest. I peered at the surrounding trees. If I didn't reduce my body temperature soon, it would be too late to make it back to the cabin.

Feverish, I struggled to my feet and headed in the stream's direction. It was closer than I thought. I removed my boots and peeled off my clothes.

When I stepped into the shallow water, I lost my balance on the slippery, moss-covered rocks. Recovering, I lay in the ice-cold water until my body temperature stabilized. Packard was right. I couldn't keep this up forever. At some point, I'd overheat and die.

After thirty minutes, I was fine. I got dressed and made my way home. By now, it was well past noon. My body was weak—I needed sleep.

I woke up sometime after three. Gathering my stuff, I loaded up the car and headed northwest. Once I reached Tres Marias, I'd figure out a way to track down Dave Pulaski.

And then, I would ask him what happened to his town.

IT WAS dark when I pulled into the Gas-N-Gut in Los Banos. On high alert, I kept an eye on everyone who came and went. It had taken me a little over three hours from Lake Isabella. I'd be on the road another four and needed something to eat.

There was nothing interesting near the 5. Driving east, I found a little Mexican joint in a strip mall that looked like something out of *Grand Theft Auto*. Inside, the smell of food brought to mind John and Consuelo's café. I missed them.

The place was tiny. Mexican music played in the background. Tables with turquoise Formica tops stood close together. Travel posters of Jalisco hung on a wall next to a sign for Modelo beer. Local farmers ate in silence, their eyes like slits on grim, weathered faces. A Latino man in a straw cowboy hat ate dinner with his wife and two noisy kids.

Behind the counter, a Latina with curly hair and a mole kept a sharp eye on me as I perused the menu on the wall. I guessed strangers were few in these parts. Or maybe it was because I towered over her.

"Any way I can get breakfast?" I said.

"Sure. We serve it all day."

"I want something with no meat."

"You like to try chilaquiles?"

I waited for the explanation. Blushing, she covered her mouth, and I realized she was ashamed of her crooked teeth. I liked her, though, and gave her a smile.

"It have eggs, tortilla, and salsa rojo," she said. "Or you can have salsa verde."

"Sounds good. The rojo. And coffee."

"Avocado? Is extra."

"¿Cómo no?" *Why not?*

I handed her more than enough cash. The rest went into the tip jar. As I took my seat, I had a strong temptation to get in touch with Kersey. I pictured the carnage in Perro Negro. *Stick to the protocol.* When the food came, I inhaled it. Before leaving, I ducked into the restroom.

When I returned to the dining area, I noticed a commotion outside. Some dude in a flannel shirt and work boots stood there, yelling at a teenager. He was lanky, with stringy hair and an acne-scarred face. Forty, maybe.

Dressed in jeans and a white crop top, the frightened girl couldn't have been more than eighteen or nineteen. Inside, the farmers paid no attention. When a kid pointed at them, her frowning mother grabbed his hand. A sudden feeling of déjà vu came over me. Then a flashback…

Now the girl was me, and I was eleven. The man yelling stood next to the corn maze with his back to the sun. As he raised his hand, I tried to see his face.

The blow to my cheek stung, propelling me to the present.

I left the restaurant and found the girl huddled against the wall. Holding her knees and staring at nothing, she shivered. Though I felt for her, I didn't want to get involved. But when I saw the blood leaking from her nose, I crouched beside her.

"Your dad's a dick," I said.

She wiped her nose. "He's my boyfriend."

She was pale and pretty, with long blonde hair and delicate hands. She should've been in school, not mixed up with some sad excuse for a human being.

"Where is he now?"

"Waiting for me in the truck. Said I needed to apologize."

"For what?"

She scoffed. "Disobeying."

"You try telling the cops?"

"Once—the first time he hit me. They said I could file a complaint."

"Do you live around here?"

"No. We're on our way to Medford, to his brother's farm."

As I stood, she grabbed my arm. Her piercing blue eyes were shiny with tears. "I don't want to go."

"Tell him to forget it."

"Like it's that easy."

I didn't need this. But the girl was in trouble—the kind that's not easy to get out of.

"Maybe you don't have to go."

I scanned the parking lot. The swartwood was nowhere in sight. Maybe he'd driven around back.

"Wait here," I said.

A near-new white GMC Sierra was parked next to a dumpster. The piece of shit who'd beat on the girl sat behind the wheel, smoking. A country station blared, competing with the rancheras playing inside the restaurant. As I walked toward him, he turned down the music. Glaring, I stood near his door.

"Get out."

"What?"

"You heard me, asshole."

As I grabbed the door handle, he aimed a girl gun at me— a Smith & Wesson stainless steel revolver.

"Bitch, you messed with the wrong man."

He fired once. The .22 slug struck me under the rib cage. When I didn't flinch, his eyes got huge. I yanked the door open and dragged him out. He dropped the weapon, and I sent it skittering under the truck.

When he tried taking a swing, I kicked out his knee, and he dropped. I beat him until he couldn't walk. He lay on the ground, gurgling blood. Both eyes were swollen shut, and he had a busted nose. I thought about killing him, but the last thing I needed was to draw attention.

"Who are you?" he said.

"If you ever lay a finger on another woman again, I'll kill you."

When I turned, the girl was standing there, staring at her broken boyfriend. Her eyes drifted up to the bullet hole in my sweater. I walked up to her and laid a hand on her shoulder.

"Need a ride?"

"He shot you!"

"I can take you as far as Redding."

She nodded and followed me to my car. A sudden surge of rage coursed through my body, making my limbs tremble.

"Are you okay?"

"It's the adrenalin," I said.

FORTY-ONE

FOR A LONG TIME, the girl stared out her window at the bleakness of January. We were on the 5 heading north, and I was bored af. Could've used some company. Uncontrollable weeping would've been preferable to leaden silence. Fine. I'd kick things off.

"What's your name?" I said.

"Stella."

"Jane."

"Aren't you, like, bleeding right now?"

"I'm okay. How'd you get mixed up with that loser?"

Over the next few miles, she told me her life story. Which was fine because it made the time pass. Stella Dane was from Bakersfield. She had two older brothers and a younger sister. When she turned eighteen, she left her parents' home and moved in with a girl she'd gone to high school with. She got a job waiting tables at a local coffee shop called Pappy's.

One day, the roommate announced she was moving in with her boyfriend, leaving Stella on her own. Unable to afford the rent, she considered moving back home. Then she met Emmett. Like most predators, he was nice at first. Offered to help her out of a jam—no strings. Next thing she knew, she'd moved in with him. Soon after, the beatings started.

"He warned me that if I ever tried leaving, he'd make me sorry," she said.

"Sounds like a stand-up guy. What'll you do now?"

"Dunno. I have no money and no clothes. Everything I owned was in my backpack in the truck."

"I can help you out, but…"

I glanced at the rearview mirror. A pair of blindingly bright high beams bore down on us. I recognized the grille. It was Emmett's Sierra.

"Great," I said.

Stella craned her neck. "What is it?"

"Looks like your boyfriend didn't learn his lesson."

"Oh God, he'll kill me!"

"Not today."

By now, we were somewhere near Gustine. I took the next exit and headed east on a dark, narrow farm road. Whatever the moron was planning, I'd make sure it happened some-place remote—where there were no witnesses.

I didn't see the truck, but I figured Emmett knew where I'd gotten off. We were surrounded by farmland. I needed somewhere to hide long enough for me to prepare. There was a barn to my left, illuminated by floodlights. Decelerating, I turned onto a dirt path and pulled up behind the structure. No one was around to bother us.

"What're you going to do?" Stella said.

"End this. Come on."

Outside, I opened the compartment in the trunk, revealing my weapons cache. The girl was awestruck.

"Are you some kind of assassin?"

"I'm a Marine."

I pulled out my Glock, a Ruger 9mm, and a Kel-Tec bullpup. After loading and checking the weapons, I handed Stella the Ruger.

"Use this if you have to," I said.

"I've never even held a gun before."

I gave her a lesson, instructing her to keep her finger on the trigger guard. She was a quick study.

"All you have to do is aim and squeeze. The weapon will do the rest. Watch out for the kick." I walked her back to the passenger side. "Stay in the car. I'll be back soon."

She held onto my hand. "Please don't die, Jane."

The gesture touched me, and I gave her a smile. As I made my way to the main road, the door locks engaged. I sensed a toughness about the girl from the way she held the gun. But I hoped she wouldn't have to use it.

On the road, a clip-clopping echoed from somewhere. Out of the darkness, an old Latino wearing a trucker's cap walked toward me, leading two burros. A few minutes later, a car carrying a man and a woman passed. They were arguing. Loudly.

The white Sierra appeared in the distance. I waited in the middle of the road. As the truck got closer, I noticed two men in the cab. Some stranger was driving. A worse-for-the-wear Emmett was in the passenger seat. Spotting me, the driver accelerated. I raised the bullpup. The truck didn't slow down. I figured these numbnuts wanted to play chicken and stood my ground.

When they were close enough, I began firing. The vehicle swerved into a field and came to an abrupt stop. Though I'd shattered the windshield, the occupants were unharmed. Marching toward them, I fired again. This time, I hit Emmett in the shoulder as he climbed out. Screaming and cursing, he went down fast.

Now the driver emerged, holding a shotgun. When he tried aiming it at me, I let go another blast. The buckshot burst through the driver's side window and rearranged his face. Holding the weapon, he stood for a beat, then crumpled.

I continued toward the vehicle. Emmett lay on his back,

nursing his shoulder and gripping the silver revolver he was too weak to point.

"I don't deserve this," he said.

Pointing my Glock at his head, I shot him and waited for him to stop moving. After making sure the other man was dead, I retrieved Stella's backpack from the truck bed.

Inside my car, the girl clutched her weapon, her eyes darting from side to side. When she saw me, she unlocked the doors. I handed her the backpack, and she cradled it in her arms.

"Are you all right?"

"We need to get rid of the bodies," I said.

We found shovels inside the barn. Luckily, it was a moonless night. One by one, we dragged the dead to a barren area away from the crops. It had rained, and the ground was soft.

Two dumpsters stood in the middle. After pushing them aside, we started digging. We had to make sure the hole was deep enough for two. Working together, it took us a little over four hours.

We rolled Emmett in first. I grabbed the second man by the arms.

"Do you know this guy?" I said.

"He's a buddy of Emmett's. Owns a bar in Lakeview."

"He should've picked better friends."

We covered the corpses with dirt, patted down the area, and repositioned the dumpsters. Though it was cold, we were sweating.

One last thing to do—ditch the truck. I gathered the tools and returned them to the barn. The girl stayed behind, her head bowed. When she returned, I handed her my keys.

I looked past her. "What were you doing back there?"

"Praying for them."

"Why?"

"Maybe now they won't burn in hell," she said.

• • •

While Stella followed me in my Challenger, I drove the Sierra to Great Valley Grasslands State Park, which was a little farther east. We wore work gloves to ensure we wouldn't leave any fingerprints. On a fire road, I stopped and got out. I put the truck in neutral, and we pushed it over the embankment into the dense brush below.

"Someone will find it," she said.

"We'll be miles away."

Instead of backtracking, I took the 33 north to Patterson and west to the 5. Though I was tired, I thought it best to continue all the way to Redding. Stella fell asleep next to me.

The Marines had trained me to kill without hesitation. But then circumstances dragged this young girl into the life. She deserved better. I blamed that sonofabitch Emmett. Before closing her eyes, she asked me a question I had no answer for.

"Do you believe in God?" she said.

WE REACHED REDDING AFTER TWO. Though I was hungry, I needed sleep more. I drove through town, looking for an out-of-the-way motel. On a back street far from the main drag, I stumbled onto a quaint little place called Owlie's Lodge. A vacancy sign greeted us, glowing white under a blue neon barn owl with shifty eyes.

After checking in, I parked the car next to our room. Though the property was old, they kept it up nice. Inside, I found a room painted off-white with burnt orange curtains and brown carpeting. The twin beds looked serviceable.

While Stella got ready for bed, I lurked near the front window, scanning the parking lot. I imagined Zeddemore hiding out there like a dire wolf in shadows. So far, the only visible threat was a drunk in a bathrobe with his junk hanging out. He got ice from the machine and disappeared.

"Which one do you want?" the girl said, pointing cheerfully at the beds.

"Doesn't matter."

She chose the one nearest her. "You don't have a favorite side?"

"I forget."

After using the bathroom, I left the door open while I brushed my teeth. Somehow, the girl had gotten under the sheets without disturbing the hospital corners. There were purple bruises on her arms. She caught me looking and slid them under the covers.

"When my sister was little, we shared a room," she said. "My mother decided who would sleep where."

"Don't tell me. Your sister got the side nearest the bathroom."

"Wow, how'd you know?"

"Lucky guess."

"Do you have any siblings?"

"An older brother."

"What's he like? Is he a soldier too?"

"Enough with the questions."

I got my bag and, removing our handguns, gave the girl the Ruger.

"Keep this under your pillow." I showed her how to work the thumb safety.

"Are we expecting company?"

"I like being prepared."

I placed the Glock under my pillow and turned out the light. She turned on her side toward me.

"Night, Stella," I said.

"Jane?"

"Yeah?"

"Thank you. For saving me, I mean."

"You're welcome. Your taste in men needs work."

"Tell me about it. I hope I don't have nightmares. You know, Emmett's ghost haunting me."

"I don't believe in ghosts, just bad actors."

"The people you've killed, it doesn't bother you?"

Emmett's face materialized before me, floating in the darkness like a wraith. *I don't deserve this.* I blinked, and the image vanished.

"I focus on the job."

"Oh. I guess I would think about it too much."

"Don't. Only makes it harder."

"Are you sorry you picked me up?"

"Stella, I'm tired."

"Are you sorry, though?"

Groaning, I rolled onto my side and faced her. Vaguely, I could make out her pale features in the faint light coming through the curtain.

"No, I'm not sorry," I said. "I'm glad I could help you."

"Neither am I. Because he hurt me." Tears rolled down her cheeks. "So much."

"He can't hurt you anymore. Try and get some sleep."

As she drifted off, I lay in the still darkness. I wasn't thinking about Stella anymore. A single thought played in my brain like a looney tune version of what you told kids at bedtime. It was something that would continue to plague me most nights.

Good night.
Sleep tight.
Don't let the hyper karma bite.

The night passed without a fever. I'd planned on sleeping in. No such luck. My roomie was an early riser. A little after seven, I heard running water. Thankfully, Stella didn't sing in the shower.

When the bathroom door opened, she found me in the middle of doing walking jump push-ups. I'd moved the beds aside to give myself more room. As the girl dried her hair, I worked my way across the floor and back.

"I'll bet you're strong," she said. "I'd like to get in shape."

"I can show you."

After I'd showered and dressed, we walked across the parking lot to a diner advertising *the best blueberry pancakes since Noah*. Each of us ordered a stack. When the food came, we dug in.

"I noticed you didn't get the bacon," I said.

"I'm a vegetarian."

"How long?"

"Since I was eleven. This one night, my mom fixed hamburgers for dinner. Those used to be my favorite. You know, with lots of ketchup. I was chewing and felt something hard in my mouth. It was a piece of bone. I showed it to my dad, and he laughed. Said it made the beef taste better. It's hard to explain, but something in me clicked. I couldn't touch meat ever again. What about you?"

"I was kind of like you. Used to eat meat all the time. Something changed, though. Even the smell makes me sick."

When the server came by with coffee, Stella asked her for more milk. In some ways, she was like a young girl. A thought crossed my mind. What would happen to her once I was out of the picture? I had to remind myself she wasn't my responsibility.

On our way to the room, I kept thinking about the girl. She'd gotten to me, and I wanted to protect her. It was curious her appearing at this moment. Except for Raul, I was pretty much a loner.

"There are some things I need to do," I said. "It's why I came to Redding."

"Oh, okay. I'll pack my stuff."

"Where will you go? Back to your parents?"

"I'm scared to return to Bakersfield. What if the cops come looking for me?"

"Why would they?"

"Dunno. Maybe someone saw us last night. I can't take a chance on this coming back to my family."

When we were inside the room, I motioned for Stella to take a seat on the bed. I began pacing.

"I know you have a ton of questions about me," I said. "The thing is, I've seen a lot of—"

"Violence?"

"And obviously, you know I've killed people."

Suddenly nervous, she gripped the blankets.

"I would never hurt you, though. You know that, right?"

She looked away, her cheeks flushed. "Are you, like, a lesbian?"

The question took me by surprise. I started laughing and couldn't stop. As she gawped at me, I pulled myself together. "Oh Stella, you're the best."

"What did I say?"

"I'm straight, okay? I'm worried about you, is all. Look, I think you're a strong young woman. And in other circumstances, I'm sure you'd make a good Marine."

"Thanks, I guess."

"But you need to learn to defend yourself against the Emmetts of the world. And anyone else who might try and harm you."

I sat next to her. At first, she looked uncomfortable. We stayed there, neither saying anything. When she turned to me, her eyes were determined.

"What do you want me to do?" she said.

We spent a couple of hours at a local indoor gun range. I showed Stella how to properly aim a firearm. The kid was a natural. After a half-hour, she consistently hit the silhouette target in the innermost scoring rings. And after an hour, she was getting headshots.

When we were done, we removed our safety glasses and earmuffs. Then we unloaded our weapons and put them away.

"I've decided," she said. "I'm going to be a badass like you."

In our motel room, I showed Stella how to disassemble, clean, and reassemble her Ruger. At the range, I'd purchased a cleaning kit and showed her which parts to oil. As soon as she put the gun back together, I made her take it apart again.

I grabbed my phone and my gun. "I need to go out for a while. See if you can improve your time."

"Are you coming back?"

"Of course."

Before I could get out the door, she stopped me. "Jane? Thanks for the shooting lessons."

"Don't mention it, kid," I said.

I'D PASSED Tres Marias on the way to Redding the previous night. Traveling south, I got off the 5 and followed a road leading downtown. There were enormous trucks everywhere, some carrying steaming asphalt. Others towed flatbeds piled high with fresh lumber.

Continuing toward City Hall, I drove past Staples. Crews were busy replacing broken windows and repainting. The town resembled a war zone after they signed the peace agreement. Debris everywhere. Volunteers in bright yellow T-shirts and face masks gathered together trash. They placed it in the many dumpsters lining the parking lot.

Past City Hall, I entered a residential area, where I found similar damage to people's homes. Ruined furniture lay in defeated piles on the sidewalk, awaiting pickup by an army of trash trucks. Many houses were covered in graffiti.

A Humvee was parked along the street up ahead. Painted on the side was a black-and-red logo with the image of a dragon—Black Dragon Security. I pulled over. A man and woman in uniform directed a group of eager young volunteers who looked like counselors at a bible camp. Everyone wore face masks. I walked up to the security people.

"Excuse me," I said.

The woman, who was way shorter than me, scowled. "Where's your mask?"

"I'm a visitor."

"You still need one. There's contamination everywhere. Come with me."

I followed her to the Humvee. She got out a fresh mask from inside and handed it to me. Reluctantly, I put it on.

"Who's in charge?" I said.

"Our supervisor, Nathan Warnick."

"Is he around?"

"Try one block over. How tall are you anyway?"

"Thanks for your help."

On the next street, volunteers repaired windows and roofs. Others piled broken furniture and trash into dumpsters. The organizers had set up a snack station along the sidewalk. There were water bottles, energy bars, and fresh fruit.

A Black Dragon employee emerged from a house. He was of average height. Heavyset with short, sandy-colored hair. As he gave instructions to a volunteer, I approached him.

"I'm looking for Nathan Warnick," I said.

"You found him."

"I'm Jane." I extended my hand. "I need to talk to you. It's about John Zwick."

Blanching, he stepped back. Side-eyeing the others, he guided me away from the house.

"Not here," he said.

"Tell me where."

"Do you know Lake Redding Park?"

"I can find it."

"There's a gazebo. You can't miss it. I'll meet you there in an hour."

As I walked away, he trotted after me.

"Who else knows you're here?"

"No one," I said.

Walking to my car, I noticed a group of volunteers removing the damaged siding from a ranch-style house. One of them was watching me. He was lean and muscular, with close-cropped hair. Gripping a claw hammer, his intense eyes bored into me like a diamond drill bit.

I tore off my mask and glared at him. He turned his back on me and kept working. I'd gotten looks before, mostly because of my height. But this was different. This guy had suspicions. *Why?* I got into my car and drove off.

The park was nice. I found the white gazebo with the blue roof and gazed at the Sacramento River. Far off, people crossed the bridge on bikes. In a few minutes, a nondescript blue Chevy Malibu pulled into the parking lot.

Nathan Warnick approached me, wearing street clothes. I'd stopped for coffee on the way. When he stepped inside, I handed him a paper cup.

"Thanks," he said. "Tell me about John."

Squinting, he took a sip and gazed at the river. Watching him, I wondered how much I could trust him.

"He's dead. So's his wife."

"What happened?"

"The gray-suits happened."

The news must've hit him hard. He remained silent. Walking east, we found steps leading down to the river and sat at the top.

"You must know about that night," he said.

"John filled me in."

"I haven't seen him since. We agreed not to contact each other, in case…"

"In case the gray-suits came looking for you?"

"John was a good man. Was he a friend of yours?"

"He helped me after I escaped from Hellborn."

The supervisor scrambled to his feet like I'd farted. "Where did you hear—"

"John said it's what Dave Pulaski calls Baseborn Identity Research."

"What do you mean, you escaped?"

"Take it easy, Nathan. I'm not what you think I am. Come on, sit down. I'll explain everything."

Reluctantly, he obeyed. I ran the whole thing down to him. The alphas. Zeddemore. All of it. I even added the part about my Hyper program abilities. But I didn't tell him I was mixed up with a guy in LA who may or may not be a criminal.

"I was lucky," I said. "I made it out."

"The things coming out of Hellborn—those cutters didn't heal."

Rolling my eyes, I dug into my pocket and pulled out a penknife. Showing him the flat of my hand, I sliced my palm straight across. The blood ran. He blinked hard, watching the wound close.

"I remember you," he said. "Lying in one of those tanks. And the others. Dead. How is it you're alive?"

"I shouldn't be. My unit malfunctioned, and I woke up."

"Why did you go back?"

"To get answers."

I mentioned Harry Packard and the shootout in Simi Valley. Though he listened, I wasn't sure he believed any of it.

"Tell me something, Nathan," I said.

"No one calls me that. It's just Warnick."

"The outbreak in Tres Marias? I'm guessing it wasn't hemorrhagic fever."

"It was way worse. I'm surprised we survived."

He told me about Hellborn and about Robbin-Sear Industries. Everything he said jibed with my research. The scientists believed a rabies-based vaccine would prevent PTSD.

But, as in any great horror movie, something went wrong. The virus got out of the lab in Tres Marias, courtesy of an infected dog. It spread fast, making people ill with an affliction known as *the jimmies*.

In days, the sick turned into flesh-eating *draggers*. As the hordes grew, they overran the town. Though Black Dragon gained control of the situation, many were lost. The mutants evolved into early versions of alphas—or *cutters*. And the man responsible for the program? Walt effing Freeman.

The final blow came with Operation Guncotton, or *How to Get Rid of the Evidence*. Black Dragon evacuated the uninfected just before the gray-suits released lethal gas. The poison killed everything in Tres Marias, including wildlife. And the official story? They stopped the outbreak. It was a bedtime story for the apocalypse.

"Did Freeman terminate the hypers?" I said.

"We thought so."

"Harry Packard doesn't."

"Why did you come here?"

"I already told you, to get answers. Wilson Zeddemore wants me dead. It's why he went to see the Zwicks—to get to me. But now, I think he's after something else."

"Like what?"

"That's what I can't figure out. Before she died, Consuelo warned me they knew something. She…"

The Russian girl is missing.

That's Zeddemore's problem.

I was an idiot—how could I have missed it? This whole time…

"Sasha's alive," I said.

"She died."

He got up and headed for the parking lot. *Dude, what's your hurry?* Unwilling to let this go, I followed him.

"Take me to meet Dave."

"I can't ask him to get involved in another mission."

"Why? Because he's too busy protecting the Russian girl? Look, I get why John told me she was dead. But things have changed, and I need to warn Dave."

We stood next to Warnick's car. Two cyclists had put away their bikes and were leaving. When we were alone, he turned to me, his eyes small and cold.

"You need to drop this. Sasha is dead."

"You're lying."

"Whatever you say."

"Wanna know what I think? The Russian girl is alive, and Dave is looking after her until the child is born. Everyone here is afraid Hellborn will find out and take her—I get it."

"It's a nice theory. But you're wrong."

"Wouldn't be the first time."

I decided to drop it. For now. Warnick climbed into his car and rolled down the window.

"That's it?" I said.

"Good luck avoiding the gray-suits."

"Thanks. Hey, where'd you serve?"

"Afghanistan."

"Thought so. Marines?"

"Army."

Bullet-catcher. "I'm a Marine."

"You're young. Where did you serve?"

"Never got the opportunity. Hellborn took me before I could…"

"Yeah."

"Okay, look. Forget about Sasha. You need to warn Dave. Zeddemore will come for him either way."

"We'll see. Hey, you never told me your last name."

"It's not important."

I let him know where he could find me, in case he changed his mind.

"Maybe we'll see each other again," I said.

"Be careful."

"You do the same."

I walked back to my car and happened to turn around. Warnick had stopped at the end of the parking lot. It looked like he was on the phone.

It didn't take a genius to know who he was talking to.

STELLA SAT ON HER BED, reading. When I walked in, she smiled with embarrassment.

"I hope you don't mind," she said. "I feel like I never get to read anymore."

"Not a problem. Which one did you pick?"

She held up the paperback—Bulgakov's *The Master and Margarita*. "I've never read any Russian authors before. This one's hilarious."

"It's one of my favorites. Everyone gets what they deserve. Have you eaten?"

"I sort of got caught up in the story. I'm hungry, though."

"Let's go to the diner."

Outside, we'd gone only a few feet when I spotted two men walking toward us. One was Warnick, and the other I didn't recognize. Both armed, they had on Black Dragon uniforms. From the look of them, this was no social call.

Warnick addressed Stella. "Who are you?"

"A friend," I said. "She's fine."

The girl grabbed my sleeve. "What's going on?"

"Nothing. Go back to the room."

Behind us, another uniformed man leveled his gun at us. Furious, I pivoted to Warnick.

"I trusted you."

His expression didn't change. "You need to come with us."

A Black Dragon Humvee screeched to a stop. I thought about running. I could survive getting shot, but Stella was another story. Copying me, she raised her hands. The man with the gun frisked us and confiscated my Glock. He waved us toward the vehicle. When the girl freaked, I patted her arm.

"We'll be okay," I said.

She nodded and followed me to the Humvee. We got in the backseat. The other men climbed in after us, one on either side. They kept their weapons on us. I glared at the one nearest me.

"Is this really necessary?"

Warnick got in up front on the passenger side and signaled the driver to take off. When we were on the road, I leaned toward the fat traitor.

"Where are the blindfolds? You wouldn't want us telling anyone where your hideout is."

He remained silent as we got on the freeway and headed south. In a few minutes, we were in Tres Marias. We drove past downtown to a narrow service road leading to an industrial park. The road dead-ended, and we turned into a driveway, pulling up in front of a long, flat building.

I got out and stared into the distance, where I spotted an old property, freshly painted gray and yellow. There was a crane truck parked next to it. The operator guided a sign toward a group of men waiting on the roof. The words read Happier Times. No one wore masks.

"I wonder what's over there," Stella said.

"Looks like a strip club."

Warnick started toward the door. "It's an ice rink."

We followed him inside. The interior was vacant, and they'd ripped out the carpet. Long rows of holes crisscrossed the bare concrete floor. I guessed the room had once been a cube farm. The other men left us as Warnick led Stella and me to a conference room. Someone was waiting for us inside, also wearing a Black Dragon uniform.

It was the man with the short hair who'd been giving me the ojos when I went to find Warnick. Though he was close to my age, he seemed older, like he'd seen some serious shit. We sat at the conference table. Warnick grabbed water bottles from a cabinet and handed them out. He took a seat next to his pal.

"Nobody's wearing a mask," I said. "They're for show, right?" Then to Hard Eyes, "Are you Dave Pulaski?"

"Why are you looking for him?"

"Didn't your friend tell you? I came to warn him."

"Did you kill John and Consuelo Zwick?"

"I already explained what happened. Zeddemore killed them."

"Zeddemore. Like in *Ghostbusters*?"

"Don't you assholes care that the gray-suits are after Dave and the Russian girl?"

"That's another thing. Why do you keep insisting she's alive?"

"Consuelo told me before she died. Not in so many words. It was the way she said it, like she was protecting someone. I figured it out on my own."

"She figured it out," he said to Warnick.

"Yeah, because I'm not an idiot."

My blood was boiling. If I'd had a weapon, I would've put down these ass clowns.

"Look. She could've told me to warn Dave. But that's not what she said. Her exact words were *They know*. I'm pretty sure she was talking about the Russian girl."

Hard Eyes sat there, ruminating. He looked at me for a long time, then side-eyed Warnick.

"Sasha is dead," he said.

"Okay, that's it." I got to my feet. "Let me know when you get tired of punching the ice bag. I have business elsewhere."

"Sit down."

When I wouldn't comply, he pointed a handgun at me. I gave him the finger and turned to leave. The bastard fired, striking me in the leg. The sound was deafening in the smothering confines of the conference room.

"Sonofa-*bitch*!"

Stella shrieked as I went down on one knee. Rolling his eyes, Warnick got up and crossed to me while glaring at his friend.

"Really?" he said and helped me into a chair. "Let me take a look at it."

"I'm fine."

When he poked his finger through the bullet hole, I yanked his hand away.

"I said I'm fine."

In another beat, the slug slid down my leg and landed on the carpet. Warnick picked it up. The trigger-happy buttmunch examined the bloody bullet and laid his weapon on the table. I looked at the blood, then glared at the shooter.

"You owe me a new pair of jeans, needle dick."

"What are you?"

I rubbed my wound and took a long swallow of water. I wasn't going to get anywhere fighting with them. Might as well play ball.

"They call us *hypers*. More of Hellborn's crazy-ass experiments in terror."

"Does that mean you go around hunting—"

"I'm not a cutter, okay? Jeez, I'm trying to help you people."

"Okay, clam down," Hard Eyes said.

"Did you just tell me to *clam down*?"

"Friend of mine used to say that." He pointed at Stella. "What's her story?"

"Someone I met. I got her out of a dangerous situation."

The man who'd shot me sat quietly, looking at his hands. That's when I noticed the wedding band. Warily, I eyed him as he approached me and put out his hand.

"Good to meet you, Jane," he said. "I'm Dave Pulaski."

FORTY-FIVE

DAVE HAD GONE OUT, leaving Warnick to babysit. When he returned, he had a laptop. Another Black Dragon employee followed him, carrying plastic bags of takeout. Dave took a seat while the other guy set up the food on the credenza.

"I made a call," Dave said to me. "Wilson Zeddemore checks out."

"You thought I made him up?"

"I had to be sure."

"I knew a Pulaski in boot camp." Then to Stella, "He was an asshat too."

The girl jammed a fist in her mouth to keep from laughing.

I gave Warnick the stink eye. "You told him about the self-healing?" Then to Dave, "What? You wanted to see for yourself?"

He thought about it for a sec. Then, "Pretty much."

"Well, eff me. Glad I could entertain you."

He opened the laptop and showed us a video. As soon as he clicked play, I recognized the phone footage from the Simi Valley shootout. When it was over, he looked at me.

"That was you, right?" he said.

"How did you—"

"I have friends in high places."

"I don't understand," Stella said. "How are you not dead?"

Smiling, he pushed the laptop aside. "Kind of a badass, aren't you? I'm impressed."

"This isn't funny. Innocent people could've been killed in the crossfire."

"You're right, it's not funny. When I fought the draggers up here, then cutters in LA, I thought I'd seen it all. But you're something altogether different. Where do you come from?"

"I can't remember." Then on his expression, "Something happened to my memory. Jane is a name I go by."

"What is it you want to do?" Warnick said.

"Stop Zeddemore. Then I'm heading to Virginia."

"What's there?"

"Hellborn's headquarters. I intend to find out what the Hyper program is. And who I am."

"And this woman who runs the whole show?" Dave said. "What's her name again?"

"Caroline Sheldrake."

"What makes you think she's any better than Walt Freeman? Maybe she's the one who sent Zeddemore after you."

"Wrong. He worked for Freeman. Harry Packard reports to Caroline."

"And this Packard guy. You trust him?"

"About as much as I trust you. But he's all I've got. And he didn't shoot me."

"Fair enough."

Leaving the discussion aside, we grabbed our food. As we ate, Dave looked Stella over, making her blush.

"Jane rescued you, is that right?" he said.

"I was having boyfriend trouble."

When the others turned to me, I gave them a tight smile. "He was beating on her, so I took care of it."

Dave nodded with approval. Though I didn't know him, I suspected we had a lot in common. Neither of us liked putting up with bullshit. He addressed the girl again.

"What are your plans now?"

"I don't know. Jane told me I needed to learn to protect myself. We went to the gun range earlier."

"Kid's a crack shot," I said. Then to Warnick, "You guys would be lucky to have her."

"You mean, working for Black Dragon?"

"Why not? You must have some kind of intern program."

Warnick glanced at Dave. "We do." Then to Stella, "How old are you?"

"Nineteen."

Dave punched his friend in the arm. "There you go, Warnick. Fresh meat."

"So, Stella," the supervisor said. "Are you interested?"

"You guys do security, right?"

"All over the world. Since the outbreak in Tres Marias, we've gone on a hiring spree. Most of our people are ex-military, but it's not a job requirement."

"You should do this," I said to her.

"Yeah, for sure." Then to Warnick, "How do I, like, apply?"

"I'll pull together the paperwork."

"Don't I need to interview?"

"I'm the supervisor, and I do all the hiring." He glanced at me. "You seem to come highly recommended."

Stella grabbed my hand. "I can't believe it! If we hadn't met, I would've never…"

"Looks like all that praying paid off."

"We can get started tomorrow," Warnick said. "I'll need a

valid ID like a driver's license. If you pass the background check—"

"Wait, what?"

"Don't worry, it's a formality. But we're required by law to do it."

The girl's face fell, and the color drained away. Patting her shoulder, I got to my feet and gripped Warnick's arm.

"Can I see you in my office?" I said.

We stood in the parking lot. It had turned cold. Gray, rain-swollen clouds darkened the sky.

"Look, Warnick," I said. "When I told you I took care of Stella's boyfriend problem, I meant it."

"You killed him?"

"Stella had nothing to do with it." When he looked away, I grabbed his arm. "Dude, she's the victim here."

"Yeah, but murder."

"The guy was a violent shitbag. You wanna talk about killing someone? What about Walt Freeman? That helicopter in the desert didn't just spontaneously combust. Someone fired an RPG at it."

"Did anyone see you?"

"No. And I didn't leave any prints."

"And the girl? She was nowhere near—"

"When it was over, I gave her a ride up here. She's a good kid, Warnick."

"Okay. But if we do this, and the background check turns up anything…"

"It won't."

I started toward the building when he called to me. He seemed remorseful.

"You were right about Walt Freeman," he said.

"It was you. You're the one who fired the missile. Never mind, I won't hold it against you."

I left the ex-soldier in the parking lot. When I got to the doors, I glanced back. He was holding a small, black book. His lips moved as he read.

The words seemed to bring him comfort.

FORTY-SIX

ON THE RETURN TRIP, Stella was moody. She marched into our room and began stuffing her few belongings into her backpack.

"What are you doing?" I said.

"What does it look like?"

Sounding surly, she acted like a dumbass middle schooler. She grabbed her book, then hesitated.

"You can keep it."

"Thanks."

"Where will you go?"

"Friend of mine goes to college in San Diego. I'm hoping she can help me get set up down there."

I placed my hand on hers. "Is this because of the background check?"

She stared at the floor, then burst into tears and sank onto the bed. I sat next to her and, putting my arm around her, let her cry herself out.

"Everything in my life is shit," she said.

"That's what life is. You try and make the best of it. I think working for Black Dragon would be good for you."

Anger flashed in her eyes, and she pulled away. "Haven't you been listening? They'll never hire me."

"I had a talk with Warnick. As long as what happened the other night doesn't lead back to us—and it won't—you'll be fine."

She glared at me, defiant. "You don't get it. That's not what I'm worried about."

"What, then?"

She refused to look me in the eye. Instead, she continued packing. I made her stop.

"Stella, what did you do?"

"I'm such an idiot. I…stole a car."

"When?"

"I was fifteen. Technically, it wasn't me. It was my stupid boyfriend Derek."

Why are Dereks always douchebags? "Did they arrest you?"

"Right after he crashed the car. My parents had to bail me out. And my dad, he wanted to kill me. It was the worst night of my life."

"Well, not the worst." I was smiling, and it made her laugh.

"It's not funny. My parents grounded me for, like, a year. I had to work in my dad's repair shop every day after school, even on weekends. The thing is, after a while, I got to like it. When he saw how serious I was, he started paying me. I've been earning my own money ever since."

"Sounds like a valuable life lesson to me," I said, getting to my feet.

"If Black Dragon does a background check, they'll see—"

"You were a minor. Those records can be sealed when you turn eighteen. File a petition, and it goes away."

"What? Who says?"

"The State of California. I'm betting your parents already took care of it for you. Wait."

I found my laptop and googled *california criminal records.*

In no time, I found a website where I could look up arrest records. When I keyed in Stella's name, I got one hit. Sitting next to me, the girl gasped.

"Hang on," I said. "This woman is from Slab City. She was arrested and convicted of murdering her father. And she's twenty-seven."

"Oh my God, all this time. You're right. My parents must've petitioned the court."

She hugged me. Not knowing what else to do, I patted her back.

"Of course, they did. They love you. Now, come on. Let's forget all this running away nonsense. You need to focus on getting hired. And stay away from Slab City."

Laughing, she went into the bathroom and washed her face. Someone knocked on our door. I grabbed my Glock off the nightstand and went to answer. I peered through the peephole and opened the door.

Dave Pulaski stood there, wearing a flannel work shirt and jeans. He looked past me at Stella.

"I apologize for the pop-in," he said.

I let him through. Brushing back her hair, Stella slipped past us and out the door.

"Going for a walk."

I closed the door and stood there, my arms folded. He knew I was pissed at him. It was easy to tell because he shifted his eyes from side to side.

"We don't have a lot of seating choices," I said.

Shrugging, he sat on the bed. "I came to apologize."

"For?"

"Shooting you. It was a dick move."

"Ya think?"

"Warnick told me about your abilities. But that's not why I did it. What I went through these past few months changed me. Everything that was bad in the world came out of Hellborn."

"And when I showed up…"

"I assumed it was more of the same. Look, I know you're not like the others. And I—"

"Let's forget about it."

"Does it hurt?"

There was a plain chair in the corner. I placed it opposite him and sat.

"I wanna ask you about Sasha," I said.

"What makes you think she's alive?"

"I know she is. And you're risking your life to protect her."

"Why would I do that?"

"Because it's what I would do. Who looks after her when you're away?"

"A friend. Her name is Maritza."

"What's her story?"

"I met her in LA."

"What were you doing down there?"

"Looking for Walt Freeman."

"Because of what happened in Tres Marias?"

"And because he was responsible for Holly's death. She was my wife."

"And the Russian girl? How did you get mixed up with her?"

"Total accident. But it turned out okay because she led me to Walt."

"While you were in LA running around with two women."

He got to his feet and began pacing. "It wasn't like that."

"With men, it always is."

He stood beside the nightstand and thumbed through my book collection. "There's some good stuff here. I used to read. Haven't for a long time."

"Go ahead and pick something."

"Maybe later."

He returned to the bed and sat across from me.

"The night we raided Hellborn to rescue Sasha, I saw you," he said. "We had no idea Walt would kill all those test subjects. If we had, we might've…"

"It's funny. When I woke up, I heard shooting and an explosion. Thought I'd dreamt it. But it was you guys, right?"

"We were fighting—what did you call them?"

"Alphas. Dave, if the gray-suits ever find Sasha… Where is she now?"

"Someplace safe."

"Do you think maybe I could meet her? I feel like we're connected. I've spent all this time trying to find answers. She's another piece of the Hellborn puzzle."

"I can't—it's too risky."

"But I can help."

"What happened to Sasha and me and all the rest, it's not your story."

He was right. I'd stumbled into his world and found a whole other shitshow having nothing to do with me. The one thing our lives had in common—the only thing—was Hellborn.

"These gray-suits—Zeddemore's people," I said. "They're headed up here."

"We'll be ready." He got up and went to the door. "Warnick mentioned he'd stop by tomorrow with the paperwork for Stella."

"I'll let her know. Hey, I figured it out. *Clam down.* Holly used to say it, right?"

He gave me a sad smile. "That and some other stuff. I used to call her *Mrs. Malaprop*."

"She must've had a great sense of humor. I mean, look who she married."

"Nice. Oh, I almost forgot." He pulled a hundred-dollar bill from his pocket and handed it to me. "For the jeans."

"Thanks, I appreciate it."

I opened the door for him. Outside, Stella walked toward us carrying two to-go cups from the diner.

"See you later, Jane," he said. "Stay safe."

"You too." I followed him to his vehicle. "Tell the Russian girl about me, okay? Tell her…I hope it's a girl."

He didn't give me an answer. Instead, we shook hands, and he left. It was clear to me he was worried. About the gray-suits. About me showing up. But there was also a sadness about him. I was right all along—he'd lost someone dear. Though I wouldn't have minded getting to know him, I was carrying my own load. I was sad I would never get the chance to meet Sasha. We were both victims of some mad scientist plot. And no one deserved that. Not her or me. Not the alphas. Not anyone.

"Look," Stella said, handing me a cup. "Milkshakes."

"We can drink them on the way."

"Where are we going?"

"The mall. Warnick's coming by tomorrow, and you need to look professional. We're going clothes shopping."

"Awesome! Hey, can you be my big sis?"

"Thought I already was," I said.

FORTY-SEVEN

IN THE MORNING, I packed my bags and waited for Warnick to show. I'd done what I came to do—warn Dave about the gray-suits. It was up to him and his friends to protect the Russian girl and her unborn child. Me, I had other business. It was time to hunt down Zeddemore. And end him before he did the same to me. I'd already paid two weeks ahead on the motel room and left Stella some extra cash until she got her first paycheck. I told her she could return the money when she was a bodyguard to the rich and famous.

The girl emerged from the bathroom, wearing a black three-quarter sleeve sweater dress and matching sandals. She'd tied her hair back and put on makeup.

"Well?" she said.

"You look interview-ready to me. Hold on a sec."

I reached into my crossbody bag and took out a small silver gift box.

"I saw this and thought of you. Maybe it'll bring you luck."

Opening it, she found a small golden angel on a chain. "Oh my God, it's… It's beautiful."

"Something to remember me by. Though I'm no angel."

Tearing up, she hugged me. I fastened the chain around her neck. She returned to the bathroom to see herself. When the knock came, I went to answer the door. Warnick wore his uniform and a sidearm. He carried a laptop and a stack of paperwork.

"Hey," I said. "She's ready for you."

Stella shook the supervisor's hand. It was the first time I'd ever seen him smile.

"Wow. The guys I hire usually don't dress this nice."

"I wanted to make a good impression."

"You absolutely did."

I held my hand out to him. "I'm leaving now."

"Oh? Well, it was good meeting you, Jane. I hope it all works out for you."

"Me too." Then to Stella, "See ya, kid. Good luck." I grabbed my bags and headed for the door.

"Wait. I wanted to say goodbye."

She followed me outside and waited as I tossed my bags into the trunk. Playing with her necklace, she seemed unsure what to say. I went first.

"You're gonna do great," I said. "They're lucky to have you."

"What about you?"

"There's something I need to take care of."

"I wish I could help you."

"The best thing you can do for me is to help yourself."

"Take care, Jane. Don't let the bastards win."

A tear fell. Brushing it away, she hugged me. "I feel like we were just getting to know each other."

"Me too."

She grasped the angel and rubbed it. I worried she might have doubts about working for Black Dragon.

"I want to ask a favor," she said. "It's pretty obvious I've got the job. And I want to thank you. You know, properly."

"What did you have in mind?"

"I was hoping you'd stick around so we can have dinner. It would mean a lot to me."

"I don't know, Stella. I was planning to get on the road."

"We won't ever get this chance again. Please?"

"Okay. Anyway, there's less traffic at night."

She hugged me again. "Thank you."

"I'll be back later," I said. "Better get inside before Warnick changes his mind."

Laughing, she walked confidently into the motel room, closing the door after her. I stood there for a bit, watching. A squirrel scampered halfway up a tree and froze, giving me a WTF look.

"Shut up," I said.

With the change of plans, I now had the entire day. Plenty of time to follow through on an idea that had been brewing since my last hyper karma episode at Lake Isabella. Hopping on the freeway, I headed south.

From my research—and from talking to Warnick—I'd learned Robbin-Sear Industries, the company responsible for the outbreak, had a lab in Tres Marias. This was where the nightmare had begun. Though it was a long shot, maybe they had the drug I needed.

Exiting the freeway, I discovered a shortcut that would take me to Old Orchard Road. It was cold and dry. The rotting carcasses of deer, squirrels, and a million birds littered the landscape. All thanks to Walt Freeman and Operation Guncotton.

At the edge of the property, fencing made from logs lined the road. And there were floodlights in the trees. I arrived at a series of one-story unmarked buildings. Pulling up to the gate, I read the sign. PROSPECT CORRECTIONAL FACILITY. My ass.

I parked and walked up to the gate, which fronted the main building. An electrified fence surrounded the property, and I wasn't sure if it was hot. But the place looked deserted. Scanning the area, I spotted bunch grass across the road. I pulled up several long blades.

Standing next to the fence, I poked one blade through and rested it on the chain link. Slowly, I pushed the blade forward, waiting to detect an electrical charge. There was none. Checking my weapon, I scaled the fence and dropped to the other side.

The building had no windows. But there were security cameras everywhere. I hoped they were off. I tried the front door. Locked. Stepping back, I kicked at it. After three tries, it burst open.

Inside, it was dark. The carpet and walls gave off a noxious odor, making me cough. Someone had attacked the site using CS gas. Covering my nose and mouth, I made my way through offices and labs. In the rear, there was a stairwell leading down. I descended.

In the basement, I arrived at an unlocked door. I went through and ran my hand along the wall, looking for a switch plate. Locating it, I flipped on the lights. Like the rest of the facility, the room was a mess. Lab equipment and broken glass everywhere. A reek came from the next room. In there lay dozens of dead lab animals in cages.

I kept going and found a hermetically sealed room that stood in darkness. There was a keypad on the wall, and next to it, a sign that read STOP! PPE IS REQUIRED BEYOND THIS POINT. I'd brought a small flashlight and used it to scan the room. Inside, there were metal racks all labeled RS-6160, but no actual drugs.

Frustrated, I continued searching. I was aware Robbin-Sear had developed the formula that eventually became Surrelis. It was unlikely I'd find anything relating to the

Hyper program, though. Disgusted, I gave up and turned to leave.

A gray-suit stood there, pointing his weapon at my head. His face was one big gap-toothed grin.

"Looks like I found the hyper," he said.

CHAPTER
FORTY-EIGHT

HE WAS MAYBE THIRTY, with short blond hair. Pudgy and way shorter than me. Though he tried projecting confidence, anyone could see the fear in his eyes.

"Gun on the ground," he said.

"Or what?"

"Three to the head. Don't make me."

I needed to buy time. If this mook was supposed to kill me, he would've done it by now. I laid my Glock on the floor and kicked it toward him. His eyes never leaving mine, he pocketed it.

"I don't want any crap," he said.

He motioned for me to continue past him. The whole time, he stayed out of striking range. Smart.

"Where are we going?"

"Mr. Zeddemore would like to meet you."

At the top, I stopped and looked at him. He was close enough now, I could've kicked his fat ass down the stairs. He knew it too and held his weapon with both hands.

"Not sure I wanna see him," I said. "I'm thinking he looks kind of uglified with that bullet hole in his cheek."

"Oh, yeah. He's lucky to be alive."

I opened the door and walked through. This time, I didn't look back. "He's gonna need luck when I get through with him."

"That's not going to happen. Keep moving."

I remained compliant as we made our way to the front of the building. The residue from the CS gas made it hard to breathe. The closer we got to the exit, the more we coughed. Between gasps, the gray-suit waved me outside.

"Someone attack this place?" I said.

"Local cops got into it with Black Dragon. That's all I know."

The gate was open. Beyond the fence, there was a black Escalade parked behind my Challenger. I didn't see any other hostiles. Standing on the steps, I glanced back.

"What now?"

"We wait. Mr. Zeddemore is en route."

"*En route?* Are those the kinds of words they teach you in strum school?"

He stuck his gun barrel in my back and pushed me forward down the stairs. I pretended it was all good.

"For a hyper, you've got a mouth on you."

"Oh, yeah? How many hypers have you met?"

"Get over by the fence."

I did as he asked. While he made a call, I glanced at the open gate. He must've seen me because a bullet whizzed past my ear. *Damn, the prick's an excellent shot.*

"Next time, I won't miss," he said. Then into the phone, "I got her. Right. No problem. See you in a few."

He brought out a pair of handcuffs from his jacket pocket. I rolled my eyes.

"Why do fat guys always wanna get kinky?"

"Shut up."

He walked toward me, pointing the gun with his right hand. I thought about taking it away from him, but he wasn't close enough.

"Turn around. Hands behind your back."

There was no way he could put handcuffs on me and handle the weapon too. Luckily, he hadn't figured it out. Spinning, I grabbed the gun and, jamming it against his jaw, retrieved my Glock. I butt-stroked him and held onto him before he could fall. While he was still dazed, I cuffed his right hand to the fence and trained my weapon. When he came to, he looked frantically from side to side.

"Shit shit *shit*!"

"Why does Zeddemore want me dead?"

"I don't know."

"You work for him."

"Ever since that night when you escaped… It's like he's obsessed."

"Enough to shoot up a quiet neighborhood?"

"That was a mistake. We warned him not to—"

"How far away is he?"

"Maybe twenty minutes."

I could see he was lying and shot out his kneecap. He cried out and started blubbering. I poked him in the stomach with my gun barrel.

"How far?" I said.

"Ten minutes. Maybe less."

"You know about the Hyper program, right? The drug they used on us?"

Tears streaming, he nodded fast. "Riactis."

"Where do they keep it?"

"Used to…" He was going into shock.

I slapped him twice to keep him focused. "Where?"

"Used to be at our facility in Rosamond. With the hypers dead, they moved everything to LA." He looked at his leg. "Don't let me bleed out!"

"How do I get in?"

"My ID badge works."

Digging through his pockets, I found the card and

pocketed it. I couldn't risk him describing my car to Zeddemore. There was no other way—I had to get rid of him. And then, a noise.

I turned for only a sec. Damn squirrel in a tree. The gray-suit grabbed me by the hair with his free hand. He was strong and pulled me close. I dropped my weapon. He bit me on the cheek as hard as he could. Warm blood streamed down my face.

Struggling, I punched him repeatedly in the solar plexus until, at last, he released me. I fell back and touched my face. The bleeding had stopped, and the wound was closing.

Breathing hard, he grinned with satisfaction. Getting bit did something to me. Instinct told me to shoot the worthless mook. When the adrenalin rage hit, I marched to the guard shack. Inside, there was a switch that controlled the electrified fence. I glared at my attacker.

"No," he said as I reached for it.

As electricity surged through him, he jiggled like Elmo in heat. I considered returning to the building to make sure the security cameras were off. But there wasn't time. Zeddemore would be here any second. I ran past the gate to my car. As I pulled forward, I took another look.

The gray-suit had stopped moving.

FORTY-NINE

I USED the backroads all the way to Redding to make sure no hostiles could follow me. When I entered the motel room, Stella wasn't there. She'd left a note saying Warnick wanted her to meet some people. She'd be back in the late afternoon.

My hair and clothes carried the stench of dead gray-suit and CS gas. I examined my face in the bathroom mirror. The bite mark was gone. I probed my neck. The scar from the older bite remained, a dark reminder of something evil from my past. The slurry voice in my head sounded mean and drunk.

Good girl.

Standing under the weak stream of warm water, hyper karma overtook me. The episodes occurred more frequently now. Soon, as Packard pointed out, I'd be unable to control them. I switched off the hot and let the cold rivulets run down my trembling body. After awhile, my temperature stabilized.

And then, he walked into my head—Raul. I couldn't remember ever needing anyone. But there he was. Close. Naked. For the first time since waking up in Hellborn, I gave in to my urges. It wasn't the same—not without him. But at the moment, I was all I had.

Feeling better, I walked to the diner and ate a cheese omelet and toast. I returned to the room and tried reading *The Postman Always Rings Twice* by James M. Cain. As good as his prose was, I couldn't keep my eyes open. Setting the book aside, I lay on the bed and let myself drift into a dream...

The gray-suit I'd killed in the forest floated toward me in a fog. His hair smoldering, his eyes resembling cooked eggs. His tongue lolled out of his mouth and twitched obscenely back and forth. Rhythmically, like the pendulum on a grandfather clock. The ticking hurt my ears.

He held something in his right hand—a glass syringe filled with a luminous blue liquid. Looking up, he grinned with teeth made of jagged metal and offered me the needle. Unable to resist, I moved closer and reached for the syringe. He grabbed my wrist and pulled me in. The ticking got louder.

The monster fed my fingers into his mouth and chewed everything down to nothing. It didn't hurt, and there was no blood.

I was up to my wrist in his face when I awoke. Stella stood near the bed. I rubbed my eyes and sat up.

"Nice nap?" she said.

"I didn't hear you come in." I yawned loudly. "What time is it?"

"Almost five."

"How'd everything go with Warnick?"

"Amazing. They let me sit in on one of their meetings. Did you know Tres Marias was a ghost town after the outbreak?"

"Yeah, I heard. Sounds like you're all set."

"As soon as the background check comes through, they'll onboard me. I get to do my training in San Francisco."

"Sounds great, Stella. I'm excited for you."

She sat on the bed. "What've you been up to all day?"

"I had a meeting. When's dinner?"

She glanced at her phone. "I need to freshen up. We have a

six o'clock reservation. I thought you'd want to get on the road early."

"I appreciate it. You can have the bathroom first. You know, to make up for your mother."

She laughed. "I can't wait for our dinner."

I'd never seen anyone that happy. So, that's what it looked like.

Our reservation was at a fancy restaurant named View 202. There was some big event going on, and we were forced to park all the way down Hemsted Drive. When we got inside, they had our table ready.

Though it was early, the place was packed. The decor was rich with blues and purples. There was a fireplace inside and a bar resembling something out of the movies. The host led us to the patio, which overlooked the Sacramento River.

"You must have connections," I said as we took our seats.

"You can thank Warnick. He did it all."

"I will. The next time I see him."

The host handed us our menus. Stella perused hers, studying each item. A server appeared, ready to take our drink orders. I wanted wine, but the girl wasn't twenty-one yet. We settled on iced tea. The restaurant featured mostly meat and fish. We ordered salads, followed by the vegetarian ravioli.

Dinner with Stella was nice. With all the violence in my life, I felt like I'd done one useful thing since leaving Hellborn. No matter what else happened, I'd hang on to that.

"What's it like?" she said when the food came.

"What's what like?"

"You know, being indestructible."

"I'm not. Just hard to kill. I can't remember being any other way. Anyway, it makes me a better soldier because I don't fear the enemy."

"Where will you go now?"

"Back to LA."

She touched my hand. "But that's where—"

"Zeddemore is. Or will be soon."

"I want to help you."

"You already have. My life is complicated. I don't have friends. People are after me. And I can't remember who I am. You're like… You're something special."

"I am?"

"You may not see it, Stella. Maybe because of some mistakes you've made. But there's goodness in you. And I, well…"

"You're good too. No, I mean it. You helped when you didn't even know me."

"Sure, but—"

"And you showed me how to stand up for myself. I meant it when I said I wish you were my big sister."

"I'll be that for you," I said. "Wherever you are. Wherever I am. Now let's order dessert."

A cold moon shone as we walked to my car. Nearly there, we stopped and took in the view. I wasn't sure I'd be alive to look at another river, and I wanted to remember the moment.

"I have one last favor to ask," Stella said. "Don't laugh."

"What is it?"

"I know I got to drive your car once. But it wasn't under the best circumstances."

"You wanna drive it back to the motel?"

"It's such a badass car."

"Well, I am the big sister, right?" I dug out my keys and handed them to her.

"Okay, don't move. I'll come to you. Tonight, I am your personal chauffeur."

"There'd better not be a scratch on it when—"

"Stop. I'm a very careful driver."

She ran ahead like a little kid with a balloon. One thing I came to appreciate was, it didn't take much to make her happy. She was guileless and genuine. Before climbing in, she pumped her fist in the air.

"Whoo-hoo!"

The engine didn't catch right away. Thinking she might flood it, I started toward her. She tried again. And again. Then…

Time slowed as the Challenger exploded. The force of the blast knocked me to my knees. It blew out car windows in every direction and set off alarms. When I could get to my feet, my ears were ringing.

I ran, hoping somehow the girl had survived. By now, angry flames engulfed the vehicle. And inside—still wearing the seat belt—Stella's slender body lay charred beyond recognition. A dozen yards away, something on the ground glittered. I hurried toward it.

It was the angel necklace. Amazingly, it had survived the blast, intact. I picked it up and slipped it into my pocket. Someone must've called 911 because in another beat, sirens wailed. They weren't far away.

As I walked into the night, a surge of adrenalin came over me. Not knowing what to do with it, I wavered toward the nearest car and pounded the hood until I broke my hand.

Then, I slipped into the darkness before anyone saw me.

PART FIVE

HERE COMES REVENGE

WARNICK STOPPED at the motel with the engine running. I sat next to him, nursing my broken hand. He'd come as soon as I called. No questions. No excuses. Couldn't ask for more.

"She wasn't a part of this," I said. "You'll let her family know?"

"I'll take care of everything."

"She died because of me."

"It's not your fault. This is on Zeddemore. And Hellborn. How's the hand?"

I showed it to him. "Like you'd expect. Getting better."

I tried smashing it against the Humvee's dash, but he grabbed my wrist and held it tight.

"Don't," he said.

"Thing is, I can't even cry. How's that for effed up?"

"You'll grieve when you're ready."

"How do you do it, Warnick? You've seen horrible things —I know you have. Been in situations that would destroy a regular person. Tell me your secret."

"Faith."

"Guess that's my problem. I'm faithless."

"You need to find a purpose. A reason to go on."

"Killing Zeddemore is a good start."

"I don't know. After Holly died, Dave made it his mission to kill Walt Freeman. It's what kept him alive."

"But you ended up killing him."

"He got the chance, but he let it go. Maybe Sasha and her baby had something to do with it, I don't know."

"And the rage? For what they did to his wife? And the town?"

"He's learning to deal with it. Slowly."

"So I shouldn't kill Zeddemore?"

"All I'm saying is, make this about you, not him. You are what's important."

"Thanks for the advice. But no. Next time I see him, he's effing dead."

I climbed out and came around to the driver's side. He was about to leave when I laid my hand on the door.

"I appreciate you coming to get me," I said. "You're a good guy. For a bullet-catcher."

"Thanks. Be careful, Jane. Revenge—"

"I know, dig two graves."

"Rely on your friends. That's what we did in Tres Marias. It's how we survived."

"I don't have any friends."

"You have me," he said.

I remained there, staring into the darkness as Warnick drove off. All I had now was the clothes I was wearing and my Glock. But if history teaches us anything, it's that battles can be won with less.

In the morning, I arranged for a rental car and headed south. My plan was to drive straight through to Lake Isabella. There, I'd contact Kersey to see if he would help me track down

Zeddemore. Once the murderous gray-suit was out of the way, I'd reconnect with Packard, and we'd go to Virginia.

The closer I got to my destination, the more I thought about the Colombian. And I'm embarrassed to admit, I wondered if he thought about me. I knew there was no future for us, but I wanted to see him—be with him—one last time.

Near Sacramento, hyper karma hit me like a red tide. My vision blurred, and I was sweating. Soon, I'd be in no shape to drive. I had to get off the freeway and find someplace cold. Nothing came to mind. Struggling to focus, I exited and took a road leading away from the city toward an upscale residential area. There were few cars in the driveways. I found a secluded place next to a park and pulled in behind the dumpsters.

My legs wobbled as I left my car. From here, I could see backyards—some with pools. I scoped out a property to make sure no one was home. *Clear.* I entered through the gate. The pool looked like it hadn't been used in a while. Dead leaves floated lazily on the surface. I dipped my fingers in the water. Ice cold. I found a coiled-up blue-and-white pool rope and brought it with me to the shallow end.

With the fever raging, I stripped to my underwear and positioned myself on the second step. I wrapped the rope around me and secured it to the stainless steel railing. I needed to keep my head above water, in case I passed out. A memory burst through the fever in another flashback…

It was my twelfth birthday and hot af. Bo and I had on our bathing suits. We were playing soldier and chased each other in the backyard with super soakers. I slipped and fell, skinning my knee.

When I looked up, a man was standing there, his back to the sun. He wanted me to follow him into the corn maze.

The last thing I heard was my brother warning me not to go.

· · ·

Opening my eyes, I found a young boy and girl staring at me. Twins, maybe.

"Why are you sleeping here?" the girl said.

"I was sick. I'm better now." I stared at the house, on the lookout for parents. "Isn't it dangerous, you being out by the pool?"

"We know how to swim," the boy said. "Want to see?"

"Maybe later."

He tested the water. "Brr. I'm not going in today. Do you like cold water?"

"Sometimes."

I got dressed and put away the rope. When I reached the gate, I looked back. The kids stared at me like two Lladró figurines. I gave them a wave and walked out. Lake Isabella was still five hours away.

By Los Banos, I was starving. I didn't want to take a chance someone would recognize me and kept driving. At Avenal, I exited and found a Mexican restaurant across the street from a Gas-N-Gut. The potato tacos were good. After I'd eaten, I walked outside. That's when I spotted them across the street at the gas station.

Black Escalades.

Two hostiles stood next to one of the vehicles, talking to someone sitting in the backseat. After a beat, they returned to their car and got on the freeway heading north. Soon, the other Escalade left. But instead of going the same way, the driver took the south on-ramp.

As the second vehicle passed me, I caught a glimpse of Zeddemore, sitting in the backseat and holding a phone to his ear. I was convinced those first two were on their way to Tres Marias to track down the Russian girl. And Zeddemore? He was headed to LA to look for me.

I texted Warnick to let him know the gray-suits were coming.

CHAPTER
FIFTY-ONE

IT WAS LATE when I reached John's cabin. This time when I stopped for clothes and supplies, I purchased mescal. For the last hundred miles, I relived Stella's death. Could I have done anything differently? Checked the surveillance cameras at Robbin-Sear? Inspected the car before letting the girl get behind the wheel? Woulda, coulda, shoulda. She was dead, and no amount of self-pity would fix it.

After putting everything away, I got a fire going and made a drink. I sat on the sofa and stared at the orange flames licking up the back of the fireplace. The bricks were black, like my mood. I imagined Stella inside the fire, her arms flailing. Begging for someone to make it stop. *Walk it off.* That's what Bo used to say.

I needed Kersey's help and decided to call Chico's Money Transfer. It took a long time for them to answer. Maybe because by now, they were closed. I disconnected and tried again. This time, someone picked up. It was the forger, Perry Rochambeau.

"What?" he said.

He didn't sound pleased. Like I'd interrupted him pushing a rope in the bathroom.

"I need to speak to Crispin."

"Crispin, huh? Never did like that name. Sounds like a Nancy-boy from Yuba City. Wait, is this the skirt who came in the other—"

"Yeah, it's me."

"You don't sound so good, darlin'. Everything all right?"

"Peachy." I gave him my number. "Tell him, will you?"

I dropped the phone, tears streaming down my face. Warnick was right—I was ready to grieve. Angry at myself for being such a girl, I fixed another drink. I hadn't planned on getting wasted. But after the third one, I told myself, eff it —I'd earned it. Still, I needed to be sharp for when Kersey called, and I stopped at four shots.

Cried out, I lay on the sofa, listening to the fire and watching the sparks rise. Somewhere in the forest, a nighthawk screeched. Warnick had advised me to rely on my friends. Besides him, who did I have? Kersey? He was my employer. Raul? Definitely the Colombian. But I worried about bringing him into the situation again. He might end up dead. Like Stella.

When my phone buzzed, I checked the number. It wasn't one I recognized. I thought about letting it roll into voicemail. Still, it might be Kersey with a new burner.

"Hello?" I said, trying not to sound drunk.

"It's me."

The sound of Raul's voice filled me with a warm glow that had nothing to do with the alcohol. Clearing my throat, I sat up straight.

"Hey."

"Kersey's tied up. How are you?"

"I'm a mess."

I started crying again. This was getting ridiculous. How was I supposed to take out Zeddemore when all I could do was sit here, blubbering like a nerd girl on prom night?

"Friend of mine was killed. Guess it hit me hard."

"I'll come to you. Tell me where you are."

"I don't know…"

"Whatever you're going through, you don't have to do it alone."

"What if you're followed?"

"Give me the address."

It wasn't that I didn't trust the Colombian. But Zeddemore might put a tail on him. He was right, though. I needed help and gave him the address. He promised to be there in a few hours.

By now, it was almost seven, and I hadn't eaten. The mescal was wearing off, and I no longer felt like drinking to blackout. I put more wood on the fire and lay on the sofa to wait for Raul. I didn't remember falling asleep.

Someone was knocking. In my dream, it was Bo pounding out a fender on his latest piece-of-shit restoration project. Grabbing my weapon, I went to the door and looked out the peephole. It was the Colombian.

When I let him in, he brought me close and pressed my head to his shoulder. I thought I was all cried out, but I was wrong. He walked me inside and over to the sofa. For a long time, he sat there, holding me.

"Have you eaten?" he said.

Like a child, I pointed at the empty glass on the floor.

"I brought food. Give me a minute."

"Pull your car around back."

After bringing in the groceries, he plopped me on a bar stool next to the island and got to work. Before I knew it, he'd made us pasta primavera with crusty bread. We ate at the kitchen table. I took another sip of a delicious chilled white wine.

"'Ornellaia Bianco,'" I said, reading the label. "Is this expensive?"

"Very."

I reached across and took his hand. "Thanks for coming."

"After I clean up, I want you to tell me everything."

"I can't—not tonight."

"First thing in the morning, then."

"Okay, promise."

Instead, we talked about Kersey. The cops had been sniffing around his offices, asking lots of questions. Worried someone might've flipped on him, he cooperated with the authorities. I pictured the kid—the vaper. But I didn't think the dilrod had the cojones.

"Have they arrested him?" I said.

"Not yet. But soon."

"What about the operation?"

"Griselda will take over."

"Maybe she was the one who snitched."

"Not likely. She has too much to lose."

Together, we cleaned up the kitchen. Sitting by the fire, we finished our wine. I no longer cared about Zeddemore or Hellborn—or even Caroline Sheldrake. All I wanted was to remain in this fairyland in the forest. Disappear forever with my unremembered name.

Raul let me make the first move. I took his face in my hands and kissed him. Soon, we were devouring each other without words. In the middle of it, he stopped. Flushed, I gaped at him. He threw a log on the fire and dug through the closets until he found blankets. We made love there. Again and again until I could no longer stay awake.

And then, we slept. Me in his arms. The fire crackling. The forest as silent as eternity.

FIFTY-TWO

I AWOKE to the smell of fresh coffee. The fire had long gone out, leaving the room chilly. Raul was in the kitchen, as usual. I wondered what his life would've been like if he hadn't gotten mixed up with criminals. For one thing, he'd be living in Medellín. Probably own a restaurant.

Stretching, I joined him and, wrapping my arms around him, kissed his neck. He pretended to be busy.

"So, who was she?" I said.

"Who?"

"I'm not the first girl you've cooked for. There must've been someone in Medellín."

He handed me a steaming cup of strong coffee. "There was."

"What happened?"

"Nothing. I left Colombia and never saw her again."

"Was it serious?"

"Why are you asking all these questions?"

"Was it, though?"

With precision, he rolled yellowish dough into little uniform balls and arranged them on the cutting board. "We were going to be married."

"Wow. I'm trying to picture you with a dad body. Taking out the garbage…"

"With the kind of life I was in, I was worried something would happen to her. I broke it off."

"She could've left the country with you."

"She'd never go." He sounded bitter. "Loves her family too much."

"What's her name?"

"Valeria."

I kissed his cheek. "Thanks for being honest. What'cha makin'? Those don't look like pancakes."

"It's called Arepa Boyacense."

"A grapey what now?"

"Ah-reh-pah Boya-cen-se. It's a traditional Colombian breakfast dish."

I stood next to him, watching as he flattened a dough ball and placed it in a pan of sizzling butter.

Leaning over, I took a whiff. "They smell amazing."

"They taste even better."

When they were ready, we sat at the table, and I took my first bite. These things were sweet and salty, filled with gooey white cheese. Heaven.

"Okay, I've decided," I said. "After I take care of Zeddemore, I'm getting another apartment and hiring you as my personal chef."

"Does this include night duties?"

I tossed a blueberry at him. "What do you think?"

"I'm in. Okay, time to get me up to speed."

I told him everything. All except the part about the Russian girl. Afterward, he collected the dirty dishes and cutlery. I sipped my coffee while he loaded the dishwasher.

"Too bad about Stella," he said. "Sounds like she was a nice girl."

"She was."

"We need to score you some Riactis. Or, as you said, game over."

"A gray-suit told me they're storing it in LA. Do you think I should call Packard? Maybe he can get me some."

"I don't see what else you can do. But he might make you go to Virginia."

I left the table and paced in the living room. After wiping down the counter, Raul joined me. I took his hand and kissed it.

"I'm not going anywhere until Zeddemore is dead," I said.

"Maybe Packard won't see it your way."

"What if I break in and take what I need?"

"Too dangerous, even for you. You'd need a team of hypers."

I sighed like Griselda. "Which we don't have."

"Besides, how much could you get your hands on? At some point, your supply will run out."

"All I need is enough to complete the mission. Then I'll go to Virginia."

He looked away, disappointed. I wondered what he'd been thinking, driving up here. Did he actually believe we could have a happy ever after? What I'd said earlier was a wish. And unless I was wrong and Jiminy Cricket was real, wishes didn't come true. Especially not for someone like me.

"Let's take a walk," I said.

I led the Colombian into the forest. I'd hoped to see the fawn again. But everywhere we looked, she was nowhere in sight. The air was brisk. Birds sang, making me believe for a moment that life could be sweet. I led him to the brook, where I kissed him and took his hands in mine.

"You know there's no future for us, right?" I said.

"I hoped maybe somehow… But you're right. We could never pull it off."

"Wait. Pull what off?"

"Escaping together out of the country."

When I laughed, he tore his hands away. I grabbed them again, forcing him to stay put.

"No, no," I said. "I'm not laughing at you. I'm happy you'd even think of something like that. With me, I mean. I'm too hot to handle, remember?"

"Not to me."

He kissed me and held me close. The babbling of the brook and the birds singing bore into my brain like a message from a snow angel. Was it even possible?

I wasn't your average girl. Hellborn had done something ungodly to me. And in doing so, they'd erased my memories. Whatever my past, I was a trained killer—a soldier in the service of…what? Going away with Raul was a little girl's dream. A fairytale requiring tiny tea sets with homemade cookies and music boxes.

"Guess I'd better call Packard," I said.

We headed back, neither of us wanting to talk about the future.

The security chief had been expecting my call. I let him know Zeddemore was getting close.

"You should've come with me when I asked," he said.

"If you recall, there were about fifty gray-suits shooting at us."

"Okay, what about now? I can have a plane ready in a couple of hours."

"I have a more pressing problem. And I can't wait for Virginia."

"Hyper karma?"

"I need Riactis. Can you get it for me?"

"I'd have to go to the LA office. Zeddemore would know it's for you."

"I knew I could count on you."

"Jane, what do you want me to say?"

"It's all right. I'll find another way."

"Don't tell me you're thinking of breaking in. That little stunt you pulled in Rosamond won't work again. They'll be expecting you this time."

"I'll figure something out."

He was still talking when I disconnected. In another beat, he called back. I let it go to voicemail. Later when I checked, there was no message. *Time for a new burner.* I looked at the Colombian.

"Looks like we're doing it the hard way," I said.

"Don't try it by yourself. I'll see if Kersey will loan me a couple of guys."

Raul stepped outside to make a call. In the meantime, I grabbed my new laptop and tried digging up info on Baseborn Identity Research in LA. A thought came to me. When I first met Dave Pulaski in Tres Marias, he'd left the conference room and returned with fresh information. *Wilson Zeddemore checks out.* Who had he spoken with? I called him.

He'd heard about Stella and offered his condolences. I asked him if he could help me gather details on the layout of Hellborn's LA location. Entrances and exits. Security. The times people got on and off work. Having broken in there himself, he told me what he knew and gave me a name and number. According to Dave, this woman could find out the President's underwear size, if she wanted to. After disconnecting, I stared at what I'd written.

Karen Rothberg.

CHAPTER
FIFTY-THREE

IT WAS ALMOST lunchtime when I contacted Karen Rothberg. The call went to voicemail on the first ring. Raul had gone out for supplies. The man was determined to win me over with food. The fact that it was working I would take to the grave.

I spent the next half-hour tidying up the house. Though John and Consuelo were gone, it was my way of honoring them. My phone vibrated, and the screen displayed *Private Number*. I picked up.

"This is Karen," a voice said. "Who am I speaking with?"

"Jane. Dave gave me your number."

"Are you alone?"

"Yes."

"Do you have a computer with VPN software?"

"Affirmative."

"Get it and key in the IP address I'm about to give you. I'll wait."

I brought my laptop to the kitchen table. After connecting to the VPN, I opened a browser window. She read off the address, and I entered it. A login prompt appeared, with a company logo at the top—CYBERALLES.

"Okay, I'm on the login screen," I said.

She gave me a username and password. As soon as I was in, a woman's face appeared. She was in her early sixties. With dark-brown hair and blue eyes. She wore an expensive suit, with a necklace and no earrings. She looked like someone who was better suited to hosting charity events for wealthy donors.

"How are ya, doll?" she said. "It's nice to see your face. The last time, you wore a helmet when you took on Zeddemore."

"You saw the video?"

"Everyone saw it."

I wasn't sure how to start. "What's Cyberallz?"

"It's pronounced cyber-all-es, as in *Cyber über alles*."

"German?"

"Rock-solid security protocols. I've used them for years. What can I do for you? Dave said you were in trouble."

I ran down the situation for her. Rather than typing on her computer, she took notes in longhand. I noticed she wore a white glove on her other hand. Nothing I said seemed to bother her, even the part about electrocuting the gray-suit. When I asked her why, she mentioned she'd had her own run-in with them.

"Quite a story," she said.

"How does Dave know you?"

"We have a mutual friend."

"He told me you helped him when he and Sasha were in trouble."

"Correct. And her brother as well."

"You already know about Wilson Zeddemore."

"Nasty piece of work. I gather you want him out of the picture?"

Relieved, I almost laughed. "I do. But first, I need to get into Hellborn. There's this drug—"

"What's wrong with you?"

"I have a condition. They call it hyper karma. Comes on suddenly, and I end up with a raging fever."

"And what happens if you can't get the drug?"

"I'll die."

"I see. How have you been coping?"

"Cold showers, ice—anything to bring down the temperature."

Karen told me about the security system at Hellborn. After Dave broke in, they beefed it up. Worse, the facility was crawling with additional security guards. And there were cameras everywhere.

"The only way to get in is for someone to compromise the security system," she said. "Even if we do manage it, you won't know where they keep the stash."

"Can we hack in?"

"Just what I was thinking. By the way, it's not Surrelis you're after, is it? Because that drug is dangerous."

"I'm part of the Hyper program. They gave us something called Riactis. It stabilizes our systems."

"Hacking into their security won't be enough. Someone needs to go there ahead of time and scope out the place. Find out where they're hiding the drug."

"Someone?"

"I have an idea. Give me two hours, then log back in."

Before I could say goodbye, she ended the video conference. I closed the laptop and got a beer from the fridge. Raul walked in through the back, carrying groceries. I smiled at the bottle of Old Faithful.

"We're having popcorn tonight?" I said.

"Absolutely." He kissed me. "After which, I plan to rip off your clothes."

"Promise?"

I let him know about my conversation with Karen while he made us vegetarian sandwiches. As soon as he set them on the table, I tried one.

"Mm, this is incredible," I said.

"Simple. Avocado, feta, apple cider vinegar, and other secret ingredients I can't divulge."

"What do you think? About Hellborn, I mean?"

"Sounds like it's going to be impossible to break into."

"Karen is working on it."

"I heard from Kersey. With everything going on, he can't spare anyone. I think he's pissed off about me being up here with you."

"It's just you and me then."

He stroked my arm with his finger. "How's the hyper karma?"

I took a swallow of beer. "I haven't had another attack. Weird. The last one was outside Sacramento."

"Maybe your body's adapting. Or…"

"Or what?"

"It might be all the amazing sex."

"I wish. Listen, when I talk to Karen later, I want you there."

"Sure she'll agree?"

"She'd better," I said.

We sat together in front of the laptop and waited for Karen to start the session. When she appeared on the screen, she looked Raul over, and giving him a smile, raised an eyebrow.

"I see you have a partner in crime," she said. "Always been partial to Latin men. Anyway, down to business."

She took us through a rough plan. Karen knew a young hacker who went by the handle *V. Kulla*. I'd read Stieg Larsson's *Millennium* series and knew the name was a reference to Pippi Longstocking's house, Villa Villekulla.

The plan involved V disguising herself as a gray-suit and, using a fake ID, walking into the LA facility. Once inside, she'd search the building until she determined where they kept the Riactis.

Later at night, she'd gain access to the security system so

we could enter and take the drug. V advised Karen she needed a day to prepare. The researcher seemed pleased with the plan. I was skeptical. After we ended the session, I turned to the Colombian.

"Some girl dressed as a gray-suit running around the building?" I said. "What if she gets caught?"

"You did it, remember? Have a little faith."

"Right. Semper Gumby."

"I don't know what that means."

"Always flexible," I said.

MY PLAN WAS to stay one more night before returning to LA. But after speaking with Karen, I wanted to get moving. We drove down to the lake and hiked near the shore. Though the sun was out and the sky clear, it was too cold to go in the water. Instead, we climbed among the jagged rocks near Wofford Heights and found an enormous flat boulder to sit on.

I looked out at the water and tried not to think of anything else except today. Most likely, I'd be dead soon. But I didn't want to say it in front of the Colombian. The difference between him and me was, he had hope. I didn't even have my memories.

"What's your best day ever?" I said.

"I was five. The cops had arrested my father for inciting violence."

"Wait, this is your best day? What did he do?"

"Handed out bibles. The police detained him for four days. As a kid, it felt like four years. One day, he walked through the front door. They'd beaten him, and he never even complained. I remember him smiling at me and my brothers and sisters. Like everything was normal, and he was coming home from work. I'll never forget that day."

"Is your dad alive?"

"He passed a few years ago. My mother died soon after." He took my hand. "You can't remember your best day, can you?"

"And I don't even remember my parents."

"It sucks. About your memories, I mean. Maybe when you get to Virginia, they can help bring them back."

"There you go being all positive again."

He kissed me. "I'll try harder next time."

"There she is!"

Raul looked at where I was pointing. It was the fawn. Standing like a statue, she waited for us to make a move. When we didn't, she lingered awhile and scampered into the forest.

"See?" I said. "I do have friends."

Dinner was a total surprise. Raul made potato tacos from scratch—even the corn tortillas. They were superb. We washed them down with Mexican beer. And for dessert, he'd followed through on his promise to make bourbon and salted caramel popcorn.

The rest of the evening, we spent in front of the fire, sipping mescal and pretending everything would come out all right.

"Best donuts," I said.

"Donut Friend. Best coffee."

"How should I know? Wait. There was this one weekend when I took a drive. I ended up getting lost in Huntington Park and found a place. Their coffee was so good."

"Do I get to hear the name?"

I jabbed him with my elbow. "I'm thinking. Civil Coffee.

Okay, worst movie—and you can't say *Plan 9 from Outer Space*."

"Anything with Pauly Shore. Worst pickup line."

"Hey, girl!" we said together.

We laughed over that one a long time. I'd had my fill of mescal and fell asleep next to Raul. Somewhere far away, in a dream, I thought I heard the Colombian say *Hey, girl*.

When I woke up, it was morning, and I was in my bed. Alone and wearing my clothes. I sat up and stretched. Another night had passed without hyper karma. Was it possible I was no longer afflicted?

I wandered into the kitchen, expecting to see Raul cooking. He wasn't anywhere in sight. I picked up the new burner he'd given me and saw I had a voicemail.

Jane, I didn't run out on you. There's something I need to take care of. I'll be back—don't leave without me. Te quiero.

I wasn't sure what I'd heard and played it over. Te quiero. I couldn't remember anyone ever telling me they loved me. And the Colombian? We hardly knew each other. Hell, I didn't even know me.

Dammit. Why did he have to lay this on me now, when I'd already accepted the inevitable? No use stewing over it. After my morning routine, I made coffee and ate the leftover Arepa Boyacenses I found in the fridge.

Raul walked in through the back door. I wanted to be angry at him for ruining my resolve. Instead, I held and kissed him.

"That was some message," I said.

"It's how I feel. I get that we can't be together, but I wanted you to know. It's something you can keep with you, inside. I sound like an idiot."

"No, you don't. I… I don't know what I feel."

"That's okay. It's enough one of us said it."

"Maybe when all this is over—"

"We should go soon."

He poured himself coffee and sat beside me on a bar stool. From his expression, he was a million miles away.

"I went to LA to see Kersey," he said.

"Which means last night we didn't…"

"You fell asleep. I carried you to the bedroom."

"Not an easy job, my friend."

"My back still hurts."

"Shut up. How is he?"

"They arrested him in Santa Monica last night."

"Where is he now?"

"Home. He made bail."

"What's he being charged with?"

"Violating the Federal Immigration and Nationality Act."

"Let's hope he has a good lawyer. I feel like there's something you're not telling me."

"I didn't drive all the way down to LA because of the arrest. I told him I was quitting."

"The outfit? Why?"

He didn't answer for a long time. Whatever was on his mind, he didn't want to say.

"I'm going back to Colombia."

Though we'd talked about not having a future together, I hadn't expected this. Anyone could see the decision hadn't come easy. He couldn't even look me in the eye.

"I'm happy for you," I said. "You'll return to Medellín and marry the girl—what's her name?" I knew her name.

"Valeria. By now, she's probably fat, with six screaming brats."

"Or not."

I stroked his cheek. He took my face in his hands and kissed me with a smoldering passion that honestly? It made me swoon. The feeling was intense and brought tears to my eyes. But I didn't cry. Instead, we made love.

When it was over, we packed our things and got on the road, taking separate cars. Coming down the mountain, a single thought plagued me like a housefly on a mission.

Medellín is too damn far.

CHAPTER
FIFTY-FIVE

AFTER DROPPING off the rental car, we headed south toward LA. We'd made it through Tejon Pass—Angelenos call it *The Grapevine*. In Gorman, I started watching for drones. Didn't spot any. I'd spent much of the trip thinking about the Colombian. I didn't want him to leave, but what choice did I have?

Today, V would make preparations. Tomorrow morning, she'd arrive at Hellborn during the shift change at around 0800 hours. If everything went smoothly, I'd show up later with Raul. I didn't like the idea of him going with me. The gray-suits would shoot first and ask questions later. I'd be left with bullet wounds, no drug, and a dead Colombian I had feelings for.

"Where are we staying until tomorrow night?" I said. "Can't go back to The Borgia."

He kept his eyes on the road. "I asked Kersey. Thought we could hang out at his place. He said no—too many feds lurking."

"Maybe we can find some out-of-the-way motel."

"We're staying with Griselda."

"Are you sure that's a good idea?"

"Why not? Babić's security team watches the place twenty-four seven. Anyway, she insisted."

"I'm worried about her daughter, is all. What if the gray-suits show up and start shooting?"

"We'll be fine."

I didn't know whether it was anxiety over our mission or worry about Lily. But as we got closer to LA, hyper karma threatened to take me down. By the time we reached the 405 interchange, I was burning up.

"You need to find us a gas station," I said.

"Bathroom break?"

When he saw my eyes, he understood. He exited the freeway and drove along San Fernando Road until he found a Gas-N-Gut. A cop cruiser was parked next to the mini-mart. No one was inside.

"We'd better try somewhere else," he said.

"I can't hold out. You have to stop."

He parked in the rear. "What do you want me to do?"

"Wait here. I'm gonna use the restroom."

"What about the cops?"

Feverish, I made my way to the entrance. Two police officers were buying Gutbuster dogs with the works. Those things had more filler than a Dickens novel. I was glad they were distracted and headed straight for the back.

I tried the door to the family restroom. Locked. Inside, a mother spoke some Asian language to a small child. I propped myself against the wall. In another minute, the toilet flushed, and mother and daughter walked out.

Locking the door after me, I ran the tap and tore off my sweater. Cupping my hands in front of the sink, I poured cold water on my face and neck. Outside, someone tried the door.

"Ocupada," I said.

A man said something faint. Another man answered him.

I couldn't understand why the hyper karma had gone,

then returned with a vengeance. As I continued dousing myself, I tried thinking what I might've done to prevent the fever. Maybe it was the food I'd eaten. Or I'd gotten enough sleep. I thought of Raul's suggestion—*all the amazing sex*. Despite my discomfort, I let out a laugh.

After ten minutes, my temperature dropped. In another few, I was back to normal. I took several slow breaths to calm myself. When I opened the door, the cops were waiting for me, holding their uneaten Gutbusters.

"Is one of those for me?" I said.

The tall one answered. "Can we see some ID?"

"Sure. What's this about?"

Though I had a concealed carry permit, I was glad I'd left my Glock in the trunk of Raul's car. They waited while I got out my driver's license. Each of them examined it, then looked me dead in the eye.

"You need to come with us," the short one said.

"Why?"

"There's a warrant. You're wanted for questioning."

"Regarding?"

But I already knew. Someone must've identified me from the Simi Valley video. I had a choice. Go with these bozos peacefully. Or run. In my peripheral vision, I saw a dad buying candy for his two boys. If I bolted, I'd put them in danger.

"It's fine. I'll go with you."

Though I was cooperating, they cuffed me anyway. They walked me past the father and his kids. A boy looked at me, a little scared. I gave him a smile. Outside, Raul watched us from the corner of the building. I side-eyed him, telegraphing a message I hoped he would receive—*Get the hell out of here*. In another beat, he was gone.

"What's this about?" I said. "Come on, you're obligated to tell me."

The tall one wiped his mouth. "Robbery-Homicide division wants to talk to you about a shooting in Echo Park."

I didn't say another word the rest of the way. As they pounded down their food, the reek of mustard, relish, and onions filled the car's interior. I almost hurled.

They drove me to the Rampart station on 6th. Because they wanted me for questioning, they didn't fingerprint or photograph me. Instead, the tall one escorted me to an interrogation room the size of a janitor's closet.

Water-damaged acoustic tile covered the walls. A video camera mounted on the ceiling pointed at a small table with two chairs. The fluorescent lights were bright enough to hurt my eyes. Some stiff in an off-the-rack suit waited for me to sit. He introduced himself, but I wasn't listening and didn't get his name.

"Have a seat, Ms. Doe," he said. "Is that your real name?"

"I changed it."

"From?"

"Karla Nowak."

"Polish, huh?" He brightened. "Where are your parents from?"

"Laski. I came over when I was a kid. Is this why you brought me here?"

"Dlaczego są wy w Los Angelesie?"

"I don't speak the language."

"I asked what you're doing in LA."

"I'm a security consultant."

"And the gentleman who was found dead in Echo Park? Vincent Luong? You knew him, right?"

"Don't think so. Is he Polish?"

The detective smacked his hand on the table. "Being a smartass won't help your case, young lady."

"Case? I thought I was here for questioning."

He leaned in. There was a stain on his tie. Looked to me like he'd gotten a little too generous with the Coffee-mate.

"Listen," he said. "This investigation—"

A knock interrupted him. When the door opened, Harry Packard's daughter stood in the hallway, wearing her uniform and carrying a manila folder.

"Can I help you, Officer?"

"I'm here to escort Ms. Doe."

"I'm in the middle of an interview."

Maggie stepped into the room, avoiding eye contact with me. Turning red, the detective watched morosely as she removed a sheet of paper from the folder and handed it to him. After reading it, he glared at me, his eye twitching from caffeine.

"This is a judge's order," he said to me. "It says you're employed by Hermes Security Partners and that your work is classified."

As he reread the order, I side-eyed Maggie. She gave me a quick nod.

"That's correct," I said.

The detective sighed. "Guess I owe you an apology."

I got up and joined my friend. "No problem. See ya around."

We left the room and proceeded down a long hallway leading to the front entrance.

"What just happened?" I said.

"Not now."

Outside, I spotted Harry Packard walking toward me. He didn't look happy. Behind him in the distance, a black Escalade slowed. The backseat window went down. As the vehicle continued past, I caught Zeddemore glaring at me, one eye effed up beyond recognition. It gave me pleasure to know I was the one responsible for his new look.

"That was Zeddemore," I said to Packard.

"I know. He's the reason they brought you in."

"And you showed up to save me."

He gave his daughter a hug, and she returned to the station. His eyes were on me now, his expression grave.

"Whatever it is you're planning, I want you to stand down," he said.

CHAPTER
FIFTY-SIX

A CRAPLOAD of Starbucks stores surrounded the police station. Worried about Zeddemore finding me again, Packard drove us across the freeway to Andante Coffee on Grand. The place wasn't crowded. We got our drinks and found seats toward the back, facing the entrance.

"Should I be jealous about Raul having Maggie's number?" I said.

"The plan was for that detective to hold you until Zeddemore showed up to take you into custody. I used my contacts at the Justice Department to get an emergency court order."

"How'd you get it so fast?"

"You don't want to know."

"A lot of bother for little ol' me."

"I'm convinced Zeddemore would've taken you to an undisclosed site and—"

"Which is why I need to kill him first."

"Not a good idea."

"How can you say that? After what he's done?"

"Jane, you're angry. I get it."

"Angry? He's trying to effing end me."

"Keep your voice down. Look, I can keep you safe. But

you have to promise to stay away from Zeddemore and Baseborn."

I hated to admit it. What Packard said made sense. The key to me finding out who I was lay in getting to Virginia and meeting Caroline Sheldrake. Sure, Zeddemore needed to pay for his crimes. Maybe someday he would.

"What about Riactis?" I said.

"I promise you, I'll get it. Once we're in Virginia."

I swallowed the last of my coffee and tapped the side of the paper cup. All our plans were in place. Karen...V. Kulla... Raul. I wasn't ready to call off the operation.

"I have to think on it."

"Don't take too long. Zeddemore is looking for his next opening."

"Why can't you guys stop him?"

"We tried, but his people are loyal. They'll do anything to protect him."

"Even killing innocents? I can let you know in the morning. Can you take me to see Raul?"

We left the store. Packard exited first and did a sweep of our immediate surroundings. No other gray-suits. I stayed close as we made our way to the car.

I didn't want Packard to know where we were staying and asked him to drive me to Griffith Observatory, where Raul would be waiting. The security chief got on the 110 going north and cut over to the 2. No one followed us, and there were no drones visible in the sky. We exited on Los Feliz Boulevard. From a side street, a black Escalade identical to ours sped past a line of cars and slipped in behind us.

"Your guys?" I said.

"No."

"Looks like Zeddemore found his next opening."

"Where to now?"

"Stick to the plan."

I made a call to let the Colombian know what to expect. While I was on the phone, Packard got on his, asking for backup. We took North Vermont Canyon Road and continued all the way up the hill. As we closed in on the observatory, another Escalade joined our pursuer. Now two more vehicles appeared, using a different road.

"Those are my guys," Packard said.

Lucky for us, the building was closed for repairs. No civilians to worry about. Raul's car was parked next to a vast lawn in front of the entrance. Packard swung close to him and let me out. I scrambled to the rear, where my partner waited with a trunkful of weapons. He'd already put on body armor. I stared at the trunk. There was only one ballistic helmet.

"That's for you," he said.

"What about you?"

"No time—put it on."

After I suited up, he handed over a Kel-Tec bullpup and kept an AR-15 for himself. Packard covered us as we raced past a monument with a sundial on top toward the entrance. The doors were locked. We headed to the side. Behind us, wave after wave of gunfire echoed as the two sides fought each other. We ran up the stairs and found a narrow walkway surrounding the building.

All of LA lay before us. Past the railing, there was a sharp drop leading to the rocks below. We backed up against the building and waited. If we were lucky, Packard's people would take out the other gray-suits—including Zeddemore. From around the corner, two hostiles appeared. My partner killed them both.

"I changed my mind," Raul said, checking his weapon.

"About going back to Colombia?"

"Pauly Shore. I liked him in *Encino Man*."

"Thanks for letting me know. Now I have to kill you too."

A weapon appeared from around the corner on my side.

Exhaling, I waited for the hostile to show himself. When he did, I fired the bullpup at his chest. He went over the rail, screaming. Then Zeddemore's voice with an echo that made it hard to tell where he was.

"It's no good, Jane," he said. "Packard and his people are dead. Time to call it a day."

"Bite me, Zeddemore."

"Don't be like that. You sure liked me when I was Tyler Berry."

I side-eyed my partner. He inched his way toward the opposite corner. I checked my weapon. Plenty of ammo.

"I don't hear any more shooting. Does that mean your guys are dead too?"

"Ask me no questions, and I'll tell you no lies."

Slowly, I worked my way closer to my corner, hoping the shitbag would show himself.

"Why, Zeddemore?" I said. "Because of what happened to Walt Freeman?"

"The Alpha program would've worked. But hypers? Sure, you heal fast, but… Ain't hyper karma a bitch?"

A hand appeared next to Raul. My partner had been looking in my direction and didn't see it. By the time I warned him, it was too late. A gray-suit who resembled me had him by the throat. As I aimed my weapon, someone grabbed me from behind, jamming his gun against the side of my helmet.

"It's over," Zeddemore said.

He shoved me against the wall and took my weapon. I could see my partner out of the corner of my eye. As I turned, the hostile fired. Raul dropped to his knees and fell over sideways, blood pooling around his head.

"No!"

"Looks like, for once, you ain't got this," Zeddemore said, and laughed.

I'm not clear on what happened next.

Time slowed. My temperature spiked, but not from hyper karma. The sound faded as my field of vision shrank to a pinpoint. And the rage—the intensity was like nothing I'd ever experienced.

Strange hands were on me now—rude, unwanted hands. More gunshots. A dull thudding as multiple rounds struck me in the arms and legs. I can still recall Zeddemore trying to shoot me in the head. The helmet saved me.

Blind with fury, I flung him aside and grabbed the bullpup. As a reflex, he waved his arms defensively, his right hand still gripping his weapon. I fired at it once. And again. And again. Until there was nothing left but a gored, bloody stump. Staring at it, he wailed. And then, he ran.

The woman gawped at me, frozen in a tableau of stupid. Her dark hair was short like mine. For a second, I pictured myself hunting hypers for Zeddemore. Then I shot her in the face and pushed her over the side. To oblivion.

For a long time, I stood near the Colombian, asking myself the same question. Over and over. *What brought us together?* From the first time I saw him in John's café, I knew we had something. Something intangible—spiritual. And I knew in my soul I'd never have it again.

The adrenalin rage burned inside me like a torch. Shaking it off, I picked up Raul and carried him to the car. All around me, Harry Packard and the rest of the gray-suits lay dead. The security chief had promised to protect me, but that was a lie. Once again, I was on my own. After laying Raul in the back-seat, I went to retrieve the weapons.

Driving down the hill, I was unsure what to do next. In the rearview mirror, I looked at my partner. My lover. My friend.

"You were right," I said. "I am dangerous."

CHAPTER
FIFTY-SEVEN

I TOOK Sunset all the way and made it to Bel Air in less than an hour. When I arrived, I found two Serbians guarding the gates. One was the smartass I'd met the last time I was here. Expecting a repeat, I rolled down my window.

"Griselda invited me," I said.

He glanced at the body lying in the backseat, and saying nothing, signaled his friend to open the gates. I gave him a nod and drove through. As usual, armed men patrolled the grounds.

Clutching a bag, I approached the entrance where Griselda was waiting. I hardly recognized her. She had on minimal makeup, with her hair in a ponytail. Wearing a cashmere sweater and jeans, she folded her arms tight against the cold.

"Where's Raul?" she said.

I looked toward the car.

Speaking in German, she instructed a security man to take care of the body. Another carried the rest of my stuff inside. She took my hand—the way a mother might—and walked me in.

The study was sparsely furnished, and there were more

books than furniture. A black-and-white photo hung on the wall. Griselda's daughter in riding clothes, standing next to a bay wearing an English saddle. We sat next to each other on a long, blood-red leather sofa, waiting for the maid to finish arranging the tea things. The girl closed the door on her way out. Griselda poured.

"Milk?" she said.

"Black is fine."

"Tell me what happened."

Feeling numb, I ran it down to her, beginning with the police station. Afterward, she offered me cookies. Her eyelids were red, and I wondered what had upset her. She couldn't have known about the Colombian. *Kersey's arrest—she does have feelings for him.*

"You're lucky to be alive," she said.

"I don't wanna trouble you."

"Nonsense. I'm pleased you're here. Lily has been asking after you."

"Why?"

"She insists you and she are friends. You must have made quite an impression at the party."

"I'd like to see her again."

"You will at dinner. Listen, about Raul. I wanted to say that—"

"And the body?"

"We'll take care of it."

"I heard about Kersey. Will he be all right?"

"We have the best lawyers." She sounded unsure. "We'll see."

"Did someone inform on him?"

She cast her eyes down to her cup. "It was Marta, his sister."

"What? But I thought the family—"

"She blames him for her son's death. When she asked who

was responsible, he refused to say. She's punishing him—and me."

Kersey was no saint, but he didn't deserve this. He might go to prison because of me. I had nothing left to lose. Clearing my throat, I looked the German in the eye.

"It was me," I said.

"You? Why?"

I told her about my escape from Hellborn and how those vicious men almost killed me in the desert. She put her cup aside and folded her hands.

"Don't worry, Jane. I'll see to it."

She took me upstairs, where my room was waiting for me. I lay on the bed and thought of Raul, dead in my arms. His scent all over me. When the tears came, I couldn't stop them. I buried my face in a pillow and sobbed. I kept on crying until I couldn't anymore. Wiping my eyes, I turned onto my side.

The afternoon sun poured through the large windows. Birds sang. Somewhere, a child laughed, and I slept.

I awoke in the evening and discovered all my clothes washed and ironed. After a quick shower, I came down to dinner. The dining room felt gloomy and looked enormous without all those partygoers. There were three place settings at one end of the table. And in the center, a winter floral arrangement.

The German entered from the kitchen as I walked in. She motioned for me to take a seat. In another beat, her daughter skipped in, wearing designer jeans and a Bangles sweatshirt. She ran to me and hugged the air out of me.

"Jane!"

"How are ya, kid? I like your sweatshirt."

"Lily is a big fan of the old music," her mother said.

Griselda remembered I was vegetarian and fed me a pasta primavera. It made me think of Raul. Though my grief hadn't resurfaced, I could feel the tears hovering in silent storm clouds of emotion. Soon, they would burst.

Lily dominated the dinner conversation with her little girl chatter, which took my mind off things. I didn't realize kids were so busy. Books, concerts, Italian lessons, horses. And very little television.

After dessert, the uniformed older woman I saw the last time appeared in the doorway. Lily gave me a hug and a kiss, then excused herself. Griselda doted on her daughter, and I could see why. She was a treasure.

"Let's go to the study," the German said. "There's something I want to discuss with you."

I sat on the sofa next to a bar cart filled with expensive liquor.

"Can I fix you a drink?"

"Do you have any mescal?"

"Of course. Ice?"

"And lime, if you have it."

She handed me my drink and poured herself a cognac. Sitting beside me, she patted my knee. "I remember seeing you for the first time in the restaurant."

"Honestly, you were a little scary."

"I'll tell you a secret. I was a little drunk." She sipped her drink. "And perhaps, jealous."

"Of me?"

"Kersey and I… It's complicated."

"You get that he's in love with you, right?"

"Yes. And I love him too."

"Then why the divorce?"

"There is a word in German. Willensstark. It means strong-willed. That's Kersey and me."

"But if you love each other."

"Also, there's history between our countries. Imagine Germany and Poland getting married. We knew it would be a problem." She laughed. "We fought—a lot. When Lily came to us, we thought *yes*. Now we will put aside our differences and raise our daughter. But neither of us was willing to change. Understand, we love Lily. But this business of ours…"

She gave me a sad smile. For a sec, I thought she might cry.

"You and Raul," she said. "How do you Americans say it? You were a thing?"

It's not easy to make me blush. I finished the mescal and made a show of looking for a refill. She got up and freshened my drink, her back to me.

"I knew it the instant I saw you two at the party," she said. "The way he fawned over you when you had your episode. To my knowledge, he's never done that with anyone."

Not even you? I accepted the glass and, taking a sip, told her all about hyper karma and my quest for the cure.

"Raul and me, we started out as partners—Kersey's idea."

"Something happened between you? Tell me."

Feeling the effects of the mescal, I couldn't help snorting. "I don't know. He cooked for me, I guess."

She laughed at a joke I had evidently missed. "My dearest Jane. Don't you know?"

"Know what?"

"There's nothing sexier than a man in the kitchen."

Especially when he isn't wearing clothes. "What did you wanna talk to me about?"

"Your mission. You're a clever girl. But what you're planning is stupid. I want to help."

"Help? How?"

She took her phone from her pocket and texted someone. In another beat, there was a knock. It was Babić, wearing his expensive European suit and pointy black shoes. I didn't like him and wondered what he had to do with the situation.

"I won't permit you to do this without backup," the German said. "Lily would never forgive me."

I STARED AT THE SERBIAN, unsure whether to leave or stay and listen. He poured himself a drink—vodka neat. Grabbing a chair, he sat across from us.

"Jane, I'd like you to brief Mr. Babić on the operation," Griselda said. "Don't leave out a single detail."

"I'm not sure this is a good idea." Then to Babić, "No offense."

"Don't you think my team can handle it?" His accent was less harsh than the goons who worked for him.

"The place I'm breaking into has ties to the government. Security is high."

"May I ask how you plan to get in?"

"We have a hacker."

"We?" Griselda said.

"Friend of mine set it up."

"Surely, they know your face," the Serbian said. "What if you're caught?"

"They'll kill me." Then on Griselda's reaction, "Look, it doesn't matter. If I don't get the drug soon, I'm dead anyway."

She laid a hand on my arm. "I'd like you to give Mr. Babić a chance."

"I can provide four men," he said. "Ex-military. Highly trained in weapons, explosives, and surveillance."

Other than V, it was just me now. I may not have seen combat, but I knew in my gut they were right. A well-oiled team beats a lone wolf any day of the week. Besides, even with an authentic ID badge, they'd make me the second I walked in. I decided to tell them everything.

"Good," he said when I'd finished. "Two of my guys will go in and retrieve the package. The others will cover the outside."

"And what am I supposed to do?"

"This hacker. He'll be monitoring the operation, yes?"

"It's a she, and yes."

"You will stay out of sight—with her."

"Agreed," I said. "But I need to let my friend know."

I hadn't spoken to Karen Rothberg since Lake Isabella. When she heard Raul was dead, she was furious and advised me to abort the mission. I explained about the resources Babić brought to the table. We went back and forth until, finally, she relented. But I could tell the researcher was far from pleased.

Previously, we'd arranged to meet at 2200 to finalize our plans. Griselda had no interest in military-style planning and went to bed. I set up my laptop in the study. Babić stood beside me, out of view of the webcam.

We waited to be connected to the video conference. Karen appeared onscreen. In another beat, her image shifted to the side as a new person joined. I assumed it was V. Instead of her image, a yellow smiley face with a black eye patch filled the frame.

"Good, we're all here," Karen said.

After introductions, the researcher turned the meeting over to the hacker. The smiley face disappeared and was replaced by V. She was younger than I'd imagined—maybe twenty. African, with smooth skin and large, dark eyes. Her hair was short. A tiny crescent and star pendant hung from her neck.

Hellborn maintained three shifts at eight, four, and midnight. At 0800 sharp, V walked into Baseborn Identity Research in East Los Angeles, posing as a gray-suit named Abby Hoffman. Cute. She carried a firearm identical to those issued by the company. Earlier, she'd uploaded her fingerprints and retinal image into their system. Armed with a verified ID badge indicating she was based in Virginia, she got past security without a hitch.

In LA, Hellborn operated out of one building in an industrial park. V wandered the halls for four hours. She carried an electronic device that disrupted the signals from the video cameras. Wherever she was, the monitor displayed a rolling, staticky band until she was out of view. No one caught on.

During her rounds, she concentrated on low-level employees, looking for a mark. She found one. Around lunchtime, she met a vulnerable gray-suit who appeared to have the hots for her—something she encouraged. She told him she'd heard about the escape in Rosamond. She said there was credible intel indicating the hyper was coming to steal Riactis.

By the time she finished winding him up, the hapless idiot ran from the lunchroom to check on the drug. She volunteered to go with him, and he took her to a room marked First Aid. Inside, there were boxes of syringes containing Riactis—enough to last years.

"Can't be too careful," she said to the gray-suit on the way out. As a flourish, she promised to mention him to her superiors back in Virginia.

While on her tour of the facility, V planted small devices

wherever there was a camera. When activated, they would piggyback undetected onto the signal so we would have eyes. The hacker planned to be at her computer the whole time, guiding the team via comms to the room where they stored the drug.

When the briefing was over, Babić grinned. He pulled up a chair next to me and peered at the screen. "Hello again, V. Kulla."

Long silence. I didn't know what was going on. Karen was equally puzzled.

"No greeting for your old friend?"

"Hi." V looked nervous.

"Don't worry. I won't divulge your identity." Then to me, "She and I go way back."

"May I ask what the connection is?" Karen said, visibly irritated.

"My team was smuggling refugees out of northern Sudan." He looked at the girl. "You were a scrawny little thing. Only twelve, if memory serves. Anyway, we got you and the others safely into Greece. Then Italy. Didn't we?"

"Yes," the girl said. "You saved my life."

"But I thought your plans were to settle there. You'd always talked about…what was it? Culinary school."

"Things are better in America. More opportunities."

"And you've lost your accent. Shame."

"Reunions are fun," I said. "But we have work to do." Then to the hacker, "What time do we show?"

"It's after ten now. How long will it take you to reach the facility?"

"Traffic should be light. Less than an hour."

She gave us an address where we would rendezvous. There, she'd provide the clothes and electronics we needed. Babić's men were in charge of weapons.

"Better get a move on," V said. Then to the Serbian, "Nice talking to you again."

After disconnecting, I turned to Babić. "What about a vehicle?"

"Outside."

"Then what're we waiting for?" I said.

THE RENDEZVOUS POINT was a vacant lot on North Evergreen near the cemetery. We arrived in the black Escalade Babić had provided. V wasn't there yet. I asked my men to line up. They were older than me—much older—and a little intimidating. I addressed the first man in line.

"What's your name?"

"Vartolomej Dimitrijević."

"Yeah, that's no good. I pointed at each in turn. "Larry. Moe. Curly. And Shemp."

Larry gave me the greasy eye. "You are serious?"

"Look, I don't have time for this."

"I vant to be Moe."

Rolling my eyes, I redid the order. In a few minutes, V arrived in a used white Chevy G20 van with tinted windows and antennas on the roof. The girl was way shorter than me and whisper thin. She had on camo pants, Doc Martens, and a black commando sweater. I guessed she wanted to be as badass as the rest of us. I took a beat to admire my team. Four hardened mercenaries and a wicked-smart hacker. Doing it Babić's way had been the right call.

We followed V to the back of the van. I noticed something

peculiar embedded in the high-mount brake light—a miniature camera. Inside, there was a narrow desk along one side. On it were three monitors. And below, computers and other electronics bolted to the underside. In front stood two black captain's chairs.

"Where did you find this thing?" I said.

"Government fleet auction. It's an old FBI surveillance van."

She handed out gray suits and shoes. We stripped and changed. My suit was ill fitting—inferior to what Nate would've made me. The girl gave each of us an official Baseborn Identity Research photo ID and weapon. Then she grabbed a long black cardboard box. Inside were tiny black earpieces and microphones sitting in a foam cutout. She distributed them to everyone but me.

"Those have a range of 1.2 miles," she said. "The mics go on the inside of your lapel."

"I'm afraid to ask where you got them."

"Right, don't ask. They're military grade. Not even on the market yet."

"You stole them," the new Moe said.

"In America, we say they fell off the truck. By the way, Baseborn uses jammers inside the building. They won't affect our comms, though."

"What about eyes?" I said.

"Gotcha covered. Who's going inside?"

"Alpha Team."

"Okay," she said. Then to Moe and Larry, "Those devices I planted earlier? I'll direct you to each of their coordinates."

From her pocket, she pulled out a rectangular black device the size of a deck of cards. She handed it to Moe.

"The devices are identical to this one. You enable them by pressing that button on the side. Once activated, I can use their cameras to track you throughout the building."

"They vill know you are tapping in," Larry said.

"These ride their signal. To detect them, they'd have to do a full scan of the network, which they have no reason to do."

Confused, Larry looked at Moe, who translated.

"And you're sure we have a cart?" I said.

The girl nodded. "There's one inside the first-aid room. Put it there myself. It's big enough to load a lot of boxes. Also, before I forget. There's an exit at the end of the hallway. It'll be a straight shot to your vehicle."

"What about the drones?"

"Right. Earlier, I tapped into those video feeds and made my own recordings. As soon as you're onsite, I'll play them back through the security system. They won't know the difference."

"Wow, you are good."

Babić had provided us with Blackhawk Advanced Field Operator watches. Before getting underway, we synchronized them. V had never done this before and wore a satisfied grin as she followed our instructions.

"It's 2352 and counting," I said. "The next shift change happens in less than eight minutes."

In another beat, we were on our way, the two teams in the Escalade, and V and me trailing in the van. As we approached the industrial park, we encountered a line of LAPD cop cruisers. The Escalade slowed.

"Pull in there," I said, pointing at an abandoned gas station.

We watched as the Escalade cruised past the cops. Moe was driving. Like a tourist, he waved at the officers.

"What in hell are you doing?" I said.

I checked my watch. We had less than five minutes. My mouth fell open as the cops in the lead cruiser waved back. The police accelerated en masse and continued out of sight.

At one minute to midnight, V drove us to the opposite side of the industrial park. She found a spot behind the building next to Hellborn. The Escalade continued to its destination and parked in the rear. Soon, workers coming off their shift would pour out of the building.

Between the front seats of the van, there was a door leading to the rear. Climbing through, we took our seats at the monitors and put on our headsets. I spoke into my mic.

"Radio check." The responses came back quickly. "Alpha Team, position?"

"Approaching front entrance," Moe said. "Vill let you know ven ve are past security."

"Bravo Team?"

"All good here."

"Roger. Be careful, boys."

I side-eyed V, who rolled her eyes. Nothing to do now but wait. The hacker leaned sideways and grabbed a Costco-size tub of Red Vines from a shelf. She jammed one in her mouth and let it hang there like a limp cigarette. She caught me watching her.

"Want one?" she said.

It was now two minutes past midnight. Waiting was hard —anything could've happened. I checked my watch. Another minute had passed. I couldn't take it anymore and spoke into my mic.

"Guys?"

"Ve are in," Moe said. "Approaching first device."

In another beat, the main monitor lit up, showing a hallway with Alpha Team moving away from the camera.

"Take a right at the next intersection," V said. "The device is hidden in a planter."

They continued out of sight. Soon, they were visible again, heading away from us. The pattern repeated, with my team proceeding to each device, and another video feed coming online shortly after.

"First-aid room is around this corner, yes?" Moe said.

V glanced at me. "Correct. Your ID badge should work."

They approached the door. Before opening it, Larry trotted

to the end of the hallway and stood near the exit, waiting for my signal. V cycled through the video feeds until she found the camera watching the rear parking lot.

By now, the shift change had completed, and the area was quiet. Among the vehicles, there were several Escalades, including ours. She typed something on the keyboard, then stopped abruptly.

"What is it?" I said.

She pointed at the left monitor. "See the guy standing by his car, smoking? The parking lot needs to be empty for me to make a good recording. If I do it now, there'll be a loop of him standing there. The guards will get suspicious and investigate."

Moe's voice came over the comms. "Team Leader, vaht is happening?"

I gripped my headset. "Alpha Team, Bravo Team, hold. We have a situation."

"Look!" V said.

After stubbing out his cigarette, the worker got into his vehicle and drove off. V made the recording and keyed in a command to switch feeds. The image glitched, then stabilized to the new video loop.

"Bravo Team, in position," I said. "Alpha Team, open the rear door."

Larry did as instructed. Bravo Team was already waiting outside, packing four AR-15s. They handed him two and entered. While the others guarded the hallway, Moe swiped his badge and entered the first-aid room. I heard him mutter to himself—it sounded like he was swearing.

"Team Leader, ve have a problem."

"What's wrong?"

"The room is empty," he said. "There are no drugs here."

GLARING AT THE HACKER, I coughed up every obscenity I could think of. Then into my mic, "Are you sure that's the right room?"

"Coordinates check out," Moe said, unfazed.

V cycled through the video feeds, her fingers flying over the keyboard. "I don't understand. They're in the right place."

All of a sudden, the rear door slammed shut, and a deafening alarm sounded while security lights flashed. Both teams ran toward the exit.

Moe tried opening the door—locked. Signaling the others to stand back, he fired his weapon at the lock. A bullet ricocheted and struck Shemp in the leg, sending him down on one knee. Still, the door wouldn't open.

Now there was new activity on the other monitors. Gray-suits and security guards with shotguns were on the move.

"I count eight tangos headed your way," I said. "Take cover."

The men disappeared around the corner, with Shemp's blood leaving a trail. The video feeds showed they had seconds until the hostiles arrived.

Grabbing my gun, I flung a rear door open and looked at V. "Get as far away from here as you can."

"I'll be out of range—we'll lose our comms."

"Go."

"What are you going to do?"

"Something incredibly stupid," I said.

Outside, I slammed the door shut and pounded it twice as a signal. The girl started up the van and peeled out. Up ahead, I could see the rear entrance at Hellborn. I ran full out toward it.

Four security guards waited by the door, shotguns ready. Scanning the parking lot, I didn't see any more hostiles. Keeping low, I made my way to the back of our Escalade and opened the power liftgate. Inside the vehicle, I found more AR-15s—and an M72 rocket launcher. A box of earplugs sat next to the weapons. Babić had thought of everything.

Recalling my training, I grasped the sight and extended the launcher. While the guards focused on the door, I loaded the rocket and grabbed an AR-15 and extra mags. Positioning myself for a clear shot, I armed the weapon and aimed.

"Fire in the hole, fellas."

They turned as I squeezed the trigger. The missile pierced the metal and exploded. The resulting fireball disintegrated the door.

I picked up the AR-15 and ran toward the entrance. Nothing left but dead guards and a gaping hole. Inside, billowing smoke made it hard to see. Light fixtures dangled. The walls were charred. And there was debris everywhere.

Distant gunfire got my attention. As I moved toward the end of the hallway, I glanced at the first-aid room. It was as Moe described it. Only the cart remained.

Shouting and more gunfire. I raised my weapon and turned the corner. There in front of me, Bravo Team lay dead on the floor, twisted and riddled with buckshot.

"Alpha Team!"

Moe peered out from a supply closet. When he saw me, his eyes narrowed. "Behind you."

Pivoting, I fired. Two guards dropped in front of me. I sprinted toward Alpha Team, and they joined me in the hallway. Moe found the keys to the Escalade and pocketed them. Then, we ran.

Zeddemore was waiting for us when we reached the exit. He looked bad. Eye all effed up. And the bloody stump I'd given him, now wrapped in surgical gauze. Behind me, two short gunfire bursts. I heard two bodies drop, one on either side of me. Moe and Larry. A guard relieved me of my weapons.

"Let's you and me have a chat," Zeddemore said.

I felt a prick in my neck, and everything faded to black.

When I opened my eyes, the windowless room was quiet. No alarm sounded. I was tied to a chair, suffering from a raging headache. There were two exits—one across from me and one behind. Boxes of Riactis lay stacked haphazardly along the wall.

Zeddemore spoke quietly to a muscle-bound behemoth of a gray-suit with a brush cut. He noticed me staring at them and nudged his boss. The juice pig departed through the rear door, leaving me alone with the sociopath.

"Nice nap?" the security chief said as I struggled against the nylon ropes. "That won't do any good."

"How's the hand? Too soon?"

Bravely, he laughed and backhanded me. I ignored my stinging cheek.

"You didn't have to kill Stella."

"That was a mistake." He made a frowny face. "Aw, she was your friend."

"Why am I still alive?"

"Don't worry, you won't be much longer. I'm going to try a little uncontrolled experiment. Should be interesting."

He crossed the room and lingered beside a stainless steel table. When he returned, he was holding a syringe filled with black liquid.

"The boys in the lab call this Nite-Trane. We're marketing it as a better lethal injection drug. You got a little taste earlier."

"That's what Walt Freeman used to kill the other hypers."

"Too bad your unit malfunctioned."

"It is too bad. Just think. You'd still be able to play the piano."

"For the next several hours, I'll administer small doses to see what it does to you. You might experience some discomfort. I apologize in advance."

"You are a sick motherf—"

"Language," he said, clucking his tongue.

He brought the needle close to my neck. I twisted my head back and forth, trying to avoid it. Ignoring me, he found a spot he liked and injected a small amount of the poison.

Everything went red. My headache intensifying, I almost passed out again. He removed the needle and stepped back.

"So? How are we feeling?"

"Bite me."

"We'll give it a few minutes, then go again. At some point, your organs should fail, and your heart will stop. I can't wait to see if I'm right."

"I'm gonna kill you, Zeddemore."

"That's the spirit," he said.

His voice had become an echo. I was floating, unable to see clearly. Somewhere far away, a burst of gunfire got my attention. I tried focusing on the door in front of me.

The deranged security chief had dropped the syringe and struggled to pull out a handgun. Pointing the weapon at my head, he watched the door. The knob turned a couple of times, and the door burst open.

Moe stood there, covered in blood, his AR-15 raised. Before my captor could execute me, the Serbian fired. Zeddemore fled through the rear door. I thought I was dreaming as the last man on my team limped toward me and cut the ropes.

"I thought you were dead," I said.

He pointed at the boxes. "Is that the drug?"

Wobbly, I ripped open a box and grabbed a glass syringe filled with the luminous blue liquid. I found a clean needle and looked for a vein. Before jabbing myself, I held the syringe up to the light.

Concerned, Moe grabbed my hand. "How much are you taking?"

"All of it," I said.

When I injected myself, the result was immediate and extraordinary. It was as if someone had flipped a switch. All of Nite-Trane's side effects vanished in a burst of light, and my head was clear. I was stronger than I'd been since escaping from Hellborn. I felt truly alive.

Outside in the corridor, distant gunfire. I handed Moe two boxes and took another two for myself. A weapon in one hand and the drug in the other, I followed him out of the room and into a dark corridor. There were stairs leading outside. He went first, leaving a trail of blood. At the top, he peered through the small window. I waited for his signal. Then, we exited.

We found ourselves in the rear parking lot at the edge of the building. Our Escalade was parked across the way. Moe leaned on me as we made our way toward it. No longer able to stand, he clung to the door frame. I took the key and flung the passenger door open.

Zeddemore and Brush Cut fired at us. As bullets rained all around, I tossed the boxes of the precious drug inside. I tried getting Moe into the vehicle, but he'd collapsed. Round after round pinged off the bulletproof glass. One struck me in the shoulder. I shook it off.

"Come on, get your ass up."

As I helped him to his feet, a bullet tore through his neck. He fell. Clutching his throat, he pushed me away. I knew there was no way to save him and considered my options. There were only two.

1. March toward the gray-suits, firing at will until they're dead. No good. Zeddemore knows how to kill me.
2. Flee.

Scrambling inside, I shut the door and took off. My pursuers ran toward another Escalade. How long could I expect to outrun them? Zeddemore had made it his life's work to kill me.

This time, he might succeed.

A VOICE in my head screamed *Get out of the city!* If I could make it to a freeway going north, I'd hole up somewhere and regroup. Find another way to end Zeddemore. I didn't know where I was. Somewhere on 1st Street heading west. I spotted the 10. But there was no effing on-ramp. I kept going straight.

It didn't take long for the drones to find me. Up ahead on the street, there were blinding lights, heavy equipment, and orange cones everywhere. Damn night crews.

I couldn't go fast. The UAVs had no trouble keeping up. I spotted the other Escalade in the rearview mirror. Brush Cut was behind the wheel, with Zeddemore next to him on the phone.

We passed the LA River, entering Little Tokyo. At Alameda, they accelerated and rammed into me, pushing my vehicle into the intersection.

Out of nowhere, a second Escalade plowed into me on the driver's side. The force sent me skidding sideways across the intersection. Screeching brakes now as other cars collided in the street. Though the impact was bad, my head remained clear thanks to the drug. I checked the rearview mirror.

Zeddemore's Escalade had stopped, and the two passengers got out.

The AR-15 was jammed tight under the dash—I couldn't free it. All I had was my handgun. The sociopath was getting closer. I'd have to leave the drug behind.

A crowd had gathered in the street. Other drivers yelled accusations at each other. In the confusion, I exited through the passenger side. The gray-suits who'd taken out my vehicle were waiting. One tried shooting me in the head. I bobbed, keeping my hands in front of me. While they stopped to reload, I killed them and fled into the night.

I was lost again. All I knew was I had to continue west—away from Hellborn. I sprinted down 1st until I reached Main. Up ahead, cop cruisers lined the street. And the tall building next to them? LAPD Headquarters. Perfect. I took a left, running as fast as I could.

The drones were directly over me. If I tried shooting them down, I'd attract some beat cop's attention. I needed a place to hide so I could think. As I continued south on Main, my surroundings became familiar. At West 5th, I turned right and kept going until I reached The Last Bookstore, where I ducked into an alley.

I needed help. Ignoring the smelly stewbums, I pressed myself against a brick wall and made a call. When Griselda answered, I told her what happened. She went to get Babić.

"Jane?" the Serbian said.

"Your men are dead. I tried to—"

"Where are you?"

"Downtown LA."

I gave him the address, and he put me on hold. While I waited, I noticed Zeddemore's Escalade slowly cruising past. I moved deeper into the shadows. A stewbum tried petting me, and I smacked him.

"Okay," Babić said. "You're near Angel's Flight. I can pick you up there." He gave me directions.

"Listen. This is important. I need someone to retrieve the drug."

I told him where to find my disabled vehicle. It would take him thirty minutes to reach me. I scanned the sky—no drones. Exiting the alley, I continued west on 5th. When I got to Pershing Square, I spotted a homeless camp and passed through the middle to keep from being seen from the street.

A young mother sat huddled with her two children—a boy and a girl. She was younger than me. All three were cold, and they looked hungry. The children gazed up at me, their gaunt little faces dirty and their clothes thin. I wished I had food to give them. Instead, I waited until no one else was watching and slipped her some cash.

"Get something to eat."

She took the money and clasped my hand in hers. Things must've been bad for a long time because she had no more tears to shed.

"I'll pray for you," she said.

From South Olive, it would be a short walk to the top of Angel's Flight on Grand. When I emerged from the homeless camp, two black Escalades were waiting. Zeddemore climbed out of one and, drawing his weapon, came toward me.

Weaving my way through the homeless camp, I ran until I found the public restrooms. As I rushed toward them, two gray-suits appeared in front of me and fired. A stray bullet struck and killed a homeless man.

I hid behind a tree and waited. As the hostiles closed in, I leaped out and returned fire. Four quick bursts, and they were dead.

Heading east, I took a left on Hill Street. Bullets struck me from behind, catching me in the back and legs. Fighting off the intense pain, I used parked vehicles as cover. When I had the chance, I darted into an alley.

Brush Cut was the first to catch up with me. He was ripe with roid rage. When I shot him, he kept coming. He grabbed my arm and threw me against the wall. I dropped my weapon.

He tried swinging at me—useless for a bodybuilder. Standing back, I gave him a roundhouse kick to the head. Instead of going down, he just stood there, only slightly dazed. Approaching footsteps now. Timing my move, I grabbed muscle boy by the lapels and forced him out of the alley. A stream of bullets hit him. As he fell, I came out, weapon up, and fired.

The rounds caught Zeddemore in the side and leg. Screaming, he went down on one knee and returned fire. A bullet struck me in the chest. I aimed at his head. Before I could squeeze the trigger, a police siren wailed close by. I ran.

The sociopath was nowhere in sight. I hauled ass until I reached the Angel's Flight stairs on Hill. Next to them, bright orange funiculars stood like dark sentinels. Out of service and still. With the pain from my injuries almost gone, I climbed the incredibly long flight of stairs to Grand Avenue. This was where Babić had instructed me to wait. When I got to the top, I turned around and saw Zeddemore.

Unable to walk, he crawled after me up the stairs. How was it possible he was alive? Covered in blood, he gripped each step with his good hand and, with all his strength, pulled himself up. Pointing my weapon, I waited for him.

"I'm going to kill you," he said. "Then I'll take care of your pals in Hampstead."

"What did the hypers ever do to you?"

He glared at me, his face a mask of sorrow and rage. And then he continued crawling until he couldn't anymore. By now, he wasn't more than ten feet from me. I should've put him down, but I wanted the truth.

"I need to know why," I said.

"I begged Caroline to let me join the Hyper program. I wanted to be like you—unstoppable. Oh, she strung me along. Made promises. In the end, she said she was never going to do it. I was too old. I would've made a good soldier."

"So instead, you became Tyler Berry."

He laughed, spitting up blood. "Supposed to be my consolation prize. I think Walt felt bad for me. But being a part of the game did nothing for me. And I decided to burn it all down."

"Walt didn't kill the hypers—you did."

"Damn straight."

"I'll give Caroline your regards when I see her."

"Don't go."

"I want my memories back. And I wanna know the truth about the Hyper program."

"The truth? You think she'll tell you?"

"I'll make her."

"Don't look for it, Jane. You may not like what you find."

My hands steady, I took aim at Zeddemore's head. He stared at me, his one good eye pleading. But not for life. He just wanted it to be over.

"Go ahead," he said. "You got this."

Watching the blood pouring from his mouth, I knew he was done. And I no longer hated him. My eyes never leaving his, I lowered my weapon. He lay prostrate on the steps, taking quick breaths. Unable to lift his head. And then he was still. Behind me, the sound of an approaching vehicle. Now a car door opening, followed by rapid footsteps.

"Jane."

I recognized Babić's voice. He joined me at the top of the stairs. Together, we gazed down at the lone gray-suit. Small. Lifeless. Unfulfilled. Far off, sirens wailed as if in mourning.

"Did you get the drug?" I said.

"It's in the car. Let's go before the police arrive."

In a daze, I drifted toward a gunmetal Humvee. As we left downtown, I closed my eyes. I didn't open them again until we reached Griselda's house. I'd wanted badly to kill Zeddemore. For Stella. For Packard. For Raul. But in the end, there was no need.

Like a tragic hero, he saw to it himself.

CHAPTER
SIXTY-TWO

GRISELDA LET me sleep for most of the day. My dreams were intense. Filled with false memories of a firefight in Afghanistan that never was. Images paraded past—people and places I confused with Hellborn…

Amid the gunfire, armed security guards and gray-suits pursued me along the pathways of a dark mountain village. I ducked into a mud hut.

Raul and Packard stood at the end of a long, blown-out corridor, surrounded by smoke and fire. Wearing battle rattle, they urged me on. The hostiles had Stella, they said. And it was up to me to rescue her.

When I entered the dank, empty room where the girl had been a prisoner, I found no one. Now I was in a caged room in a parking structure. A chair stood in the center. A used syringe dripping with black liquid lay on the floor next to it. Bo appeared at my side, armed and ready.

"Sometimes, they win," he said. "You keep fighting the fight."

I looked at him—really looked at him this time. He was vague and translucent. Fading from my memory like a creek run dry.

"Where are you?" I said. "Bo, I need you."

"You'll find me in—"

A noise woke me. Turning over, I found Lily, wearing jeans, a pale pink sweater, and bows in her hair. She stood near the bed. Smiling shyly, she offered me a mug of something hot.

"What is it?" I said, sitting up.

"Coffee. I'm supposed to tell you it's almost dinnertime."

I inhaled the aroma and drank. It was strong and brought me to my senses. The little girl didn't move. For a time, she gazed at me like I wasn't real. Her lower lip trembling, she began to cry. I put the cup down and held her tight. She was warm and small and delicate. Like a bird.

"I dreamed you were dead," she said.

"Just a nightmare."

"Is it over?"

"Tell your mom I'll be down soon."

She kissed my cheek and went to the door. When she looked back at me, I thought of another girl full of promise. Softly and without words, Lily closed the door.

"I'm so sorry," I said. But it was meant for Stella.

I walked into the dining room and found Lily with her mother—and Kersey. The girl patted the seat next to her, and I sat.

"You look okay," my ex-boss said. "Considering."

He poured me a glass of red wine. It tasted expensive. I would've asked him about his case, but his daughter was there. Instead, we talked about other things. Paris in the spring. Books. Music. A horse show the child would compete in soon.

After dinner, Lily left us. Kersey brought out cognac, and we got down to business.

"I'm going to plead out," he said.

I was confused. "I was told you had the best lawyers."

"I do. But they thought it wise to avoid a trial. Certain things could come out that might implicate—"

"The mayor."

Griselda laughed. "You always were a smart one. Which brings me to the reason we're all here. We want you as our partner."

"I don't understand."

"They'll sentence me to three years in a federal penitentiary," Kersey said. "I might get out sooner. But it'll be hard for me to run my business. Too many people to pay off."

His ex-wife took my hand. "I'm taking over. But as a single mother, I need help."

I finished my drink and tapped my fingers on the empty glass. My head swam. This whole thing had come out of nowhere. No. No way—I had plans. Nothing mattered except getting to Virginia.

"Why not Babić?" I said. "He's competent."

Griselda side-eyed her ex-husband. "Babić is good at what he does. But he's no businessman."

"And you think I'm the one to help run your operation?"

"You see things clearly—without any drama. And you get things done."

"You mean, I kill people."

"That's not what I'm talking about. When you make a plan, you follow through. And when faced with a crisis, you make the right decision."

"If you remember, I made the wrong decision to go to Hellborn alone. It was you who talked me out of it."

"You're young. And yes, you have a lot to learn. That's why I'm here."

"To mentor me?"

"Why not? With your mind and your abilities, think of what you'll be like in ten years."

"If I live that long."

"We could all be dead tomorrow," Kersey said. "Doesn't mean we shouldn't plan for the future."

You keep fighting the fight. I poured myself another drink. If I agreed to stay in LA, I'd be no closer to discovering who I was or retrieving my memories. Most of Kersey's enterprises were questionable. And even if he turned over a new leaf in prison, it didn't qualify me to run his business.

"You having this kind of faith in me means a lot," I said. "But I can't accept."

My ex-boss cleared his throat. "Going to see Caroline Sheldrake?"

"Can you understand? I need to know who I am."

He jammed a toothpick between his lips, and I knew he was annoyed. I tried seeing his side of things. He'd made an investment. Took enormous risks. Lost Raul. And for what? So some little pissant could whine about not knowing her name? *Pathetic, Jane. Real pathetic.*

"Okay, listen," I said. "You guys have done a lot for me. I won't say no. But I need time."

Griselda patted my hand. "That's fair. You've been through a lot. We come along and—"

"No, it's all right. I meant what I said about your faith in me."

Kersey pushed his untouched glass aside. "How do you see this working?"

"I am gonna meet with Caroline. I don't know what will happen. She might see me as a threat. A test subject who went off the rails."

"Or a brilliant success," the German said. "The perfect soldier."

"Optimistic, but okay. Let's say that does happen. There's no guarantee she'll release me."

"You've never had a problem escaping in the past," Kersey said.

"Whatever happens—if I'm alive—I promise to return here."

Griselda squeezed my hand. "Then, it's settled."

We got up from the table. She hugged me and, taking my hands, pulled me down to kiss my cheek.

"I can't get over how tall you are," she said. "Lily will miss you. And so will I."

"Thank you. For everything." Then to Kersey, "Can we talk about me getting another car?"

Side-eyeing Griselda, he pointed a finger in my face. The more he tried to look stern, the less convincing he was.

"Fine," he said. "But this is going on your tab. And it's a big one."

CHAPTER
SIXTY-THREE

I SPENT ALL the next day with Lily. After a breakfast of Belgian waffles decorated with M&M's—not the red ones—I drove her to her riding lesson and watched her jump a series of oxers like a pro. They weren't high, but I would've been on my ass.

Later, we had a picnic lunch in the backyard, where I shared with her stories from some of my favorite books. In the afternoon, we watched *Mary Poppins*.

"What's your favorite part?" she said during the end credits.

"The song they sing on the roof."

"Mine's when everyone jumps into the painting. And they end up in a horse race."

When it was time for me to go, Lily wheedled and cajoled, trying everything she could think of to get me to stay. I told her a secret—I would return because of her. That seemed to please her.

Carrying my bags, I walked outside, where I found Kersey —and a new black Dodge Challenger SRT8.

"A bribe?" I said.

"The glass is bulletproof."

"Wow. Thank you."

"Plenty of weapons too." He opened the trunk. "And something else."

A strongbox sat mounted against the rear seats. He opened it to reveal the cache of Riactis I'd stolen, as well as a supply of needles.

"What happens when you run out?" he said.

"I'll drive off that bridge when I get there."

Griselda came out with her daughter. We said our good-byes, and I headed out, waving to the Serbians guarding the house. When I checked the rearview mirror, Lily had made Kersey and his ex-wife hold hands.

For the first time since waking up at Hellborn, I was free. No drones. No Zeddemore. And for now, no hyper karma. I waited until I was on the freeway before calling Karen Roth-berg. I asked her to dig up anything she could on Caroline Sheldrake. We agreed to a video conference later on.

I had one last stop to make before heading to Lake Isabella.

In Castaic, I got off the freeway and took The Old Road to a Starbucks. There, I met Maggie Packard. She wore jeans and a UCLA sweatshirt. Her hair was pulled back. Her eyes were troubled and distant. We got our coffees and sat in the rear. I wasn't sure how to start.

"You okay?" I said.

"Getting used to it. I'm planning to take some time off after the funeral. My mom's flying in from Denver."

"It'll be nice, the two of you spending time together."

"I want to tell you something. Dad and I didn't keep secrets. He told me about the night you escaped. A chill went through me, you know? It was like a darkness was coming. And all I could see ahead was—"

"Nada de bueno."

"Right. Nothing good. When you and Raul showed up at our house…" She choked back the tears. "Everything I feared came true."

"Maggie, I… You know it was Zeddemore, right? He did all this."

She took a swallow of coffee. "I know. Is he—"

"Dead."

"I hope you made him suffer."

I didn't have the heart to tell her he'd died on his own. "Yeah, I did."

"And Raul? I guess we both lost someone."

"He was a good guy. Put up with all my bullshit."

She let out a laugh. "Where do I find someone like that? What will you do now?"

"Heading to Virginia as planned."

"Jane, be careful. Dad would've arranged a flight for you. But now…"

"It's okay. The last place I wanna be is at an airport. I'm driving."

"Smart. Stay off the radar."

"I feel like I owe you. Is there anything I can do?"

"When you see Caroline, you tell her. My father gave his life to protect you. It needs to mean something. Tell her, okay?"

"Promise," I said.

Three hours later, I was back at John's cabin. I pulled in behind the house and entered through the rear. As a precaution, I did a sweep of the premises to make sure no one had broken in. Later, I prepared a cheap imitation of Raul's pasta primavera and ate it with a white wine I'd picked up at Trader Joe's on the way. I'd saved Raul's voicemail and listened to it again. *Te quiero.*

I was sleepy. But I had a video conference at ten. I made a

pot of strong coffee, and chugging three cups, read in front of the fire until it was time.

When Karen's face appeared on the laptop screen, a feeling of profound loneliness came over me. Truly, I was apart—separate from everyone who had ever done anything to help me. I had to remind myself I was lucky to be alive.

"How are ya, doll?" she said.

"Tired. How's V?"

"Fine. She sends her regards. You've been through hell. But you survived."

I pictured Raul, grinning as he gave me a taste of some luscious sauce he'd made. Some time must've passed. Karen had been speaking, and I hadn't paid attention.

"Jane, are you all right?" she said.

"Can you start again?"

"I know you were worried about making contact. But I think Caroline Sheldrake might be on your side."

"Might be?"

"I'm not a mind reader. I go where the research takes me. I've looked at her career, starting with the Navy."

"She's ex-military?"

"Twenty years. When she retired, she held the rank of Commander. She's also a medical doctor. She spent most of her career at the Naval Medical Research Center in—"

"Silver Spring, Maryland."

"Correct."

"What was she in charge of?"

"A classified genomics project."

"Genomics?"

"It's the study of genes and their functions, that's all I know. When Baseborn Identity Research was formed, they went in search of a chief scientist. Guess who hired her."

"Walt Freeman."

"Right again. You'd make an excellent researcher."

"What makes you think she's on my side?"

"While in the Navy, she gave several speeches on medicine and ethics. You can find some of them on YouTube. Over the years, she's given generously to charitable organizations such as Save the Children and St. Jude Children's Research Hospital."

"Does she have a family?"

"She's like me—married to her work."

I thought about what the researcher had said. Caroline Sheldrake sounded too good to be true. After what I'd been through with Walt Freeman's people, I worried she might be better at hiding her agenda. And Zeddemore made her sound like a liar. But what choice did I have? If I wanted answers, Caroline was the only one who could provide them.

"Thanks, Karen," I said. "This has been helpful."

"You're welcome. Hang on, will you?"

I waited, thinking she had brought in V. Kulla. It made sense. I would need the girl's help before showing up unannounced at Hellborn's headquarters. More time passed. Karen's image moved to the side, then dropped off completely.

The image of another woman filled the screen. I recognized her. Sixty. Shoulder-length brown hair with blonde highlights. Black designer glasses. The brown eyes kind but intense.

"Hello, Jane," Caroline Sheldrake said.

For a sec, I couldn't respond. Then like a feeb, "Hi."

"You've had quite an adventure, haven't you? I know you have questions, dear. And I can provide all the answers you need. But it's imperative we do this in person."

"Will you tell me about the program? And why I was in it?"

"Yes, and more. I'll show you the work we're doing here and what part you and the others play."

"I... I'm not sure I can trust you."

"Trust. That's something you have to earn, isn't it? Tell

you what. Ask me one question now. I promise to answer it truthfully."

An intense longing came over me, making it hard to speak. I needed a minute. Then, "What's my name?"

"Faith Regan. You were born in Bakersfield, California. You'll be twenty-four on September 7th."

She moved closer to the camera. Her expression was one of kindness. I looked into her eyes, trying to see the lies.

"What do you think, Faith?" she said. "Time to pull back the curtain? See you in Virginia."

The screen went black. And once again, I was alone.

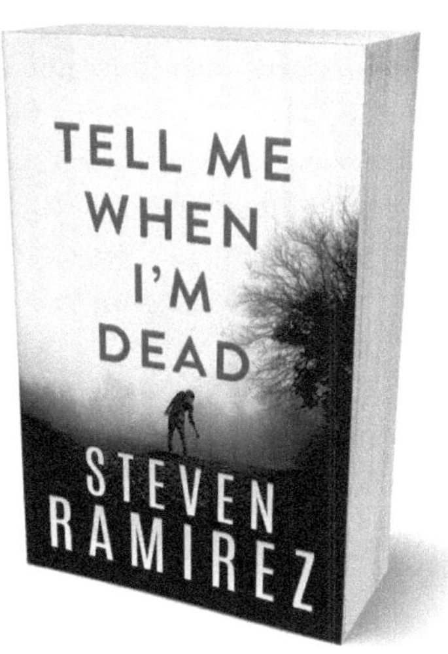

TELL ME WHEN I'M DEAD
STEVEN RAMIREZ

YOUR FREE BOOK IS WAITING...

When your boss pulls a gun on you, it might be time to quit.

Get your free copy of *Brandon's Last Words: A Jane Doe Thriller Prequel.*

BOOKS.STEVENRAMIREZ.COM/GET-THRILLER

ABOUT THE AUTHOR

Steven Ramirez is the award-winning American author of thriller, supernatural, and literary fiction. A former screenwriter, he's written about man-made plagues and idyllic towns infested with ghosts and demons. His latest novel is *Let's Get Lost*, a modern fairy tale. Steven lives in Los Angeles.

AUTHOR WEBSITE
stevenramirez.com

instagram.com/byStevenRamirez
goodreads.com/byStevenRamirez
bookbub.com/authors/steven-ramirez

www.ingramcontent.com/pod-product-compliance
Lightning Source LLC
Chambersburg PA
CBHW031628200726
48288CB00019B/368